IT'S NO[T ABOUT YOU]

Ratna Vira is a human r[esources] professional with a master's degree from the London School of Economics and Political Science, a master's in English Literature from St. Stephen's College, and an MBA. She lives in Gurgaon with her daughter and son.

It's Not About You is her second novel. Her first novel, *Daughter By Court Order*, was a national bestseller.

Also by Ratna

Daughter by Court Order

IT'S NOT ABOUT YOU

RATNA

PAN

First published 2016 by Pan
an imprint of Pan Macmillan India
a division of Macmillan Publishers India Private Limited
Pan Macmillan India, 707, Kailash Building
26, KG Marg, New Delhi – 110 001
www.panmacmillan.co.in

Pan Macmillan, 20 New Wharf Road, London N1 9RR
Basingstoke and Oxford
Associated companies throughout the world
www.panmacmillan.com

ISBN 978-93-82616-74-0
Copyright © Ratna Vira 2016

This is a work of fiction. All characters, locations and events are fictitious.
Any resemblance to actual events or locales or persons, living or dead,
is entirely coincidental.

All rights reserved. No part of this publication may be reproduced, stored in or introduced into a retrieval system, or transmitted, in any form, or by any means (electronic, mechanical, photocopying, recording or otherwise) without the prior written permission of the publisher. Any person who does any unauthorized act in relation to this publication may be liable to criminal prosecution and civil claims for damages.

1 3 5 7 9 8 6 4 2

This book is sold subject to the condition that it shall not, by way of trade or otherwise, be lent, re-sold, hired out, or otherwise circulated without the publisher's prior consent in any form of binding or cover other than that in which it is published and without a similar condition including this condition being imposed on the subsequent purchaser.

Typeset by Manmohan Kumar
Printed and bound in India by
Replika Press Pvt. Ltd.

Dear Anita,
Blessed to have you as a friend,
Big Hug,
Rahla
May 2016.

In the loving memory of my Nani
For my children Suhasini and Shauryya
For in my words you must look for the answers

'You may write me down in history
With your bitter, twisted lies,
You may tread me in the very dirt
But still, like dust, I'll rise.'

Maya Angelou

1

'At its best, life is completely unpredictable.'
– CHRISTOPHER WALKEN

Christmas was still a few days away but Gurgaon was already cold, with even the mid-morning air being distinctly chilly. Sammy was working on her laptop in the study with the usual steaming cup of tea by her side. She had decided against going to office today. A late night flight, that had been delayed getting into Delhi after a particularly gruelling work trip, had left her exhausted. Her team would not grudge 'Samaira ma'am', as they referred to her, taking a day off. She led them well. She delegated often and controlled projects through careful, directed advice and precise instructions rather than vague or confusing orders. That was who she was – a successful woman in corporate India – confident, self-assured and sensitive.

Stifling a yawn, she stretched and stood up in her favourite flannel pyjamas. As she caught a glimpse of herself in the long mirror in the corner of the room, she couldn't resist grinning and muttering, 'You're still quite hot, old girl!' Walking across to the plate glass windows overlooking the golf course next to her apartment complex, she thought wistfully about how long it had been since she had played a round. Far too long! But she didn't get time for golf any more. Being a single mother with a challenging corporate career left her playing catch up on most days, never quite being able to find time for indulgences like a three-hour game on the Arnold Palmer-designed golf course so close to home. She had to make do with yoga, dance and the gym downstairs in order to keep herself in shape.

A Paresh Maity on one wall and a Hussain on the other, she also had several of her own paintings elegantly placed across her home. She should paint and exhibit more often, her friends would tell her. Someday perhaps, but for now an occasional exhibition and the satisfaction of designing and maintaining a beautiful home would have to suffice. Carpets carefully chosen by her beloved Nani and added to over the years from Kashmir, Iran and Turkey. Contemporary furniture overlaid with cushions and bric-a-brac added dashes of colour that made her home unique and excited comments. The interiors had been featured in a design magazine a few months ago. The journalist was astonished that she had not used a professional to do up her house. It would not have been as personal, had been her comment.

And there were, of course, personal items. Some with memories of different times in her life. Some with memories yet to form around them. Photographs, too. Family holidays. Happy occasions. All candid shots because she disliked posed, studio photos. Two children, her little ones, dominated the frames – Aksh, a sporty and handsome sixteen-year old and

Tara, his elder sister, an adult in her own right, who had turned twenty earlier that month. Many of her acquaintances found it difficult to believe that Sammy had a college-going daughter. She had aged well and could pass off for an early thirty-something, a decade younger than she actually was. She was elegance personified. She celebrated her children and had never attempted to recapture her youth, but took good care of herself as she, and they, grew older.

There was no man in the photographs. Not that the absence indicated a loss or a void. Sammy was content with her life. A group of good friends, several work colleagues whom she was happy socializing with and the demands of being a single mother, kept her too busy to look for romance or a life partner. Rishi, her ex-husband, and she had built a friendship that was fairly cordial, considering their past. It was good that he was in London though, for the warmth was best maintained at a distance.

Tara, her lovely and beautiful daughter, had moved to London for her undergraduate degree and was living with Rishi. The kids had always been a part of their father's life and he loved them to distraction. But Tara's relocation had created an emptiness in Sammy's home. Aksh and she only had each other now. Like any two people who loved each other intensely, they had their disagreements too.

Aksh wasn't a baby any more. He still had his childlike innocence and warmth, his deep affection and love for Sammy. But he was a teenager and often Sammy thought she didn't understand him at all. Earlier, Tara used to play the interpreter and interlocutor but since her departure, a gulf had formed between mother and son. It almost set the tone of their relationship these days. 'It isn't only about your work and your life,' he would often tell her. 'Teenagers also have problems; don't you understand that?'

This morning for instance – the thought brought a frown on her face – even though she woke up tired and a little grumpy, Sammy sat with Aksh as he prepared to leave for school. This was their morning routine, almost a ritual, as it had been since the time Tara and Aksh had begun school. Yet, lately, the once familiar and comforting start to the day had become forced and tense. Neither Sammy nor Aksh would talk, and a cursory 'See you! Love you!' would acknowledge the relationship. It was not that there was an issue between mother and son, and they were certainly not fighting. Plans would be discussed in passing, the day's events mentioned almost as calendar entries. The depth of involvement in each other's lives was less than it had been and communication was not truly open, though the love was as strong as ever. It was difficult for Sammy to accept that Aksh was growing up faster than she had imagined and she feared that she was losing touch with him.

After-school sports had become the issue that day. Aksh had wanted to stay back at school as the team practice was scheduled for late afternoon. Jay, his best friend from preschool days, would be with him and he had asked Sammy whether their car could drop Jay home after practice. Sammy, tired and a bit disoriented, had forgotten that she would not be going to office and had said that she would need the car so Aksh would have to come home at the regular time. One thing led to another, with Aksh eventually snapping that she didn't care for his plans. Sammy, realizing her mistake, apologized and said that he could definitely have the car. Aksh left irritated and the matter remained unresolved.

Simple matters and small misunderstandings were becoming an issue with her son, thought Sammy.

There was not much that could be done at the moment though and Sammy resolved that she needed to sit down and have a proper chat with her son. Perhaps they could go out for a movie together and then to his favourite restaurant. Aksh was quite the foodie. Over a pleasant evening, they could talk and bring down the unnecessary wall that was coming up between them. She would suggest it to Aksh when he called on his way back from school, another family ritual.

They had other things to plan as well. Tara was coming home for the winter and Rishi had decided to take a vacation in India at the same time. They would arrive in a few days. Rishi, typical of him, had booked them into a hotel but Sammy hoped that Tara would stay at home instead. They would meet Rishi and do things together because the kids would want that. Sammy wasn't quite sure how much of Rishi she could handle. She would have to speak with Aksh and see what he thought. Perhaps he had already been in touch with his sister and maybe they had made plans. Anyway, it was another matter that could be discussed over dinner.

Time for a shower and then a relaxing hour in front of the telly.

Not that the world outside was giving her an opportunity to relax! The newsreaders and talking heads on television seemed to be prophets of doom; interested only in regaling viewers with all the horrific acts that humans carry out on each other. Murder, rape, molestation on the metro, shooting in an American street, militia recreating boundaries in Eastern Europe. Sammy heard a popular security analyst talk about the increased threat of terrorism on soft targets in Delhi. She remembered hearing him speak about the brutal attack on a school in Pakistan a few days ago. She had been moved to tears upon hearing the story of innocent children being gunned down. 'Senseless brutes,' he had called the attackers and had strongly advised the government to step up its security at schools across the national capital.

Sammy wanted her children to be independent but she feared for them constantly. She had tried to create a cocoon of security around them as best as she could. Tara, however, was now on her own – in a safe city, no doubt, and with Rishi looking after her – but Sammy could not help but be concerned for her. Over time, she had taught herself not to worry about Tara. However, her concern seemed to have doubled for Aksh, almost stifling him in the process.

A salad with crisp toast would be her lunch today. Carrying the tray out on to the balcony, she sat looking over the expanse of greenery in front of her and at last felt her body relax.

Her phone rang a few minutes before one. At first she thought it might be the office but she saw that the call was from Aksh's mobile phone.

Odd, she thought. The phone should still be with the class teacher and Aksh would only be allowed to use it after school hours. Slightly concerned, she tried to accept the call but the signal dropped before she could connect.

'I wonder if he's forgotten something at home?' she muttered to herself as she dialled his number.

2

'The oldest and strongest emotion of mankind is fear, and the oldest and strongest kind of fear is fear of the unknown.'

– H.P. LOVECRAFT

Sammy tried Aksh's mobile phone several times without success; the call kept dropping. After a few minutes, she called again. There was no response. She was worried now and a trifle irritated. This was very unlike her son!

'I hope it's not some new complication in the afternoon's transport arrangements,' she thought, reminding herself that she should send the car to the school in the next hour or so.

About ten minutes later, her phone rang again. It was the school's number. Finally!

'You must come to the school right now, Samaira. Aksh has been hurt ... No, I don't know the details right now but the doctor has been called. Please come right away,' said Aksh's class teacher.

No further details. Just that.

The ordinarily controlled and organized Sammy was thrown into a tizzy. Partly because of guilt at having fought with Aksh in the morning and partly, the fear of bringing up a sixteen-year-old boy alone in the sometimes dangerous and always rough North Indian city. In her rising panic, Sammy passively heard the class teacher, flung a jacket over her shoulder and grabbed her car keys from the hook near the refrigerator.

Forgetting that her driver had been resting in the shade since morning, she rushed to her car and drove to the school in a daze.

The drive across town was a blur. Sammy didn't quite remember how she reached the school or how she got inside, weaving her way through a milling crowd of domestic helpers, drivers and parents waiting to pick up the primary school children who were heading home after school. Inside the gate, she had to push her way through the crowd of children, each being checked and claimed by an adult or gathering aimlessly while the bus lists were read out. The routine was familiar to her; she too had stood there waiting for Tara and Aksh when they had been in primary school.

But today things didn't look completely normal. Sammy had entered from the main gate, close to the car park. She was now at the primary school entrance, with its curved drive where the school buses would normally have been standing. That was what was different. There were no buses in the drive today. Instead, there was a white van with a red flasher on top. An ambulance.

She could see more than a dozen schoolteachers and senior school students crowding near the side of the building, getting as close to the ambulance as they were allowed, making it difficult for her to look through them. It wasn't as if they were deliberately hiding anything, but Sammy felt that something was very wrong. Tensed and troubled, her usual confidence vanished. In that instant, she was overcome with fear. Fear because she was certain that the ambulance was there for her son.

The ambulance began to wail. She spotted Aksh being lifted into it. Sammy ran forward but it was too late. The school was rushing Aksh to the hospital!

Sammy instinctively turned to run behind the ambulance, but was pulled back by a voice calling her name from behind.

'Aksh is all right. He will be okay. Calm down,' she heard a school official say to her but the voice seemed to come through a funnel, distorted and disjointed. She heard the only four words that mattered – Aksh is all right.

'What has happened?' she asked the man, her voice quivering with emotion, almost at the edge of hysteria. 'We're still trying to figure out...' he said, belching and clearing his throat as if about to say something more. Then he noticed the lingering crowd and yelled instructions, breaking them up and jolting them to action.

Sammy saw the principal walk towards her. He greeted her warmly but offered little explanation. 'We had to send him to the hospital, Samaira. I'm sorry we couldn't wait for you. The doctor felt that time was important.'

She looked calm outwardly, but her heart was thumping against her chest and she was barely able to contain her rising fear.

The external injury had been superficial and the wounds had been dressed by the paramedics, she was told by the school doctor, who had accompanied the principal. An X-ray and possibly an exploratory MRI might be needed at the hospital, merely as a precaution to explain the disconcerting nosebleed.

The principal was distracted, seemingly more eager to get the primary school children off the premises than to speak with Sammy. Not normally a role that he took upon himself, thought Sammy, disoriented and unsure of what she should say or do. His scowling demeanour and exaggerated gestures reflected his state of mind, as if now the responsibility had shifted away and Aksh was no longer the school's problem.

'Go to the hospital, Samaira. I'll send my office boy to guide you to it,' he said and turned on his heel and left.

Sammy didn't wait for the office boy; she had seen the prominent logo of a major city hospital on the side of the ambulance. She ran to her car in the unwieldy high heels – the first pair of shoes she had found – and followed the path the ambulance would have taken, her heart in her mouth. Her mobile phone was clamped to her ear as she called Aida, her housekeeper, and asked her to send the driver to the hospital so that he could take charge of the car. She might need him around, she thought.

Reaching the hospital after negotiating the particularly dense traffic, she discovered that Aksh was in the critical care unit. She had to wait for an anxious hour, which she spent pacing up and down the emergency wing's lobby, before the young doctor on duty came out and spoke to her.

It was more serious than what the school had told her. Aksh had facial cuts, bruises, swelling, a nose fracture and possibly a concussion. The MRI had ruled out a ruptured spleen but there could still be other internal bleeding. Not willing to take a chance, the hospital had put Aksh, her little baby boy, in the intensive care's shock trauma centre.

For Sammy, the nightmare had just begun.

3

*'Promise me you'll always remember: You're braver than
you believe, and stronger than you seem, and smarter
than you think.'*

– A.A. MILNE

Three days passed. Three long days with Aksh unconscious, the school sombre and his friends tight-lipped and tense. Three days when Sammy waited anxiously at the hospital, days that turned her into an insomniac on skates. Worried and hurried, haggard and fragile.

The doctors had allowed her a brief visit each day, mid-afternoon, because they didn't encourage relatives to enter the critical care unit. When she saw Aksh for the first time – sedated and strapped to monitors, drips and other machines – it had wrenched her heart. Aksh, her Aksh, was critically hurt.

It was traumatic shock, the doctors told her, accompanied by possible internal bleeding. Soft tissue had been impacted due to a crushing injury, with the release of myoglobulins (whatever they were!). 'In simple terms,' the doctors had explained to Sammy, 'there is an imbalance in the oxygen supply and demand. The body compensates physiologically to maintain adequate oxygen delivery to tissues.' Aksh was also feeling the 'physiological effects of pain' and needed to be sedated.

The emergency medical procedures were to stabilize Aksh and give him the necessary intravenous fluid replacement and medication, while treating the underlying causes. 'We need to ensure there is no intracranial haemorrhage.'

The doctors insisted that they had sedated him as a precaution and they would wait for a few days before taking further decisions. They insisted that he would be okay but Sammy took that only to mean that he wasn't okay at the moment, and this worried her even more.

Since Aksh was not in a regular ward, there was no place for Sammy to rest while at the hospital; no requirement for an attendant in the critical care unit she was told. So, she became familiar with the seats in the reception area and would bundle herself in, tucking her feet under her and wrapping a shawl tightly around her shoulders. Some part of her rational mind told her that she should conserve her energy and look after her own health, for she would be of no use to Aksh if she were to fall ill as well. So, Sammy would permit herself one visit home every day, to shower, eat and rest for an hour before returning to the hospital. Work was forgotten for the moment and her colleagues assured her that they would look after matters until she was able to return. A few of Aksh's friends had dropped in to see him on the first day, but she had been deep in discussion with the doctors when they came. No one had come since.

She was at home in the evening when the hospital called, the shrill ring of the phone startling her. 'Aksh is awake now. He is asking for you,' the nurse said. 'I think you had better hurry.'

'I will! I am getting there as soon as I can,' Sammy replied, springing into action. The hospital, like Aksh's school, was in Delhi, quite a long way from her home in Gurgaon. She rushed into her room.

'The hospital called,' Sammy said to Aida, quickly grabbing some clothes from the cupboard. She tugged at a pair of jeans from the bottom of her closet, not bothering with the shirts that fell out on to the floor with a soft thud.

'He has come around,' Sammy continued, hearing her voice as she spoke. It was strangely soothing, a reaffirmation that all would be well. 'He will be all right, and he will make it through,' she said, wanting to believe it, repeating it again and again like a mantra.

She closed her eyes and saw her son as she remembered him last. He had looked like an oversized boy sitting in his blue pyjamas on the edge of the bed before getting dressed for school on that fateful morning. Sammy was overcome with regret and guilt at having fought with him over such a petty matter. 'If only ... if only I could turn back time,' she muttered to herself as she grabbed her car keys because the driver, too, had gone home to rest.

She drove quickly through the familiar neighbourhood, with one of the houses decorated with coloured lights. The roads were strewn with coloured paper and burnt crackers, the air heavy with smog and the visibility low, the impact of boisterous celebrations from a wedding the previous night mixed with the pollution that seemed endemic in the city. Marriages had been stripped of their simplicity, morphing into elaborate week-long extravaganzas no different from IPL cricket matches.

On the main road now, she hit unusually heavy traffic. Even though she was in a rush, she stopped dutifully at each red light, acutely aware that her precious son had no one else to depend on. She couldn't risk an accident!

Aksh had always been quiet even as a little boy, always the little man. He had never liked heroic gestures and preferred no fuss, and so she had ensured that there had been none, especially since the divorce. Sammy had thought that Aksh, now older, might have some questions and might have wanted to talk to her about the divorce but the conversation seemed to trouble him. In the end, she had resisted the need to talk about it giving in to Aksh's request for silence. The last three days had brought the memory of those troubled times back. Now she was struggling with herself, with the fear and loneliness of bringing up her son as a single mother, with the nightmare that was never quite the past.

Tara had coped with her parents' divorce differently, shutting even Sammy out of her world for a while. She had mourned the collapse of their old life and the growing distance from her father. Leaving for London, Sammy often thought, was Tara's way of connecting with her father before life took her forward.

There were only a few cars in the visitor's lot and she found a spot close to the hospital entrance. Though part of a grand and impressive building, the lobby was unusually dimly lit and eerily empty and uninviting. Perhaps just one of those days or merely an impression formed because she was distracted, but she shivered as she walked through it to the ward. She muttered, 'He will be fine, Sammy.' And then more forcefully, 'He will.'

Sammy tried to prepare herself for what lay ahead. She hoped to find her son at peace. He was not afraid. Ever. He had an astrophysicist's appreciation of life. His passion was the sky, the stars and the planets, and therefore for him nothing was daunting. As he always told Sammy, 'Mama, think of how small our problems are compared to the universe. We are but a dot, an insignificant one at that. We are one species on an ordinary planet, orbiting a small sun of an obscure solar system in one corner of a fairly mediocre galaxy.'

She had wanted to shake him awake and tell him that he was wrong. In her mind, her star, the centre of her universe and galaxy was lying in a hospital bed. And it broke her heart to think of him like that.

'Wake up son, get well and walk out of here! Make my world whole again and I will make each star in the sky shine until they sparkle,' she said to herself, remembering his oft-repeated comment that the pollution in Gurgaon caused the stars to be barely visible. 'They will shine I promise,' she told him, holding a conversation with Aksh in her mind as she walked to his ward room. She had done this so often these past three days when she was not praying, talking to doctors, slumping into a chair in the reception or hovering outside the door of the critical care unit. Trying to be next to him. Always pulling herself closer to him.

He had been moved out of the critical care unit, she had been told, and was in a regular ward room now. This by itself was a good sign but Sammy did not want to raise her hopes too much. The instant she entered her son's room, she knew that he was not comfortable. He was clearly worse than when she had seen him that afternoon and he had an oxygen mask over his face. His breathing was raspy through the mask, his skin paler and he was agitated. As he reached for her with trembling arms, he had a look of desperation about him, his handsome face crumpled with pain.

Sammy quickly bent down to kiss him and pat his hand. Then she sat on the edge of the bed and battled to reign in her fear. She didn't want Aksh to see it.

'I am here, son-shine, and you are getting better,' she said softly.

Aksh held both her hands in his weak grasp but he did not relax. He tried to speak, the words coming out disjointed through the mask. 'Should have … told…' he said.

She moved closer and strained to hear him.

'A girl,' he said. 'You need…' Her son's face was gaunt, tightened with frustration as he struggled to get the words out.

'I need to what, son?' she asked gently, rubbing his head. An old habit, something she had done since he was a little baby.

'Look…' his lips trembled from the strain. 'Talk to her,' he said.

'I will, I will, my love,' Sammy said as she sobbed silently.

She whispered, 'Son, what is her name? Where will I find her?'

'In school. Find Peasant P. Ask her!' Aksh told her.

She sat there holding his hand until he drifted off to sleep. She sat rooted to the spot for what seemed like a long time. Looking out of the window she saw a lone aeroplane fly across the sky … the universe unfriendly and aloof, indifferent and distant.

4

'Time takes it all whether you want it to or not, time takes it all. Time bares it away, and in the end there is only darkness. Sometimes we find others in that darkness, and sometimes we lose them there again.'

– STEPHEN KING

With Aksh having been moved to the regular ward, Sammy had sought and received permission to walk in and out as she desired. She had already spoken with the doctor on duty and had ensured that Rishi and Tara would be able to visit Aksh as soon as they arrived the following morning. Rishi, of course, would have a million questions but they would have to wait because Sammy didn't have too many answers to give at the moment.

Sammy had already called Rishi the evening Aksh had been admitted to the hospital but flights were sold out due to the pre-Christmas rush. Rishi and Tara eventually arrived three days later on the British Airways flight from London. Not bothering with checking into the hotel and dropping off their bags, they rushed from the airport to join Sammy at the hospital.

Tara ran into Sammy's arms and they hugged each other. A sob escaped Tara. 'How's Aksh?' she said, grappling with the thought of her brother being in hospital. 'What's happened to him?' she asked as Sammy instinctively clutched her hand to silence her.

'Hush baby, we'll go up to see him soon,' Sammy said tenderly. Tara was a part of her heart living outside her body. Having her daughter with her at this moment was the best balm for her tired body. Her children completed her and she hadn't realized just how much she had missed Tara all these months. She was looking good, her daughter, despite the tiredness of a long flight and the obvious worry for her brother.

Rishi was standing to one side, letting mother and daughter have some space to themselves for a bit. Sammy was conscious of her ex-husband standing there but was also using the time to prepare herself for what was still an awkward meeting. Eventually, she disentangled her arms from her daughter and walked the few steps to Rishi.

'Hello Rishi,' she said warmly. 'It's good to see you and thanks for coming straight over.'

'Hi Sammy,' responded the man. 'He's my son too, you know...'

The moment could have had an edge that may have led to a disagreement, perhaps a fight. There was too much history between them, even though they were regularly in touch over the phone and email these days. But Sammy chose to ignore the mild reproach in Rishi's voice, stepping forward to give him a gentle hug.

'I'm glad you're here, Rishi. I need you to be here for us, for Aksh, and I know you will be.'

The nurse motioned them to silence as they entered the ward. Aksh was sleeping, a peaceful gentle sleep it seemed. 'Come later,' she said. 'Aksh is resting now and should not be disturbed.'

Tara gave her brother a kiss on the forehead, muttering, 'I love you, kiddo!' Rishi managed a gentle squeeze of his son's hand and Sammy could see his deep concern for Aksh.

They went downstairs to the small coffee shop near the hospital's lobby.

'Let me fill you in,' said Sammy. 'Aksh is responding well to medication. Much still needs to be done. I need to figure out what happened and why. The only words I have got out of Aksh are that some girl ... Peasant P ... might be involved. Or maybe that is just him rambling and is unconnected to his injury. No one from the school has come to visit Aksh for the past few days and I haven't had the time to follow up. Perhaps with your being here, I'll be able to meet the principal and find out what actually happened at school.'

She turned towards Tara, 'Do you know who Peasant P is? Has he spoken to you about her?'

'No Mama,' answered her daughter. 'Never heard the name before.'

An incoming call on Sammy's phone cut them off. It was the day nurse from the ward. The doctor had said that he would meet them in Aksh's room in some time.

'Take your time,' were the nurse's last words before disconnecting.

'Take my time,' she repeated under her breath, as she hurried up the stairs, followed closely by Rishi and Tara, instead of waiting for the lift. Sammy almost collided into an old nurse who dropped her tray. Fluids splashed on the tiled floor but Sammy rushed past, muttering apologies.

'Is he better?' she asked the nurse as she swooped down to kiss her son's forehead.

'Yes, he is. The worst is over according to the doctor. If he continues to improve…' The nurse crossed her fingers, waving both hands in the air and mouthed a silent prayer.

As if on cue, the consulting doctor swept in followed by a team of his juniors hovering in his wake like bobbing fishing boats in the swell of a passing cruise liner. 'So how are we today?' he asked in an upbeat voice, extending his hand to take the reports from a colleague.

'Stool test – okay. Blood test – normal. Slight infection … nothing to worry about, he is doing well. There is a slight concussion but we are watching it. The wound is healing well. There are marks on his body but we are looking into it.'

'What marks?' Sammy asked in concern.

The doctor ignored the question. 'The young man will be back on the football field soon,' he said with a broad smile, all the while adjusting his shirt and balancing the stethoscope around his neck and over the errant collar. The rest of his team smiled and watched politely from a distance.

'Then why is he not up? I mean conscious yet? Why is he still asleep? He woke up for a while yesterday!' Sammy said, her face reflecting her worry. 'To play football he needs to get off the tubes and machines first. When will that be? He is a teenager! It breaks my heart, doctor.'

'Why is he not responding?' burst in Rishi. 'It seems more than a normal sleep. Please tell us!'

'Please be patient. Your son is getting better but if he senses despair in your voice he will panic. You see him in a deep sleep but remember he can hear everything. He is not in a coma. We have kept him sedated since last night. Even patients in coma, patients who we doctors believe are in deep coma and sinking, have surprised us. One woman heard her mother singing the "Gurbani" and suddenly, after three weeks in coma, she joined her hands in prayer. Her children and husband had given up on her but her mother continued to talk to her, reading the newspaper, singing prayers and then one day she responded. Some things can't be explained by science and this is one of them.'

Sammy had by now controlled her anxiety and had an expression that gave nothing away, not the pain and neither her endless optimism and hope.

'It is the power of the umbilical cord; it cannot be cut or severed. Stem cells are extracted from it to be used later –'

The almost irritating monologue was fortunately cut short by an urgent phone call, which made the doctor leave in a hurry. Much to Rishi's relief because he knew that Sammy was not a great believer in the magic of the wonderful umbilical cord. She had struggled in her relationship with her own mother who had been the anti-hero, the villain and the source of her almost insurmountable problems.

Sammy and Tara sat together near the window as Rishi drew up a chair close to his son. Mother and daughter talked, catching up on news and drawing comfort from each other. They avoided the present, what had happened to Aksh and spoke more about their past.

Her lovely daughter, Sammy discovered, was delicate but surprisingly strong. Tara's love was intense once you won her trust. As Tara explained in her typical way, 'I hated middle school, loved and abhorred everything with all passion and no reason. I burned at both ends like a candle, anything made or destroyed my day, my mood, my teacher's mood, even the traffic jam was a reason to rage and vent. It appears so trivial when I look back now.'

She pulled out a poem she had written a few years ago. A poem, she said, that she carried around with her. Reading a part of the poem, the words etched themselves into Sammy's mind, the lines showing a maturity beyond her daughter's age when she had written the poem.

> Living amidst these familiar faces
> Yet everything seems so unfamiliar
> In this cesspool of emotions
> I try to keep up but only drown
> So it is now my smile that I feign
> Just to live another day with the pain…

Tara was writing about her parents' divorce. But that was over and done with. The crisis had passed and they had survived. Or had they? Sammy wondered as she looked at Rishi.

Despite their divorce and his broken second marriage to his childhood sweetheart, Sammy and Rishi shared something that was truly special. And they had two wonderful children, one of whom was in deep sleep, induced for his safety by the doctors.

Tara and Rishi changed places a few hours later. Sammy had dozed off. As Rishi came and sat next to her, she woke up and reached across, clasped his hand in hers and looked deep into his eyes, smiling.

They talked, drawing each other into conversations that lasted several hours, well into the evening, past the time the night nurse came to check up on her patients. While Aksh slept and the night nurse dozed, as the coffee in the Styrofoam cups coagulated into mush, they spoke. Sammy talked of her home that she grew up in and about their life. The people they had met. A menagerie of sorts. The Zoo at Number Two, a story of their life as Rishi often called it.

5

'Keep your face to the sunshine and you cannot see a shadow.'
– HELEN KELLER

Sammy had asked Rishi and Tara to stay with her. It would be more convenient and would allow them greater flexibility in being with Aksh. Tara had readily agreed but Rishi had decided to remain at the hotel, so they had picked up her bags on their way back from the hospital the previous night. They would take turns to be at the hospital, while Sammy tried to re-establish contact with the school.

Sammy hadn't slept well. She got up to get some water from the kitchen. When she returned to her room, she sank down on her bed and put her hands over her face. After four soul-crushing days, she let go and cried as hard as she wanted to, tired of holding up a brave front.

She felt she was part of a circus with the principal of Aksh's school as the ringmaster and the elusive Peasant P, the trapeze artist. Someone floating high above and out of focus. Peasant P ... Peasant P ... was this a joke of some sort? A code name or a not-so-nice nickname for a friend? Which friend, she wondered because the name had barely managed to escape her son's lips.

The name rang in her ears but it did not ring a bell in her mind. She was unable to find an explanation or link it to Aksh. The deafening silence from the school was strange and annoying. How could the school be so casual and dismissive about the assault? Surely they owed her an explanation?

The school had issued an official statement two days after the incident; bland and uninformative.

'We are sorry to report that one of the students of our school, Aksh, was found beaten up and in critical condition. The incident occurred close to dispersal time. The victim is in hospital and is being supervised by his mother. The school is investigating the matter.'

The school's message to the wider group of parents didn't capture Aksh's pain and didn't even begin to answer the two fundamental questions – what had actually happened and who were the perpetrators who beat up Aksh?

Her eyes fell on a photograph on her side table – Aksh holding his first football trophy. She bit her lower lip, whispering to herself, 'I can't stand the thought of my son suffering.' The image of him in hospital flashed in her mind and she thought how different he appeared from the confident central defender that he was, with his body attached to machines.

She lay back on the bed, deeply disturbed, and pulled the pillow more comfortably under her head. 'I just need to sleep. I need to clear my mind for a little while before I go back to the hospital. Before I have to face the fact that my son, my sweet son-shine, is hurt.'

The sky was still dark. She checked the time and felt guilty. Guilty not to be the one in the hospital. Guilty to be well and at home. Guilty that she could not trade places with her son. She sat up again and reached for her phone to check for missed calls. She was a dishevelled mess, having collapsed in the same clothes she had worn to the hospital. Now she quickly shed her jeans and got into a nightgown, shook her hair out of the hastily tied ponytail and pushed her feet into a pair of slippers. She shuffled into the corridor connecting her bedroom with the rest of the apartment.

The light was still shining brightly in Tara's room and Sammy saw Rishi sitting on the bed clutching Tara's hand as she lay snuggled up to him. Both of them were just as she had left them hours ago when he had come with Tara's bags from the hotel. This time his head was bowed and his eyes were closed. She could tell that he was dozing, because every once in a while he shook himself as if trying to wake up but fell right back into a jet lag and fatigue-induced stupor, all the time holding Tara's hand tightly.

As she covered Tara with a comforter, Sammy straightened a ringlet and pushed back her daughter's unruly hair from her face, admiring her delicate features and noting her loss of weight. 'I am worrying again. She is all right,' she told herself as she walked to the kitchen.

Sammy made herself a cup of coffee, left the kettle on boil for Rishi and walked to the balcony to look out. The condominium stretched below her snug in foggy slumber. The sun was weak, struggling to rise and it was still not quite light. The early winter morning mist rolled over the lawns and crept out of the gaps between the tall buildings almost like a small bush fire making smoke signals. She frowned, wanting to understand their messages.

Below her, far down in the azure-tiled swimming pool, a man was swimming lengths. His long limbs stretched out in the water and she marvelled at his determination to swim in the inclement weather. Sammy watched him, mesmerized by his repetitive routine and the fact that he was awake when she was. There was an urgency to his stroke, a frenetic splashing but completely controlled. 'The pool is heated,' she told herself, willing his being out there to be put into context and finding excuses for herself. 'But the surrounding air isn't,' she noted and shook her head as he got out of the pool, reached for his towel and ran indoors.

She was glad to have seen him and felt less alone. His determination to beat the odds and not be held back resonated with her as she said a silent prayer for Aksh. Rishi and Tara were here for now and were going to stay until Aksh was better and they had sorted things out. But their life was now in London, in Knightsbridge and not in Gurgaon.

Mechanical and perfunctory sounds from in and around her apartment caught her attention. The normal sounds of a home waking up: ice falling and collecting in the shallow freezer bin, the coffee pot clicking as the timer went off and noisily filling with latte mixture, the kettle bubbling crossly and the newspaper landing with a soft thud in her lobby as the lift slipped down with a ping.

Away in the distance, there was an orange burst of colour and smoke. Her eyebrows furrowed and she leaned forward, trying to see more clearly. 'Is it a building on fire, or is it the curtain of fog that coats the city causing an illusion at the break of dawn? An illusion of an inferno in the far distance perhaps?' Sammy mused. The morning chill had now got to her and she moved indoors.

'Sorry, I went to sleep. I should have gone back to the hotel,' Rishi said apologetically. She smiled weakly and followed him to the kitchen. 'Can I make you some more coffee?' he asked. She shook her head. 'No, thanks. I've just had a cup.'

'You have to look after yourself, you have to…' Sammy shrugged, discouraging Rishi from continuing the conversation.

Rishi left soon after to go to the hotel, shower and then head to the hospital. Sammy went back into the drawing room. She lay on the ottoman, something she had not done in the recent past. She moved around trying to make herself comfortable as a bad headache hit her in waves. Every nerve, every fibre in her body seemed to be on fire. She grimaced in pain, while memories flooded her mind.

Sammy began to cry. She cried without making a sound, tracing with her finger the pain she felt. She felt a knotty cramp collect in the small of her back. And then, a weird tightening from her gut all the way up to her chest. The pain travelled as she fought it bravely, almost buried under the avalanche of unwelcome memories. She tried to focus her mind on happy thoughts, on her children. She had seen a documentary on BBC where a mountaineer trapped in inclement weather had survived a snowstorm, waiting for help by focusing on positive thoughts, on the warm welcome he hoped to get on his return.

But her pain just got worse. Sammy wasn't sure if it was physical. Yet it seemed to spread, tearing down her back and pressing into her tailbone. Through the pain, she saw in her mind's eye her son lying on the hospital bed.

'I will find out who did this to you, my son. I promise you that,' she resolved. 'And then they will have to deal with me!'

6

*'It's your road and yours alone. Others may walk it with you
but no one can walk it for you.'*

– RUMI

A morning call to the doctor on duty assured Sammy that Aksh was better and had had a restful night.

Rishi called soon after. She heard his firm voice as he spoke and addressed her concerns. 'Sammy, Aksh is responding well to medication and might soon be taken off the oxygen, perhaps even within the next few hours. So stay calm, okay. You have to look after yourself, too. The past few days have been stressful. You need to rest, if not for yourself then for Aksh. Go out, breathe a little, invigorate yourself and only then come to the hospital. Spend time with Tara ... I'm sure you two have much to catch up on.'

No amount of arguing helped Sammy wriggle her way out of this one because Rishi had always been firm in his ways and he was being adamant now. Besides, what Rishi said did make sense. So after another minute of arguing, she hung up and breathed her first sigh of relief in what seemed like ages. She was happy, very happy. Her son was getting better and her daughter was with her. It would also be good for Rishi to spend time with Aksh.

And Sammy had a mission. She wanted to get to the bottom of what had happened in school the day Aksh was beaten up.

Sitting next to a sleeping Tara, Sammy flicked open her iPad. Absent-mindedly, she typed Peasant P and Google came up with so many related options that she was surprised. There was a Lavish P, a Pleasant P and so on ... but no Peasant P. Lavish P drew her attention. Image after image opened up on Instagram with photograph after photograph of wealth that made her feel poor. There was this cocky young man standing next to a gold Rolls Royce and sniggering. His toilet seat cover too was made of gold. Another with him tying hundred-dollar bills to balloons and letting them fly off. His idea of charity.

Repulsed, yet intrigued, she read his posts. They were arrogant, smug and obnoxious. He called Madonna a peasant and Justin Bieber a loser. According to another post, he claimed that the band members of One Direction were transvestites masquerading as boys.

And then she saw another post on her son's account and froze. Aksh's bucket list. Why, just why, would her son think of dying at his young age? She accidentally opened a link that made her laugh despite the worry. The world's liveliest man on YouTube she discovered on reading the post. And Aksh's comment, 'He made millions laugh but got depressed; what seems is often not, bro.'

Another comment that baffled her. 'Go pro, Aksh. Get into online streaming. Get noticed by the Line sponsors. Remember, ranking matters. You can make cash, lots of it bro.'

Why would Aksh need money? What had he been up to? What is the short caster he is referring to? And how is her Aksh the coolest short whatever? League of Legends? What was that? Cinema Sins … she searched for Aksh's name and saw him demolish a movie, listing all that was wrong with it.

She acknowledged for the first time to herself that there was a chasm separating their lives. That it was the virtual world that gave her son a sense of being someone. It was his escape. That it was a YouTuber who he looked up to and not any of the icons she had admired while growing up. It was the 'hits' and 'likes' that mattered most to him and not her reassurances.

How? Just when did all this begin? How did she miss it?

The world was a different place and times had changed. Sammy suddenly felt old.

She kissed her daughter on the forehead, picked up the blanket Tara had, as always, kicked off, and whispered 'Good morning!' to the sleeping girl. The sun shone through the glass window, just a glimpse of it now as it seemed to wink before it disappeared behind a cloud. Sammy smiled, lingering in the room. She looked at Tara and noticed how grown-up she seemed. And yet there was something soft, serene and childlike about her. Perhaps a gentleness that Sammy had not seen since she had left to study abroad.

Then she noticed a photograph clutched tightly in Tara's hand. Her heart sang and cried at the same time! An old habit; Tara, when they still lived together in one home, often slept with her mother's photograph under her pillow when Sammy had to travel for work. On being asked why she did so, a wide-eyed Tara would explain that it made her feel close to Sammy, especially at night.

Sammy was glad that some things had not changed. Tara might be far away but she was still her daughter and still found comfort in her mother's photograph. Gently opening Tara's clenched fist, Sammy took out the photograph and turned it around. It was an old photograph taken a lifetime ago. It was of her when she, Sammy, was a little girl playing in a courtyard.

Some memories are good and some are not. Tara's childhood had been joyful despite the trouble between her parents. Sammy and Rishi had tried to keep the children out of their battle. But Sammy herself had issues to deal with from an earlier generation. Matters left unanswered and relationships that had drifted away. There were too many experiences, stormy mornings and memories of abuse ... she shivered involuntarily. Aksh was in hospital but no one from her family called. No one reached out. Not that she expected it to be different this time.

She picked up the papers strewn on Tara's untidy desk. Then she wandered out to the balcony again, scanning the papers in the morning light.

She thought of her fears for Tara. She was glad that her daughter was far away from the brutality that often marked North India these days, the rape and oppression of women. But things were the same the world over. Terrorists got to the World Trade Towers, others ran amok in Mumbai's Apollo Bunder.

Some things, though, were not that different. Women were raped by men all the time, if one listened to the news. But was it more in India than the rest of the world? Or was it that the Indian media seemed to revel in self-flagellation? 'My friends and I cannot relate to the rapes, but I worry about Tara when she is on the road. She says that Thomas Heatherwick's wonderful design and the new Number 9 and 10 Roadmasters in London are great and perfectly safe, but I'm not sure,' she told herself.

She wondered how the world would appear to her grandparents. She looked up at the sky and blew her dead Dadaji and Nani a kiss. The world had changed in two generations. The world she lived in would be alien to them. Her grandfather had adapted to a changing world around him. But Sammy's family had been a whole new ball game altogether. She was a product of her past, having to constantly prove herself to a mother who played favourites. And from there came Sammy's strength and her desire to protect her children.

'Some memories are best hidden away,' she thought, looking distractedly at the beauty outside her balcony, sensing a disquiet even in the gently whistling wind and the sighs of the trees beyond.

'Morning, Mama,' said Tara coming up behind her, rubbing her eyes.

They spent the morning together, talking about London. Sometime in the afternoon, they wandered into Aksh's room, with Sammy taking a short nap on his bed while Tara rummaged through her brother's desk in an attempt to find a clue, anything, that would explain Aksh's cryptic comment about Peasant P.

'Look what I found in Aksh's book,' Tara shouted in her excitement, waking Sammy up.

Sammy stared blankly, taking a minute to orient herself, then looked at the magazine in her hand. An old page from the school magazine *Happenings*.

Tara asked her, 'Did you know about this? That he wrote poetry? Under all that football mania, my kid brother is a budding poet?'

'No, where did you find it?' Sammy asked, equally surprised.

'Rescued it from the bowels of the earth it seems, given its frayed edges. From under a heap of you don't want to know what!' Tara said, crinkling up her nose. Then she read it aloud:

> She lived on the edge of impulse,
> bound she was not;
> it soon became an addiction,
> she thought it would set her free.
> She'd seen life reduced to existing,
> she wanted a chance to dream;
> today's world forces you to whisper,
> it's considered impolite to scream.
> Planning seemed so worthless,
> it's all people ever did;
> though maybe it wasn't precision,
> but thoughts from which she hid.
> Adventures gave her a thrill,
> presented distraction much-needed;
> each time her feelings re-surfaced,
> a reckless action proceeded.
> The speed at which she travelled,
> even lightning was put to shame;
> she decided to burn her past,
> her emotions ignited the flame.

Tara stopped abruptly and whispered, 'Mama, you have always wondered whether Aksh realized what you went through and the many problems. Obviously my little brother more than got it! See…'

'What does this have to do with anything, Tara?' Sammy asked reaching for the magazine, her hopes dashed. 'What is the connection with that Peasant P?'

Tara whistled softly. 'It has everything to do with the mysterious P because it shows that Aksh was more perceptive than we assumed. He was not the little man we thought him to be. Aksh had, I mean has, more depth and maturity than we give him credit for. So chill, there has to be an explanation.'

Rishi had called several times from the hospital. Nothing much to report, he had said initially, a trifle disappointed. Aksh had seemed morose when Rishi walked in, but had cheered up considerably on seeing him. They had discussed the intricacies of the English Premier League and exchanged notes on possible transfers in the January EPL window. The doctors had come and gone a couple of times and seemed satisfied with his progress. 'We need to keep him under observation for a couple of days though,' they had said. Aksh seemed withdrawn, staring at the walls blankly when he thought Rishi was not looking.

Aksh and Rishi had laughed and remembered many happy moments from the past. Of sitting on a balcony when they were together as a family, looking out of the window and thinking they must be hallucinating! A large double bed was climbing a rope past the balcony ... Reality, of course, had a simple solution. A removal company was moving furniture into one of the apartments above theirs. This process always alarmed and amazed Aksh. Heavy furniture was winched up the front of the building using makeshift pulleys, as the service lifts were not quite suitable or wide enough to take the grand pieces most residents favoured. It seemed that Aksh was able to involve himself in conversation and forget that something was troubling him, inside, bothering him.

They recalled Sammy's move into her present home. Rishi was visiting from London on an earlier trip and she had commandeered his weekend to organize it, with the assistance of Aksh. She had preferred to stay away, rather than agonize as she watched her precious belongings sway precariously in the air. Cartons, cupboards and even the washing machine had been hoisted up on the narrow platform. She was willing to pick up the pieces later rather than have a heart attack with the movement of every item. That had been her logic. And she had not been missed! Rishi and Aksh had a wonderful time together and nothing had dropped or broken.

Then Rishi said that he had used the opportunity of Aksh opening up to him to talk about the incident at the school. On being asked about Peasant P, Aksh's face had a genuinely bewildered look. He had absolutely no idea what his father was talking about! Rishi cajoled, prodded and asked in a dozen different ways but with the same outcome.

Aksh had stared back at his Dad with a blank look in his eyes. Straining, struggling, searching for answers. And it was one long, last moment before he turned to his father in near despair and said, 'Dad, I really can't remember! What has happened to me? I can't remember!'

'What can you remember, son?' asked Rishi gently.

Not much from the relevant day it seemed.

Discussions with the doctor had followed. He had confirmed that Aksh's head injury was the cause of short-term amnesia. He did assure Rishi that Aksh was going to get better, but he could offer no assurances as to when his memory would come back.

Aksh had opened the door to his past. 'Dad, get my iPad and look at it! It's in my room at home. I used to write about what I felt. Maybe you will find something there! I hope…'

Spending time with his father had tired Aksh. By early evening, the nurse bundled Rishi out of the room and said that his son would be much better off if he were allowed to rest. Reluctantly, Rishi left after adjusting the pillows under Aksh's head.

7

'Yesterday is not ours to recover, but tomorrow is ours to win or lose.'
– LYNDON B. JOHNSON

Back at Sammy's house for a drink, Rishi and she settled down in the living room. Sammy was worried about Aksh's amnesia, his not being able to remember what had happened at school. She was also concerned about the silences and blank stares that Rishi told her about.

Looking at Rishi sitting across her, she knew that she had memories of the good times but, as she poured the brandy, she involuntarily shuddered, remembering the time when her life had turned on its head. Some of it was Rishi's doing and some of it had been others'. But all that was in the past now, wasn't it? Best left undisturbed, she thought and moved on to what was more important.

Sammy stood up and decided to do something and not give up, not now, not ever. Never on Aksh. 'I will find out and we will sort it out,' she said resolutely. 'Let's look at his iPad. Perhaps there will be some information there.'

Sammy and Rishi went to Aksh's room to look through his iPad for clues, hints ... anything!

'Did you know he wrote poetry? My son writes verse!' Sammy said, amazed.

'Read this,' Rishi said. 'Absolute genius.' He pushed Aksh's iPad towards Sammy.

Every Corner Whispers a Story

The Aryans walked this land so prosperous
Civilizations settled and thrived and grew
Hunters, gatherers and nomads wandered
And centuries later we hear their echoes.

'Firangs' emerged from the shadows of the west
They were strangers to our exotic country
The threat posed was greatly underestimated
And centuries later we realize our mistake.

Sammy shut the iPad; she could not deal with her feelings. She felt so left out. This was a side of Aksh that she just did not know. 'What else is there that I don't know?' she asked herself.

'Did any one drop by today? Anyone from his school?' Sammy asked, changing the topic.

The silence from the school bothered them. Misplaced and isolated conversations resounded in the emptiness of the limited official response. The lack of information created a vacuum within which the approach of the principal appeared to be cruel and casual and nibbled at their confidence in the school. It was as if they had washed their hands off Aksh. No one had come to enquire about him, neither the principal nor the counsellor. Sammy and Rishi had other things to worry about, but the complete absence of concern from the school was troubling them both.

'No one from the staff came, but his friend Jay came with his mother just as I was leaving the hospital. I didn't recognize him at first as it's been a long time since I last saw him but he recognized and greeted me,' Rishi replied.

'And?' Sammy asked. 'Did he say something? Did you ask him if he knows Peasant P? Who is she?'

'I did ask,' said Rishi, 'And Jay did want to tell me something, but his mother was guarded. She said that they only had a short time at the hospital and she pushed Jay along.'

'You should have been more forceful,' admonished Sammy. 'Jay will definitely know what happened at the school.'

She was clearly upset now with what she saw as a missed opportunity. Upset with Rishi for not asking Jay about the incident and at herself for not having thought of this earlier, of not having reached out to Jay in the last few days.

'I know Jay's mother ... we have met at the school over the years and I have her number,' said Sammy. 'Let me call her.'

She wanted privacy in which to speak, more because she was irritated with herself for not having been focused on finding out what happened from Aksh's friends, than from any desire to exclude Rishi from the conversation.

Half an hour passed before Sammy came back to the living room. Rishi could tell from her expression that she had news, information that wasn't all good.

'Matters are quite serious,' were Sammy's opening words. 'Apparently, Aksh was getting bullied at school. He was threatened and was under some kind of pressure.'

'What kind of pressure? And from whom? This Peasant P?'

Rishi had a pained expression on his face as he quizzed Sammy. As they sat and discussed the phone call, it was apparent the reasons for what had happened still eluded them. Something had happened. Something serious. And no one seemed to be telling them anything.

'Jay's mother was hesitant to speak in the beginning. Seems she was scared of something. She tried to shrug me off by saying that Jay was not with Aksh when he got beaten up. I pressed her, insisting that Jay would nevertheless know something, would have spoken to other kids. The children at school would definitely know what was happening.

'I drew upon our old association through the school, about how close Aksh and Jay had been since early childhood ... and then I heard her voice change. Almost in a whisper – I had to strain to hear her – almost as if she were afraid of being overheard in her own home. She finally told me something. It seems that there is a gang of bullies and schoolboy thugs. Aksh has got involved with these kids in some way. There was a fight. And that was all that she was willing to say. I just can't believe it!' exclaimed Sammy. 'Aksh can't be running with the rowdy crowd at the school ... he is not that type. Not my son! This is just not right,' she said firmly, more to herself than to Rishi. 'Not right at all!'

Then turning to Rishi, she went on, 'Jay's mother was caring but scared of something. She went on and on about the school and how wonderful it is. Something just doesn't seem right! Jay definitely knows more ... I am sure of it.'

She could not help her rising anger. 'And if the school is so wonderful then why is my son in hospital?' Sammy spat out. 'Just a week ago my life was normal. The world spun happily on its axis as I chased my deadlines. It is lovely having Tara and you here. I had hoped we could spend time with Tara, discuss her summer apprenticeships, catch up on your news from London. At long last, life would be normal, despite everything. We had moved on…'

And then more softly, Sammy added, 'My brain can compartmentalize, Rishi, but not my heart. My heart breaks every time I look at my son while my brain flares up, pushing me to find out what happened. I don't know what to do. I want to murder the son-of-a-bitch who did this to him,' she said ending angrily, biting her quivering lip.

She could see that Rishi was equally disturbed and angry. He kept muttering threats to the unknown assailants under his breath. They spoke for a while, trying to calm each other down. In the end, they sat together in silence, not knowing what to do, frustrated at not having a target for their emotions.

Sammy's apartment had a large wrap-around balcony that overlooked the golf course, with its artificial lake and a wooded area in one corner. It was an oasis in the concrete, urban sprawl that Gurgaon had become. She wanted to be by herself, so there she went, on to the balcony to look out aimlessly, to think and plan.

Looking through the half-closed door a while later, she saw Rishi slumped, having fallen asleep in front of the television set.

Too tired to bother going in, she sat in the balcony, drawn into memories and events of the past. Sammy was exhausted but could not sleep. She could constantly hear her heart pounding in her ears these days. Naturally, for her Aksh was in hospital.

From her vantage point she could see the metro whiz past in the distance, matching the restlessness of her racing mind. There were cars on the street heading towards the nearby town of Faridabad as they skirted the golf course ... she saw herself in their hurry, her insomniac self. Sammy looked at the flashes of taillights on the road much like frantic strobes of flashing red and orange. Vehicles pulsing nervously as they waited at the traffic signal, their constant twitching and movement telling their story.

Sammy smiled wryly. 'The city I live in is ill, along with me,' she told herself aware of the irony. 'We would both be diagnosed with *Agrypnia excitata* because we are constantly trying to chase sleep.'

'Using big words now, are we, Mama?' Aksh would have teased her.

'*Agrypnia excitata*,' she would tell her son, 'is a rare genetic condition characterized by severe sleep disorder and anxiety. I remember reading about it.' It was an appropriate depiction of the restlessness she felt now, an apt description for the city she lived in. The millennium city, a city that was always awake, always anxious. A city that never ever slept. 'Like me these days,' she thought.

Aksh would cheekily tell her, 'Mama you have *uhtceare*! I know big words, too. You lie awake worrying before dawn. So you have uht ... whatever.' Then they would giggle together.

But her Aksh was not there with her on the balcony to tease her and to laugh with her.

'Must go to bed,' she told herself and got up. Rishi was fast asleep where she had left him, though his rest also seemed disturbed. She adjusted the cushions under his head and covered him with a blanket, not caring whether he remained there or returned to the hotel. Reaching her room, she sat on the bed unable to sleep and heard the sounds of life all around her, unaffected by the fact that, for her, everything had changed so dramatically in such a short time.

There was a young couple who lived almost directly below her apartment. They threw lavish, loud parties regularly. Saturday night, as was the case tonight, was special and the guests flowed out into the outdoor seating till early hours of the morning. Sammy could hear glasses breaking; she imagined waitresses colliding as they rushed to serve impatient guests. She heard the clinking of champagne flutes, celebrations of events or victories, and much bonhomie. This had bothered her at first, when she had just moved in, but she now welcomed the optimism and joy. Happiness around her was a balm for her troubled soul and broken heart. There was the present, with her son struggling in hospital and there was the past, the betrayals and fights of the life she had left behind.

But sleep, eventually and mercifully, did come.

Sunday morning. Rishi had left some time during the night. Walking to the balcony again, she sat down on her favourite chair, wrapped in a fleece blanket to ward off the cold. It was freezing but the balcony was where she wanted to be. Lost in thought, she did not notice the rays of dawn break on to the sky. She saw, without quite noticing, the golden glow of the streetlights merging into an apricot hue through the fog, a hint of colour preceding the sunrise. Sammy sat through the changing tones of the early morning which was as usual more white than blue, transfixed as she reflected on the past few years, grateful for her freedom. Her life with its new privileges was a blessing and she was acutely aware that it had come about because she had taken that one big decision, the decision to break free from all those who held her back.

She wondered whether people make choices, whether it really is about free will or whether the opposite was true; that in fact choices shaped who we are and defined who we became.

The bell rang and she went to open the door for Rishi. Time to get on with the day. She went into the kitchen and made two cups of coffee and joined Rishi, handing him a cup.

He had gone to the family room and was watching the morning news telecast, as was his habit. Meaningless violence on the news as always! A Saudi Arabian spokesman was defending a controversial verdict sentencing a nineteen-year-old gang rape victim to two hundred lashes and six months in jail. Something about an appeal filtered through. 'Lucky woman,' thought Sammy, for getting an appeal in the Saudi General Court. But horror of horrors! The original verdict had been ninety lashes that were more than doubled on appeal.

The news seemed to suggest an international outcry. Sammy had seen it all and so had Rishi for she heard him switch from the morally outraged speech of a Canadian Minister to a re-run of Saina Nehwal winning another major badminton championship.

Sammy looked out of the French windows, out into the nothingness in front of her, into the vast yawning horizon as it stretched below her. She watched the first birds fly across the skyline.

There was something on his mind. He too had been deep in thought through the night. Tentatively, he broached the subject of his role in Aksh's life. 'Maybe I am to blame for Aksh becoming rowdy. I always thought that quality time with Aksh was better than being with him 24x7 through the year.

After all we had our problems. I was an absentee, a missing, long-distance father ... but I never knew Aksh had problems. You coped so well and he seemed so happy! Maybe that was a front and perhaps I am responsible for his being unsettled,' Rishi said looking over the rim of his coffee cup.

'I wish I had the answers,' Sammy responded tiredly. 'I am questioning everything. I am trying to comb through memories to find a clue.'

And then after an awkward silence, Sammy added, 'Let us take one day at a time. Let Aksh heal. Let us get to the bottom of this awful incident. One day at a time.'

They sat silently for a while and as if acknowledging that saying anything more at this moment would be inappropriate, Sammy got up to get ready for the day, leaving Rishi alone with his thoughts.

Back in the living room an hour later, Sammy sat quietly, neither of them speaking. Rishi was leaving her alone. The house was quiet. It was too early for Tara to be up and Aida came in much later on Sundays; her arthritis had slowed her down considerably. But Sammy didn't complain because Aida had brought up the children and been there for them since the time they were little mites.

The morning smells of coffee steaming, the yellow sunshine streaming in and the gentle morning breeze cheered her up and she smiled. There was something beautiful and calm as she watched the sun shimmer like a golden sequin, the skyline vast and indigo blue. An occasional aeroplane and floating clouds dotted the sky, adding beauty to a tranquil morning.

Everything was so beautiful, so calm, that it was easy to forget how bad things were. Aksh was still on his hospital bed and Sammy wondered what the day would bring. She wanted to forget the past, drown out the interloper that was sorrow. Bring her son back home. Cherish her daughter. Forget the agony as her body had forgotten the pain of childbirth. Revel in what came next, the future with a healed and happy Aksh and a glowing and beautiful Tara. And good times for her, a better tomorrow. Was that too much for her to hope for, she wondered?

8

'Avoiding a problem doesn't solve it.'
— BONNIE JEAN THORNLEY

Sammy had been angry and irritated by the school's lack of response and general wash-our-hands-off-it-all attitude, so she decided to take matters in her own hands. Even though it was the Sunday before Christmas, a note from the school had mentioned that the faculty was present in school for a training workshop so it would be a good opportunity to meet the principal and teachers.

Leaving Tara at the hospital to be with Aksh, she drove off to see what information she could get from the school. The 'Big Fight' as the school principal had called it. Sammy wanted to visit the school by herself and not have to deal with Rishi as well. She thought briefly about asking Monica, her friend and confidant, to join her but remembered that she was travelling and would return only in the evening.

After negotiating the half-excavated main road, she came upon officious security guards and high walls. It was truly a fortress, the school. Barbed wire topped their fences, with tiny security windows and grumpy guards sitting behind them. Sammy managed to convince the pair at the gate that she was a parent, neither a terrorist and nor about to run away with the school's silver, so they reluctantly let her in.

The foyer, where she had been so many times before, was not more welcoming either. The old, upholstered sofas and the grey walls made it appear even more isolated from the rest of the school. A hook-nosed receptionist sat behind an imposing desk. Security cameras surveyed the two corridors leading off from the foyer and a faint ringing could be heard in the background. These were more than the outcome of a security-paranoid culture. It emphasized the school's attitude to outsiders. Everyone who was not a student or a teacher was not welcome, it seemed! It was an artificial environment, remote and cut-off from the real world outside.

'Would it be so difficult to design a school that keeps its students secure but doesn't isolate them entirely from parents and the rest of the community that the students should engage with?' she thought. 'So different from what Tara tells me about London,' she said to herself, 'and this is supposedly one of the best institutions in the city.' In the crisis of the moment, Sammy was questioning whether she had made the right choice in sending Aksh to this school.

The peace of this supposed oasis of tranquillity was disturbed when Sammy demanded a meeting with the principal who, it seems, was busy.

After an hour, the receptionist indicated with a nod that Sammy could walk into the great man's room. Waved into a chair, she burst out, 'Hello sir, I am Aksh's mother, as you know. This will only take a few minutes and I am sorry for disturbing you. I want to check if the school has held an enquiry into the incident. And if there were any other children involved in the incident? Who is responsible? You must understand, sir, that I am naturally worried and anxious to get to the bottom of what happened on the day that Aksh was beaten up.'

The principal sat back in his chair and looked at Sammy. After a minute of strained silence, he spoke. 'You do not come to school often enough. When was the last time you came for a parent-teacher meeting?' he asked, trying to provoke Sammy and establish a position of strength but the woman in front of him was not one of his usually meek and submissive parents. 'We are responding to the concerns of the parents through improved communication,' he continued. 'My staff is focusing on meeting the academic needs of each and every one of our students. We have a new report…'

'Sorry to interrupt you, sir,' said Sammy angrily. 'I am not here about Aksh's report card. You may remember that my son was beaten up at school and had to be rushed to hospital. I am here about that!'

Another minute of silence and then Sammy was told that the school had implemented a new policy that would require parents to be called if a child is hurt. Many schools tried to 'deal with' matters by themselves and it was seen as futuristic to immediately communicate with parents in such situations. And, in any case, hadn't the school 'met its responsibilities by sending the boy to the hospital?'

Sammy was doing her best to keep her temper in check but it was getting increasingly difficult. She spoke as calmly as she could, clenching her fist under the table to control her natural instinct to get up and slap the principal. Sammy was glad that Rishi was not with her because he was quite short-tempered and she needed to maintain her cool if she wanted information. Rishi would have knocked out the condescending, smug school head with one punch.

'My son Aksh is in hospital with concussion due to a horrific beating. He nearly died. And this happened at school. And all you can say is that you sent him to hospital? Is this the responsibility that the school has towards its students? I have come here today to understand what happened to Aksh ... why was he beaten up and by whom. And any self-respecting school would care more about its students and want to get answers to the same questions!'

An instant response came with the principal standing up and glaring at Sammy. 'What do you mean that we don't have responsibility and don't show respect? We respect everyone! Everyone! And what do you know about what happened? Do you know that the school supports beautification of the area around us and the Parent-Teacher Association has a cake breakfast planned for Christmas Day and a Respect Day Open House on the following Sunday? We continue to focus on respect, responsibility and safety for all members of our school community,' he said. 'It is trouble-making parents like you who create problems for the school!'

'And how am I creating problems for the school?' asked Sammy coldly. 'There has been such poor communication between you, the principal, and me, the mother, that I wonder whether this issue will be resolved at all! What is it that happened that day?'

Sammy could easily see why teachers, most parents and students probably feared the principal. The students might well feel bullied by the school head himself and be in fear of him. Yet, bullying a resolute parent, particularly one like Sammy was quite different from shouting at a cowering teenager. She stood up to face the principal and said in a firm tone, 'You are supposed to be a leader, the head of this institution. Your responsibility is to lead. Not to bully, not to harass, not to intimidate.'

Silence again and a brief staring match where the principal saw something in Sammy's eyes that made him afraid for the first time. His mannerism changed as he switched suddenly from frosty to warm. He changed tack and smoothly told Sammy that the school loved Aksh and all the students. 'I love the students – all of them,' he said. 'They live here,' he said proudly again, patting his chest to indicate his heart but on the wrong side as he shouted out to the receptionist, 'Call the class teacher.' It didn't need to be said which class teacher was to be called. The school, it seemed, was well prepared for a visit from Aksh's mother.

The class teacher came in, a sweet-looking young lady, who was made to stand while relating what had happened on that fateful day. She looked as if she were barely out of school herself!

'It was a normal school day. I remember that Aksh had come a bit early to school. He was already in the class when I arrived in the morning. I think some other students were there ... perhaps they were practising for a play or something. It was quite an exciting play I am told. Two boys had pinned Aksh to the chair and were asking him questions ... I think he was being interrogated. They were talking about slitting his throat if he didn't cooperate. Another boy was standing around laughing, though I didn't understand his role. Anyway, they broke up the rehearsal when they saw me enter the room.'

'Are you sure, ma'am,' asked Sammy, 'that it was a play that was being acted out and not a real-life scenario?'

'Oh no, no!' exclaimed the young teacher. 'Nothing like that. They assured me that they were just acting. I asked them!'

'And what happened with Aksh after that? What was the rest of his day like?' asked Sammy.

'Well, they had the Form Assembly that morning and then Aksh had to see his Math teacher. There were three tests scheduled, I checked, and Aksh attended all of them. I didn't see him until dispersal time, when he should have been going home, but he had games I think.'

Sammy tried a different tack. 'Are you aware of bullying at the school, ma'am?' using the polite term that she normally used when speaking to the kids' schoolteachers. At the back of her mind she remembered Rishi's irrelevant comment about 'ma'am' being reserved in the UK for royalty and military officers of a certain rank, rather than for schoolteachers.

The teacher hesitated and looked at the principal before answering. 'Well, sir, you know how boys can be and parents make such a big deal of things. Just the other day, a second-grade girl was groped on the playground by two boys. It turned out that they had just been tickling her. We suspended a boy the other day for biting another kid. There were no witnesses, there was no bite mark but the principal took the victim's word for it,' she said proudly. 'And he came from such a good family, too. A rich businessman with a bungalow in Amrita Shergill Marg. We suspended the boy who bit him. He was from a slum near the school.'

'What about Aksh? What more do you know about him?' said Sammy, bringing the class teacher back to what most concerned her.

'Aksh would often get into trouble. Little things. Like, the other day he submitted a papier mâché pen stand as his class project. But when I turned it upside down, I saw another boy's name on it. Aksh was submitting his friend's project, passing it off as his own. But I didn't see him do anything that day. It was mid-afternoon when I saw him,' the teacher continued, 'at dispersal time. Aksh found his younger brother in the library and they both started heading for the bus.' She seemed to have completely forgotten her earlier statement that Aksh was staying back for sports at school.

'But Aksh does not have a younger brother,' exclaimed Sammy, quite agitated by now.

'Oh, is that so! I must be confusing him with someone else,' she said nonchalantly, getting a nod of approval from the principal. 'But I definitely remember him munching a snack with another boy. And I really don't know much else.'

The teacher left soon after, having added little to what Sammy knew. All that she had gathered was that Aksh had been at school, attended classes, managed to eat lunch with someone and perhaps head for the sports field. And then there was the issue of the 'play rehearsal' in the morning, which seemed to Sammy to be suspiciously like a real fight.

'My son has obviously been beaten up at the school,' said Sammy addressing the principal. 'To the extent that it landed him in hospital. And it took multiple phone calls before I received any response at all. Even after I had a response, the incident was blown off as an ordinary spat. Dismissed just like that. I was told patronizingly and I quote, "After all boys are boys". It wasn't until I turned up today and sat in the lobby demanding a face-to-face meeting, that you have even bothered to speak to me, leave alone giving us any help.'

'Well, I'm sorry if you feel that way, Samaira,' said the principal. 'We will try to get to the bottom of the matter and will inform you accordingly. Now, as you can understand, I have to get down to other work as well.'

'It is tragic,' Sammy went on in a conciliatory tone, hoping that this would get her some more information. 'Tragic that such an incident had to happen. But I do hope that there has now been a greater awareness about the issue of schoolyard bullies.'

Silence from the principal. Sammy understood it was time for her to leave. This was not the moment to fight. She knew too little at the moment. What if the fault lay with Aksh?

With little to be gained and having extracted a vague promise of further information from the principal, Sammy left the school. Looking back at the tall gates, she could see the big sign that glowed with the school's learning performance indicators on it. The guard saw the visitor's pass peeping out of her pocket and asked for it. That one gesture emphasized the growing sense of isolation that overwhelmed Sammy. She was, after all, just a visitor at the place where her son spent much of his day, every day. And instead of being welcomed and feeling like a part of the institution, she was barely tolerated.

Hours spent and none the wiser, she thought. The school had imposing buildings, but they were a little less impressive now that she was beginning to doubt the interest of the institution in getting to the bottom of the incident that had led to Aksh lying critically injured in the hospital.

Sammy realized that she, like other parents, had assumed that getting Aksh into a 'good school' meant having no problems for fourteen years, from nursery to grade twelve. That she had no real responsibility because the school would take care of the rest; it would keep her son safe and help him grow. That a good school was like Aladdin's lamp with a genie that would, at the end of grade twelve, deliver a perfect child with perfect marks, extracurricular activities and a football trophy. Sammy brushed her jacket as she struggled with her emotions, pent-up anger, guilt and frustration. She had begun to understand that bullying was immoral, that predators followed no rules. That often there was no purpose, no reason, no provocation for picking on a victim. That bullying was horrible, almost like the scourge of cancer. Her eyes burnt as she whipped off her sunglasses, stomped to the car and adjusted the rear view mirror. She frowned as she looked in the mirror, for she saw her son and not the road.

9

*'Do not dwell in the past, do not dream of the future,
concentrate the mind on the present moment.'*

— GAUTAMA BUDDHA

Humming to herself on the drive to the hospital to calm herself down, she felt that the day hadn't begun very well. Walking into the hospital room, she went over to sit by her sleeping son, giving Tara a hug on the way. She noted with satisfaction that some colour was back in his cheeks. The breakfast tray was still there. Although he had barely eaten anything, it was a good sign. She touched wood and mouthed a prayer.

The late morning routine at the hospital was entirely predictable. A steady parade of doctors, nurses and helpers; one could almost tell the hour of the passing day as they walked in and out in an unbroken stream.

The day passed by but it also gave Sammy time to think. Rishi had some work and would be joining them soon at the hospital. He had called her after the visit to the school but she had only given him a brief account on the phone. She would tell him in greater detail when he came over. But she was no longer sure that going to meet the principal had been wise. Something was definitely wrong. What had happened? Was she to blame for the mess that Aksh found himself in? What was going through his mind? Should the police be brought in? Why wasn't the school providing any answers? And why were Aksh's friends, even those who used to drop in every evening, staying away? There was fear in the voice of Jay's mother when they had spoken on the phone. What was happening?

So many questions and such few answers. She would have to take matters firmly in hand. Perhaps the answers lay at home, perhaps with Aksh's friends, perhaps at the school. She was determined to get to the bottom of this.

Mid-afternoon. Tara and Rishi were entertaining Aksh. So she decided to begin her investigation. She realized that she needed to do a more thorough check of Aksh's room at home.

Her talk with Rishi about her visit to the school had been depressing, bringing up unanswered questions. There was obviously more to the story but the school was stonewalling, refusing to give any information. Gulping down the last dregs of her tea, she called the principal to set up another meeting and, on getting no response, left a message asking him to call her back.

There was a determination and sense of purpose in her stride as she walked into Aksh's room. She sat down on his bed and wondered just how Aksh, of all children, could have been involved in a fight. 'He is normally the one to break up fights,' she told herself.

She tapped her fingers on the polished surface of the wooden table restlessly. A sheet of paper slipped out from under a book and she bent to retrieve it. 'Odd,' she thought. 'More poetry?' she wondered, remembering the school magazine and the scrap of paper Tara had found.

She read the lines, her forehead creased, her reading glasses perched on the tip of her nose. It was a quote. Tara loved quotes but Aksh had always laughed at his sister's obsession with what he called were dead people's words. 'Loser' he would call out behind her and Sammy often had to intervene to break up the fight. She looked at the paper, perplexed, as she clutched it. It was a clue, a key to Aksh's world, a world that she was looking into from the outside. A world that was alien to her but was her growing child's oyster.

Don't tell me this,
sucks for you too.

A killer cannot sue
For the bruises
on his knuckles

or the blood
on his shoes.

Beau Taplin

What? What was all this about?
Photographs on the desk, some old, some taken recently. All four of them together ... A few with just the two of them.

Big smiles. Was Aksh hiding something behind the big smile, she wondered?

The last thing that she would have associated with her son was poetry. 'Nothing mushy for me,' he had often told her in the past. But maybe this was new. Maybe, just maybe there was a girl involved ... and there was a scuffle over the girl.

'But Aksh confides in me. He calls me his mother and his buddy.' Even when Sammy was raging, he would tell her that buddies don't fight.

'Buddies don't hide things from each other, Aksh!' she wanted to tell him.

His iPad had not yielded any secrets or cause for concern. It had only shown her another side of Aksh, his love for poetry. However, she was now focused on his laptop, lying on the desk. She flicked it open, feeling guilty for invading his privacy but she needed answers.

'It's for his own good,' she thought to herself and continued. She searched Beau Taplin and breathed sharply. He had several hundred followers on Instagram.

Instagram was bookmarked on Aksh's Google Chrome browser and it opened directly on to his account. Her eyebrows shot to the top of her head. She came across a multitude of pictures. Some children had posted pictures of themselves, of fun times and enjoyment, youthful laughter shining through the photos to darker posts about their world crashing around them.

Aksh didn't seem to have posted anything personal at all. The photos were those of others, the posts were copied from elsewhere or tagged by Aksh. He seemed to express himself through his curation and choice of what he selected. There was a generally dark tone, almost depressive, in many of the posts in his account but not really enough to worry Sammy. She would not even have been concerned about these, she thought, if it hadn't been for Aksh having been beaten up and in hospital.

She opened a link to Tumblr and read in shocked silence. The messages were full of pent up emotions bordering on the dark.

Scrolling down further, Sammy came across a picture of Rihaan, one of Aksh's friends, and below the picture she saw Aksh's comment, 'Looking dapper, bro!'

And another comment, 'That's how we roll', left her amazed and astonished. What was Aksh trying to say? When did his English get so bad? 'Tuitions are required for sure else he will fail the school leaving exams at this rate,' she thought.

In the silent room, she could almost hear her own heart beat as she leant back in his comfy chair, hands folded neatly in her lap.

The uncomfortable silence and her dignified pose were broken by a rude growl from her stomach. She cleared her throat and called out to her housekeeper to cut an apple for her because she was too nervous to eat much else.

Sitting at her son's desk, she remembered that fateful day, the day Rishi had left them, when her world turned on its head but not in a 'nice' way. Aksh always qualified the phase with 'nice' or 'not so nice' to express his individuality. Maybe he had felt stifled in a home in which women outnumbered the men for he had only Sammy, Tara and the domestic help to deal with. She was making assumptions now but he had never complained.

And this time when the world had turned on its head, it was not in a nice way. 'Aksh, how can anything be nice with you in hospital?'

How she wished that she could wind back the clock, reset time and go back to that morning. An ordinary start to a normal and usual weekday, which had morphed into a nightmare. To have avoided the needless argument with her son, caused partly by his moodiness and partly by her being distracted.

Was Aksh depressive? She tried to think back to incidents that might have given her warning signals. Aksh's decision to skip the football finals and his declining to play in the National Championship had certainly been unusual, out of character. He had always done the right thing at the right time, his entire life. At least his entire life except this time and in all respects other than this one. Sammy had dismissed his decision as stemming from examination pressure.

Possibly also due to Tara's absence, for the two of them were like twins, sharing everything, talking, fighting and yet fiercely protective of each other. Tara was the elder one but the roles would reverse in a jiffy if she complained about anyone or anything. Aksh was insanely protective and had fought many a battle in school for her, punching and pushing guys who had shown an unhealthy interest in his sister. Tara, on the other hand, hissed like a cobra if any girl got too close to her dear brother, raising her head to strike the unsuspecting girl off the list of friends. As she had once explained to Sammy, no one was good enough for him. 'Not born yet,' she had told her mother in all earnestness.

Sammy felt her face flush. She felt like a snoop in Aksh's room, going through his things without his permission. Arguing with herself about keeping the big picture in mind, she opened his cabinet. Sammy reached into the shelves and pulled out whatever came to hand.

Photographs, old report cards, memorabilia and a few coins. Digging deeper she found more photographs, some football paraphernalia and a pile of CDs. Inspecting his school muffler in the light; she held it close and sniffed it. It smelled of chocolate cookies and this made her miss him even more.

She tugged at a drawer but found it locked. 'Damn,' she muttered, yelling for her housekeeper as the phone rang.

10

'There are three things in the world that deserve no mercy: hypocrisy, fraud, and tyranny.'
— FREDERICK WILLIAM ROBERTSON

It was the school! I must have definitely riled them today, she thought.

'I will come immediately, yes, but … but can you please tell me what…' she paused, suddenly aware that she should choose her words carefully, 'what really happened?' she asked.

'I am afraid such issues cannot be discussed on the phone,' the deputy head said. Sammy was ready with a thousand questions but had to be calm while the deputy head continued to speak. 'There are other children involved. There are confidentiality issues, rules and procedures that we follow at our school. You see, it is among the best in Delhi if not the country. We came third in the Education World ranking. I am sure, you understand. We have to be fair. We will give you the details when you come over. How soon can you come?'

Sammy turned to look at Aksh's digital watch. 'I will be there in an hour,' she said, accounting for the distance and the entirely unpredictable traffic, and buying herself some time to think. Why was the school calling her back? She hoped there would be some answers this time round.

'If that is the best you can do,' she heard the deputy head say, sounding irritated as if she really wanted to be far less accommodating but was being forced to be genial. 'I suppose that will be fine. Though it *is* a Sunday and we are staying late just for you.'

Sammy dumped the contents of Aksh's desk on the bed in her hurry. As she dropped some papers, a folder, a splash of beige caught her attention and she grabbed it without thinking.

She walked out of the room, collected her ironed clothes from the laundry room and rushed to the bathroom. A quick change of clothes, some mascara, a dab of perfume and she was out of the apartment.

'Ashok, please get the car,' she told her driver, as she did not want to negotiate the evening roads in the distracted state that she was in. Settling into the passenger seat, Sammy whipped out her mobile phone to tell Rishi that she was heading to the school again but was unable to get through. 'Network not available' sang the irritating recorded message. 'Do the telecom providers know how annoying that bloody voice is,' she wondered closing her eyes.

The traffic was heavier than usual. Visibly annoyed but stuck in the car, Sammy urged her driver to get a move on, accelerate, do what was needed! 'Jump the light,' she told him, and then bit her lip as he ticked her off. 'Madam, at this rate we will all be in hospital.'

Resisting the urge to vent, Sammy ignored him and opened the beige book stuffed in her handbag. It was Aksh's report card and took her back to when her now grown son was an adorable baby and so talkative. Spotting a camel on the road, he had excitedly called her up at her office when he got back home from nursery school. His concern had been whether 'Tamil was fine'. Confused at first, it had taken her a bit of time to figure out that in his baby talk, he was referring to the 'camel' he had spotted bleeding on the road and not the Tamilian office boy who worked for her.

She spotted her son in the class photograph, smiled at the memory, and then read:

> Maths and Science: Aksh was confident and pointed out the parts of the body. He had fun popping and counting bubbles on the bubble wrap and correctly matched pairs of coloured shoe laces.
>
> Dramatics: Aksh laughed when he walked on the bubble wrap. He felt tickled while walking on rice but hated walking on sticky tape.
>
> Language and Literacy: Aksh was made to read short sentences like 'I am a boy' and 'I study in Sunshine'.

And the name had stuck, for Sammy had taken to calling Aksh, her 'son-shine'. Sammy grinned, remembering the fuss he had made about the sticky tape.

Next, she found his third grade report card.

Aksh is an affectionate and expressive boy. Spontaneous and articulate! He speaks and reads freely, spontaneously and expressively. He can think clearly and independently and expresses his ideas in writing very well. His story, 'How the Gorilla got its Tail', was replete with wit and humour.

She closed her eyes and a kaleidoscope of memories crowded her mind. Tara and Aksh as babies. Tara, a little baby herself, was handing her the school bag with Aksh's milk bottle and little wrap. 'Mama, give him back to *Dotor* aunty, send him to the *hopeetal*,' she had told Sammy, jealous of the new baby in the house.

And the many holidays together, his tears when first Rishi left and then when Tara chose to leave, too. He must have missed her tantrums when he showed interest in girls; because no one met her exacting standards for no one was good enough for Aksh.

Finally at the school! Sammy tumbled out of the car in a hurry, dropping her mobile phone. As she bent to pick it up, she yearned to hear Aksh tick her off as he had done a million times in the past. 'Mama! It is a smartphone. You have to be smart with it. The screen can crack if you drop it like that. It isn't Sammy-proof. That phone hasn't been invented yet,' he used to tease her.

Walking into the school reception, she almost bumped into another parent who flashed his trademark smile while running his hand over his prematurely grey hair. He was tall, good looking and, as always, supremely confident in his pink-striped shirt. She had met him at the school over the years, usually on the day of the annual carnival.

'Is everything all right?' he asked.

'No, idiot!' she shouted in her mind. The words that came out were more circumspect, emphasizing merely the 'No.' She heard herself say, 'I don't know what to expect. Apparently there has been a fight and Aksh has gotten into some kind of trouble, which doesn't make sense. He is such a good boy; fights are just not his thing. Just not his nature.'

Slickly Suave Parent made the right noises. 'You know these private schools. They blame first, ask questions later. Whatever happened, I am sure there's a reasonable explanation.'

This made Sammy feel a little better. For once, Slickly Suave Parent had said the correct thing! And was empathetic in the right way, not too strong. His words came across as seemingly genuine. Sammy should have known better!

'Don't worry.' He waved a nonchalant hand.

She heard her name being called out and turned. The receptionist was almost on her heels and Sammy nearly smacked into her by accident. Regaining her composure, the lady walked Sammy down the dimly lit corridor with its security cameras.

'Like a funeral procession,' Sammy told herself but quickly dismissed the thought, cursing under her breath, the irony not lost on her. Her son, a young boy, was in hospital. No place for a sixteen-year-old.

There had been a silent handover and a junior teacher escorted her now. She heard her heels click on the polished floors as she walked behind the teacher, lost in thought. Surely, whatever had transpired would be taken as bad parenting! They would blame the parents. The more Sammy thought about it, the more she was convinced that whatever Aksh had been involved in must have been serious.

The school took pride in being modern in spirit and outlook. Child-centred. 'Was there any other kind of school?'

Sammy wondered. Founded decades ago by professionals, intellectuals and a creative community, the school had gained the respect of the city. It got its students into the best colleges. The city's elite wanted their children to be there.

But there had also been undercurrents and a reputation of a different kind. There were murmurs of access to substances and practices that came with a lot of money and less family time. There were whispers about the belief that cash could buy anything. There had been reports that the school no longer attracted the very professionals, intellectuals and creative community that had once breathed life into it.

The school was liberal for sure and shunned the rote learning, do-as-you-are-told attitude that was widely prevalent in India. Learning was experiential. Given the lack of extremely rigid rules, Sammy could not imagine what might have happened.

A door flew open and before she could compose herself, she found herself in the principal's room. 'Aah, here you are!' was the greeting she heard as the principal directed her to the nearest chair. 'Good to have you here again, Samaira, and I think we did tell you what we could do when we met earlier.'

He dived into an agonizingly detailed description of the recent massacre of school children in Peshawar. What was the relevance to what had happened to Aksh? 'We have beefed up the security, the commandoes were here. We did a mock drill, you see, your children are our children.'

'Why is Aksh in hospital?' Sammy asked, drawing him back to the matter of immediate concern.

'I am waiting for the other parents. We have to wait for the parents,' he replied, stating this as a matter of fact. He reached for the phone and mouthed 'give me a minute'. After which he looked fixedly on a spot on the wall silently as Sammy looked out of the window, wondering if Aksh's screams on that fateful day could have reached the principal.

'Have some tea, please.' He called out for tea as the door opened and a group of people poured in led by Slickly Suave Parent.

The school had been unprepared when Sammy had dropped in unexpectedly earlier in the day but they had now got their act together. Five parents, the deputy head of school, the principal and Sammy. Sitting around a rectangular glass table, the principal on a sofa at one end, two ladies on a couch near him, Slickly Suave Parent on the other side. Sammy chose a straight back chair in between the remaining two parents. The deputy head remained standing, fussing around with the principal's secretary and the tea boy.

Hot water in a kettle, porcelain cups, tea bags, a jar of Nescafe, sugar cubes in a bowl that matched the milk pot. Small spoons on a plate with salted biscuits on another. A bowl of samosas being passed around.

It took fifteen minutes to get the tea service done with, but Sammy waited patiently through it all.

'Samaira,' began Slickly Suave Parent. 'Our kids have been at school since Prep; we know each other.'

After a pause, he went on. 'And we know the school. It has been so supportive.'

Nods all around. Almost a mutual admiration society here, thought Sammy.

'How is Aksh?' said the parent, changing track abruptly. 'Do give my, I mean our, very best,' he said, sweeping his hand around to include the entire room in his wishes.

'Thank you,' said Sammy politely, waiting for the real discussion to begin. She had played this game several times in the corporate world and knew that the main purpose of the meeting had not yet been reached.

'Uh-huh.' The principal cleared his throat indicating that he wanted to speak.

'Samaira, thank you once again for coming today. I was a little preoccupied when you came earlier. And I thought it would be good for you to meet other parents as well. It would give you some perspective, calm your state of mind.'

Sammy almost reacted to the last statement but decided to keep quiet. What did he know about my state of mind, she thought? My son is in hospital, beaten badly due to something that happened in school. What should my state of mind be?

'I thought,' continued the principal, 'that we should all be aware of the facts of the matter.'

'May I ask one question?' said Sammy, ever so sweetly. 'I appreciate all of you taking time to be here on a Sunday but this is really a matter between the school and me, isn't it?'

'No,' interjected Slickly Suave Parent. 'We represent the parent body and this is a matter of the school's reputation. It affects us all.'

Sammy decided not to argue the matter and addressed the principal directly. 'Sir, could you please run me through what exactly happened that day? I got a confusing account from the class teacher I met earlier. It would be good to sort out what happened.'

The principal was prepared for this. 'The events are quite clear. Aksh, your son, came early to school that day. He went for classes I am told, had a few tests and things. When classes ended for the day, he must have wandered off somewhere. He was staying back in school for sports, football I think. Sometime around dispersal, I got a message that a boy had been hurt on the basketball courts. The school doctor reached him first. He decided and I concurred that Aksh should be shifted to hospital at the earliest. We didn't want to take any chances, as you can understand I am sure.'

'I know the sequence of events,' said Sammy. 'That is clear enough. What I really want to know is who did this to Aksh? And why? What is this kind of hooliganism that is going on in school?'

'Now, now, Samaira,' came an admonition from Slickly Suave Parent. 'You can't make such statements about the school!'

'What have I said that is bothering you?' retorted Sammy. 'My son was beaten up while at school and I want to know why this happened and who did it!'

Slickly Suave Parent looked around at the other parents. A couple of them nodded, one looked away. Slowly, he turned back to Sammy and said, 'Well, from what we hear, Aksh was part of everything in this school. And you know how rowdy some of these sporty kids can be.'

'What!' exclaimed Sammy. 'Are you trying to say that this was Aksh's fault? How dare you!'

The principal, who had been silent through this exchange, came back into the conversation now. 'We are not saying anything, Samaira. But you must understand that everyone has their own perspective.' And he nodded towards the other parents.

The next half hour was devoted to the parents taking turns telling Sammy about incidents where the school had supported them, gone out of its way to be good to their children, about how happy they were with everything at this wonderful school.

One hour and forty-five minutes from the time she entered, Sammy left none the wiser. The principal, Sammy realized, was like a walnut that wouldn't crack easily. The school was putting up a front that Sammy was not able to penetrate. The meeting had been a circus, with Slickly Suave Parent as the ringmaster. No one, simply no one, would explain to Sammy, how Aksh, a football player, had been found bleeding on the wet basketball court. Or why.

As Sammy sat in her car, she suddenly realized that Aksh and she were indeed living in different worlds. For Aksh, their home had been the haven, his refuge from the world outside, from school and teenage angst. The home environment Sammy had grown up in had been very different; she had always sought freedom outside the family and once independent, had never looked back.

11

'As a mom I know that raising children is the hardest job there is.'

– HILARY ROSEN

'Or had there been more to it,' Sammy wondered, as she walked briskly from the car park to Monica's house in a condominium where they had lived until recently.

Aksh was still in hospital and was stable. While there was no reason for concern, his recovery was not as quick and final as Sammy would have liked it to be. The short-term memory loss was worrying, for Aksh still did not remember the events leading up to his beating at the school. The maddening silence from the school about the who and why continued, which was making Rishi angry and frustrated. He wanted to find out who had beaten up their son and sort out 'things'. Sammy, in the meanwhile, was eager to understand what had been happening in Aksh's mind. She wanted to know about his life, about the bits that she as a parent did not know, the things he did not tell her.

Hence, the visit to Monica's house, who was now back in town. Monica knew Aksh well and met him almost every day when he came for extra lessons to a teacher in the apartment complex, or to play football with friends in the park. Perhaps she might have some information that could shed light on what had happened with Aksh.

Sammy blinked and raised her hand to shield her eyes from the strong sun as she walked, increasing her pace. The otherwise busy street was quiet and she was acutely aware of her inappropriate shoes. 'Damn,' she muttered, as she made her way between parked cars, her heels clicking on the concrete and slowing her down despite her best efforts to speed up.

The park where Aksh had played football with his friends from the condominium was on her left. The leaves had gathered around the drain and there was moss covering the overhang that Sammy had not noticed earlier. She had not been to that park for years. Not even when her son's team had won the local football tournament. She had been busy fighting battles that she no longer cared to remember. Fighting a mother who was also best forgotten.

As she walked on, she noticed the shabby-chic façade that had been just right until a few years ago, noticed for the first time the peeling pink walls and turquoise blue canopy. The details seemed to belong to someone else's life, something that she could not relate to, she noted with a sense of detachment.

Ahead of her were a couple of Two Tree Estate moms, attractive, slim and sexy but not overly chic or hip, giggling as they walked out of the park. They were chatting as they came out of the tiny side gate, a small child gripped in their one free hand and a jacket in the other, unperturbed by anything around them, taking in the winter sun. Watching them, Sammy felt a little envious of their seemingly uncluttered and innocent lives. 'Not complicated like mine,' her tired mind wanted to shout out aloud.

As she neared the block of apartments that was her destination and the heavy wrought iron gate jangled open, her heart picked up speed and she jogged to the landing, preferring to run up rather than wait for the lift.

Before she could ring the bell the door opened and she found herself in Monica's arms, glad to have her friend and confidante back.

'I know you are worried sick but you have to hold out. I did make a few calls. Actually many calls, and have found out from the other moms that Aksh was being bullied at school, that he was reluctant to speak about it at home and had stopped going to the park to play and that he was hanging out more and more with that not-so-nice brat, Kushal Singh.'

A long pause. The silence seemed to hum with anticipation. Sammy heard herself speak as if from a distance; like an out-of-body experience. It was a strange kind of sound as though coming from the bottom of a swimming pool, distorted and disjointed. She tried to be articulate, to talk coherently but just could not get the words out.

Monica reached out for her hand and continued, 'Aksh was having trouble coping with schoolwork and the teachers were getting tough with him. But we can sort it all out,' she added quietly, as Sammy sank into the reclining chair.

Sammy shook her head and said softly, 'Monica, not possible, not my Aksh. We had sorted out the bad grades, he was taking tuitions and was quite regular.'

'Not so, apparently,' Monica replied, acutely aware of the impact this would have on her friend. 'I have seen Aksh sitting outside, staring vacantly into space on the days you sent him here to study. After all, Mrs Khanna lives in the same building as I do and I watched over him. Not actively but as I went about my business, rushing in and out of the complex.'

And then with a pause, she continued, 'Sammy dear, I am sorry, I should have told you.' Her voice was now barely a whisper. 'But, but ... after a long time ... you seemed happy and the past was behind you, I thought, and now this. Especially since it didn't *look* so serious.'

'Aksh calls you Checkpoint Charlie, because he had to pass your apartment to climb up for his tuition,' Sammy said, smiling for the first time as she looked at her friend. 'How can this happen? My Aksh, he was always smiling. Never a complaint, nor did he throw tantrums. Always polite, so good, so happy,' she muttered, barely audible.

'That is the point! Was he as happy as he appeared?' Monica asked, thrusting a cup of coffee at Sammy. 'Drink up,' she ordered, getting up to snatch her house keys. 'We have to get to the bottom of this. Call Rishi and tell him to stay at the hospital for a little while longer. We have things to do and people to meet. We have to find out what was wrong.'

Galvanized into action, Sammy jumped up and followed Monica out of the house and bounded up the stairs, catching up with her just as she rang Mrs Khanna's bell.

A beautiful young girl opened the door, her face flushed red and her complexion almost polished and shiny. She ushered them into the drawing room, switching on the fans by mistake. Sammy looked around and suddenly wanted to hide, escape from the present problems. She sank into the deep sofa. The relaxing lighting, soft music and powerful room heater blowing in the corner gave her some respite and she suddenly felt optimistic and felt that all was not lost.

But the moment did not last for long. Mrs Khanna waddled into the room and began to speak in an odd, unsettling way. Her sharp, high-pitched, loud voice was jarring. Sammy heard without listening as Monica exchanged angry words with Mrs Khanna. Their words overlapped as their voices got an almost nasty edge and became incomprehensible. It was an avalanche of animosity.

Cleary the discussion was not going anywhere, though much was being said. Sammy realized this despite her strong pent up feelings that came down on her like a dense fog. Mrs Khanna was blaming her, Sammy, for being an absentee mother, consumed by ambition and greed.

'In Germany, we have a term for it. Rabenmutter, or crow mother. I grew up in Deutschland, my father was posted there,' she added smugly and then continued after a pause. 'Women like you, Samaira, are plagued by an undying ambition, a thirst for control, driven by money, addicted to these *rakshasas*, demons, that ultimately consume your children and you. Broken family with ambitious mother cannot sink roots. Pah, I have seen it before.'

Sammy watched, almost hypnotized, as Mrs Khanna shook her arthritic, age-spotted hand around, to cut in and make her point, ignoring Sammy and drowning out Monica's objections.

'But it is my son, Aksh, whom we want to talk about and no other child,' Sammy tried to intervene. 'Do you remember him?' she asked, hoping that Mrs Khanna had it all mixed up and was horribly wrong and that she was talking about another child.

'Yes, yes, I know Aksh. I am not that old yet but will get there sooner than my years because children these days … pah, complicated and with the attention span of a gnat,' she replied, rolling her eyes to emphasize her point.

'Good child but bad company. Quite distracted of late but I did not give up. I talked to him all the time. I had all the time for him unlike you and even overlooked his rude behaviour, his mood swings. Because my own grandson, Biltoo, he … he got depressed and lost a year, he was bullied in school. His sister, the one who opened the door, on the other hand, gave it back as good as she got. But not he. My poor boy suffered quietly. They lost their father, my son-in-law, when in school. One day my daughter's life and marriage was going well and then, pshh, he, my son-in-law, just keeled over and died. Biltoo took it very badly. Girls are stronger you see,' she added for good measure, not letting Sammy off the hook that easily.

She paused for effect and a quick gulp of coffee, before continuing, 'Aksh is a sensitive child, good boy.' Seeing that Sammy was trying to butt in, she stopped mid-sentence, visibly annoyed and made no effort to hide it.

'But Rishi is not dead! Aksh's father is very much alive,' Sammy interjected.

'But you are,' Mrs Khanna said.

The silence in the room was deafening as Monica and Sammy stared at her, stunned. What did she mean?

Sammy leaned forward. She sucked in air and wanted to cover her ears. Surely Mrs Khanna had confused Aksh with another child. This had to be a mistake, a big mistake.

She pulled out her mobile phone and swiped open her photo gallery, showing Aksh's photograph taken just a few short weeks earlier. Every cell in Sammy's body wanted to hear that it was a case of mistaken identity – wrong child, simple.

Passion, anger, fear, depression, anguish, dejection ... her confused feelings gushed out in a burst of words. Questions poured forth in a firm voice.

But Mrs Khanna's replies did not change. 'No, Aksh was not regular. He did not complete his assignments, covering it up with lame excuses. He told me that he could not speak with you and hated German ... that you forced him to study. That he was under tremendous pressure since his sister went abroad to study. That you want him to follow in her footsteps, to be like her. That you will not hear of his ambition to play football professionally and to study at the United World College (UWC) because you want him near you. That you do not see his misery because you are so determined that your children get the right qualifications. That you see life in a particular way and will not budge.'

'So,' she concluded, almost triumphantly, 'you are dead to him because you are snuffing out his dreams.'

And then, easing off a little, Mrs Khanna muttered, 'Of what use is money and a career if you don't know what your son wants. It's not about you and your challenges and your future! He is not a child any more. He is not an extension of your dreams any more, he has his own. If he is hailed as the next Math genius, the new Ramanujan, you will bask in the glory of being the force behind his intellect. But that is exactly my point; it is criminal to push children to realize one's half-lived dreams. The child suffers and grows up with a complex. You have to realize that and acknowledge his right to be different. The problem with all you working women is that you have no time for your husband, family, in-laws or even your children. Tell me; tell me when did you last see your own mother? Your father?'

She asked Sammy pointedly, 'Do you even know where they are?' Her question was almost menacing in its tone and Sammy looked away.

Sammy listened dumbfounded, in silence, suffering and raging. She felt let down again by life and by her circumstances, feeling an acute sense of betrayal and abject despair tinged with anger for being judged. For being reduced to a stereotype, a character in a box.

And looking up, she asked, 'Did Aksh tell you this? Is that what the problem is?'

'There is no need for Aksh to tell me. I listen when he doesn't speak. I taught him for two years but he never mentioned his Nana-Nani or any other relative. You tell me, what shall I make of it? He was quiet but his silence spoke when his friends showed their birthday gifts, video games given by a fond uncle, holiday with a cousin. I got the impression that all is not well with his father. What can you expect from a working mother? Always away ... leaving children with servants! Throwing money at them, buying gifts but always too busy to have a conversation. Poor Aksh.'

Sammy sat there rooted to the spot as though the sofa had been glued to her backside. She heard the refrigerator in the corner hum. Her thoughts raced, her heart missed many a beat. She wanted to argue, to protest, but could not, as Mrs Khanna hammered her point home by throwing one unfinished tuition assignment after another on the table.

She felt torn by Mrs Khanna's expression of Aksh's feelings. His helplessness and alienation clawed at her heart. His turmoil. His questions. His searching. His quest to find his own little space in the world. His unique calling, different from that of Tara and distinct from her ambition for him.

Monica cleared her throat to speak. Her words, meant to steady Sammy, disturbed her even more. 'The problem in the marriage was Rishi, Mrs Khanna, and not Sammy. I know!'

'Why? Just why did Aksh not tell me?' Sammy asked with wide tear-filled eyes, trying to make sense of all that she had heard. 'Was he scared? Scared of making mistakes? Did he have problems at school? Was it his friends? That Kushal whatever?'

'It was you,' Mrs Khanna said softly, dropping her voice almost to ease the blow, but she obviously refused to believe that the fault lay with the husband. Most people lay the blame conveniently at the woman's door.

Sammy stared at her mutely, her pain at the unfairness apparent.

'It was you. It is you; it is his love for you. He adores you and does not want to disappoint you. Aksh told me that you have had enough setbacks for a lifetime and there is no way that you can cope with more.'

The room seemed to shrink and Sammy felt uncomfortable and flushed. Her face was red-hot with emotion and her eyes welled up with tears. Brushing her eyes with one hand, she reached out for a sip of the untouched, now cold, coffee.

'Poor Aksh, my little son-shine,' she said, her voice full of emotion.

She was filled with a sudden burst of savage self-loathing. Why? Why this and Why now? It felt wrong. This was the time when she was out of the tunnel of problems and more settled in her life. So why? Just why? 'God, will you not let me be? Why? Give me a break, God,' she screamed silently, letting go of herself. Her self-control dissolved as she looked at the sympathetic but unyielding face of the tuition teacher. She remembered the argument with Tara the night before which had resulted in her daughter banging the door and stomping off in a huff. 'It is not about you! Stop being self-centred,' Tara had shouted over her shoulder. 'It is about Aksh, about how he coped.'

She had been judged and found wanting. She had joined the tribe of aggressive parents who pushed their children, wanting to live their dreams through their reluctant children. Often hoping to realize their over-vaulting life ambitions by pushing their children. Their uptight concerns about what other people thought had seemed such a waste of energy to Sammy and she had decried it until now. Sammy felt hopeless, as though she had lost out having spent life in the dark shadows of what could possibly have been a different life, albeit a happier one.

Wasn't Sammy an advocate for just the opposite? She had worked hard for her children. 'Your story will be different,' she had told them. And yet, she found herself back again where she had started, in an abyss of despair. She felt rootless much like refugees displaced from their homes did; but the irony was that she felt so in her own home. This was her creation; this mess was hers alone. This was what she deserved for trying to live life on her own terms against the established norms. It was the cost of freedom, of an independent life. Her shoulders hunched as if she was weighed down by her guilt.

Monica held out her arms uselessly as if she wanted to pat Sammy's life back into place but they were separated by something too enormous to be crossed. 'The most difficult decision in life to learn,' Sammy's soul cried out, 'was which turn to take and which to avoid.'

Monica nudged Sammy and they found themselves out in the lobby, and took the lift in silence to her apartment.

The two friends were alone and Monica tried to talk, but Sammy turned on her with a sharp remark. 'Leave me, let me be,' she sobbed, her pain apparent.

But Monica did not give up; she stood firm. She read out a Facebook post saved on her mobile phone.

> There are a lot of things in life that will drag you down and make it almost impossible to get back up again but you have to find the courage within yourself to pick up the pieces and carry on. It doesn't matter what happened yesterday, only today and tomorrow matter.

'You grew up in that Zoo as you called your parents' dysfunctional home but for Aksh and Tara you created a home. Their Zoo, Aksh's specially, was external. It was in the world outside. You cannot beat yourself up. Focus on today,' was her message to her friend.

12

'You want to believe that there's one relationship in life that's beyond betrayal. A relationship that's beyond that kind of hurt. And there isn't.'

– CALEB CARR

Back at home and almost ready to give up on life, Sammy dropped down on the deck chair in the balcony. A quick call to Rishi at the hospital to check on Aksh was her first priority. Once she was reassured that Aksh was well, her mind went back to thoughts of the past.

How she wished that she could turn back the week and get a chance to explain what had happened that summer many years ago when Rishi had left once and for all, leaving them alone and stunned. She wanted to tell Aksh that she had shut that part of her life out. That, in protecting him from the pain, maybe she had been wrong, very wrong. She wanted to shout and tell the sanctimonious Mrs Khanna that she too was wrong in judging her without the facts. Yet, deep down she knew it was not Mrs Khanna alone, the world had gossiped and she had not been spared. The agony of every single woman, every single mother is who to share the shadows with and whom to bare the reality to. So many people make assumptions, so few know the truth.

Sammy kept long hours at work but this was something that Aksh was accustomed to. He and Tara had known no other life ever since their parents had divorced. The last few years had been just Sammy and Aksh, secure in their love and friendship, knowing that they were there for each other.

At times Sammy wondered whether Aksh missed Rishi, even though Sammy had tried to plug the holes and be both mother and father to her now teenage son. Her concern had become even greater after Tara had left to live with her Dad because Aksh was now alone. He appeared to cope very well!

Instead, she thought, he was really running with the wild crowd. She needed to get to the bottom of it and she had a thread to pull on. A name. Kushal Singh.

The name was familiar, she thought. Perhaps she knew the family? Monica had done some digging … she might know.

An immediate call to Monica followed.

'Yeah, I did ask around and Aksh did spend a lot of time with this guy Kushal. Mrs Khanna told me about him and some of the moms in the colony know his mother. Not very well, but they've met. She's one of these society types and filthy rich. Used to be stunningly beautiful, I am told. Her looks beguile, she is almost doe-like and innocent. Not that she was innocent! She had many men around her all the time, if the gossip in my locality is to be believed. Somewhere along the way she got pregnant with Kushal. Now she lives with an older man – Santri they call him but I am not sure if that is his given name. Apparently, he dotes on her but she still plays the field. I don't know much more,' finished Monica, 'but am told that Kushal is a bully and a spoilt brat. And Aksh and he have been seen together many times.'

Sammy was a successful corporate woman but she had never had much time for the Delhi cocktail party circuit, preferring to spend time with her friends and her children instead. Now it seemed that Aksh had gotten himself involved with the crowd she had avoided, had become one of the arrogant, spoilt kids of Delhi-Gurgaon.

And to think that he was so different at home and that Sammy had never picked up on this side of his character!

Perhaps she should go and meet Kushal's mother, thought Sammy. And who better to look to for an introduction than Maasi ji!

Sammy smiled to herself, remembering her childhood and the hours she spent with her favourite aunt sitting on the veranda, perched on their favourite chowki, gossiping for hours. Maasi ji was the universal *maasi ji*. She was Sammy's father's unmarried sister who lived in the family house, though normally one would address one's mother's sister as maasiji. Sammy had known for a long time that she had suffered at the hands of her mother, ridiculed for being unmarried and for being an insufferable burden. So Maasi ji understood Sammy and empathized with her.

Maasi ji was quite the society woman herself. She knew everyone in town and was at all the important parties. She would know who Santri and his wife were.

'Hello? Maasi ji … yes, yes … I am well but Aksh is in hospital. He was beaten up in school.' Pause. 'He is slowly getting better.' Another pause. Listening a bit, she spoke again in response when Maasi ji asked if she knew how Aksh had come to being beaten up. 'No, no ... don't know yet how it happened,' she said, walking out on to the balcony but the call dropped. Sammy dialled once, twice, but could not get through.

Trnng! Sammy's mobile phone broke her reverie. Jumping up, she grabbed it from the table where she had just put it down and mouthed to herself 'Not the hospital' as that had been her first reaction. It was Maasi ji calling back.

'Yes, Maasi ji. Thanks for calling. I wanted to know if you have met someone called Santri. He has a wife who is much younger than him. Do you know them?'

Of course Maasi ji knew them!

'Santri! Yes, I know him. Mister Minister Mantri's younger brother.' Maasi ji seemed to hesitate on the phone before continuing, 'But what do you want to do with them? Not your type at all.'

Sammy explained, 'Aksh has got into some trouble at school and there was a fight. He seemed to be friendly with this boy Kushal, whose mother is the girlfriend or wife of Santri. I wanted to see if I could meet them.'

'No, no!' exclaimed Maasi ji on the phone. 'Not a good idea at all!'

'Let me tell you a bit about them,' she said in a gentler tone.

'Mantri ji and his brother Santri ji. Yes, I know them very well. Evil. All that piety and goodness, tut tut. All a front.'

Sammy stared out of the window listening to Maasi ji for it was unusual for her to voice such strong feelings.

Maasi ji continued, 'Yes, Mantri ji and Sadow, Santri ji, his brother.'

'Sadow?' Sammy asked quizzically.

'No one remembers the brother's name,' replied Maasi ji. 'He has always lived in his older brother's *sadow*. Arre, his whole long life he has tried to jump,' Maasi ji said.

She heard Sammy's puzzled voice and continued in a conspiratorial manner. 'Jump – not high – but jump his brother's sadow and become something.' And then lowering her voice further, Maasi ji continued, 'He is quite the bad guy so people call him Sinister Santri. But for me he is Sadow. Dark Sadow!'

Maasi ji was full of gossip but this was all new information for Sammy. Her bad English did amuse Sammy though. 'Maasi ji, /sh/ so shadow,' she corrected her mischievously in her own mind.

'He was once quite handsome; both the brothers were,' Maasi ji continued without interruption. 'Some called them Santri-Mantri while others knew them as Sinister-Minister!'

Her aunt continued, caught up in her excitement. 'Mister Mantri was quite the rage in his time. Young, idealistic, brilliant, and ready to take on the world. For that matter, he even took on the government, argued his way through the internal troubles and bickering in the party. He joined the anti-incumbency movement and was one of their most famous intellectuals. They were not the motley group of protestors we often see on the streets these days. But then, slowly, he changed. Time does that to people. No one escapes the corruption caused by time. Even idealism collapses. I have seen too much of life!'

A little wistfully, she added, 'Much like the way our country was transforming itself, Mister Mantri too got caught up with things not quite kosher. Money became his ideal and he used his power of argument to favour whoever paid him. A voice for hire, they called him!

'And then he became cunning. He would find out information about people, use any means possible to get some dirt. He kept files, meticulous records. Not for nothing was he called the Minister of Affairs, Samaira. This was an art Mister Mantri perfected later in life, ruthlessly exploiting the personal details of powerful men. He lusted for power. And women. And he was so handsome!

'We knew him. Your grandfather knew Mantri even better, as their father worked in some capacity for your grandfather a long time ago. He didn't like Mantri, your grandfather; had no time for him.'

'You know, Sammy, for that matter, Mister Minister Mantri had an affair with your mother!'

Shocked silence from an embarrassed Sammy and Maasi ji knew she had said too much. Quietly ending the phone conversation, Sammy sat down, too disturbed to think clearly.

Her mother! Her long dead mother had an affair with this Mantri ji.

Who, just who, were these people that Aksh had got himself involved with thought Sammy in near despair.

13

'They always say time changes things, but you actually have to change them yourself.'

– ANDY WARHOL

Back at the hospital, Sammy was still trying to call people, other parents of kids at Aksh's school, trying to find out what her son's life outside home had been like. The phone calls kept dropping on her mobile, so, irritated, she walked out of the hospital to hopefully get a better signal when an orange Ford almost ran her over. An agitated Sammy stomped to the car a few yards away and banged on the window.

The window slid down and the driver was not an aggressive lout as Sammy had expected but a plump woman. A familiar figure with dark skin, a sparkly oversized diamond nose ring and hastily applied mascara.

'Oh my God! Maasi ji!' Sammy exclaimed, reaching out to clutch her extended hand.

'For that matter, hello, I had to come to see the sweet boy, all grown up now,' Maasi ji, her aunt, said as she got out of her car and handed the keys to the valet for parking.

Sammy was clearly astonished and stood rooted to the spot. 'You drive? You actually drove here?' she asked, amazed, for she had always seen Maasi ji being driven around..

'Darling, just learnt,' Maasi ji told her, chuckling at her surprised expression and immensely satisfied with herself.

'But Maasi ji, how did you find out which hospital Aksh was in?' asked a curious Sammy.

'Oh beta, I know we haven't met in a while but you how can you forget my skills? I know everything,' she chuckled.

'But you could have come under a truck, the traffic is horrible these days. They should impound your car!' Sammy spluttered, steadying her elderly aunt as she helped her climb the stairs leading to the reception. She noticed the designer outfit, long kurta with cigarette pants and the Gucci clutch bag her aunt carried. Her lacquered red toes peeped out from her strappy wedge heels, as her Patek Philippe gleamed on her thick wrist.

With a twinkle and clearly enjoying herself, Maasi ji updated her niece with her travel plans. Indonesia the following week and Australia in the summer. 'I am enjoying life, for that matter. No worry, little *kharcha* – which I can thankfully afford now that the family property has been sold – but lots of fun.'

As they reached Aksh's ward, the mood changed and Maasi ji stopped outside the door. 'All will be well, Samaira. Aksh will be all right, don't worry.' And then, holding her hand, Maasi ji walked into the ward room.

Bending down to touch Aksh's sleeping face, Maasi ji said a silent prayer, anointing his head with the sacred powder from her puja room.

Visibly disturbed and a little emotional, she dabbed her eyes before addressing Sammy. 'It pains me to see him in hospital. He is such a good-looking boy. Everyone asks me about him, very good boy. Good boys are rare these days especially good boys from Bihar. Tara is so pretty so clever and so grown up. I am looking for a suitable boy for her. Marry her while she is young and doesn't have all those new ideas, *bekar* and useless ideas that the TV channels put into young impressionable minds. We don't want her to become like HER, your mother! After all the genes are there so we have to fuse them.'

Sammy immediately protested. 'You mean diffuse them, not fuse them or confuse them. And, no Maasi ji, no! Tara is still in college and I am not looking for boys for her at this moment. Not at all! She has to complete her studies in London and get started with her career. If she finds someone, that might be okay. But I am not looking around for a husband for her at this moment!'

And then after a moment's silence, Maasi ji continued about Sammy's mother. About what happened when she passed away. 'What happened is over, may she rest in peace but it was all very sudden and your brother, that Ratprick, did not let us see her body but *chhodo…*'

Sammy remembered the newspaper clipping that her brother had circulated to friends and relatives, which mentioned her mother's untimely demise. 'A beautiful life cut short,' it had read.

She smiled as she reached out for her aunt's hand. Maasi ji had not forgiven Pratik for calling himself Patrick after his stint at a foreign university. 'No change in attitude, same stale water in a different bottle, not new just different,' she had said scathingly and had proceeded to call him Ratprick to his face.

'Old age, makes *upma* of words, all mix up,' she had smartly told Sammy's mother not wanting to pick a fight.

She listened quietly while Sammy gave her the latest news about her children, Tara and Aksh. Maasi ji soaked up the information, her maternal instincts revelling in their success. Then, after a pause, she told her own stories about her struggle as a young woman, about the good old days.

Sammy was non-committal, refusing to be drawn into a conversation about her family and quickly changed the topic as Maasi ji sank into the chair closest to Aksh.

The day passed. The doctors had said that the next day would be important for Aksh, as they wanted to do a scan to check for any internal bleeding. The results of the scan would be significant in determining his recovery it seemed. A possible scan of the brain might also be required. The mood in the room was quite tense and strained.

Soon it was time for Maasi ji to leave. Cold air hit them as they opened the door.

'About that Santri ... Sadow ...' Sammy muttered while seeing Maasi ji out.

'These are strange people, Samaira, not so nice at all. With all that bowing and scraping to the gods, the *puja-path* and all that grand talk about piety! And we talk of equality ... They treat their women like slaves. Not that Sadow's wife cares ... she lives her own life. She is Queen of Bridge, arre cards. Spends day playing alone on her laptop. Bechari, no company, everything alone only. But how many girls are lost in relationships to big men, how many?' Maasi ji muttered as she walked to her car.

'Not everyone dotes on their daughter,' said Maasi ji suddenly. 'Tara is a lucky girl and you are an exceptional mother to love your daughter like your son. Give her the same opportunities. Although beta I don't agree with your decision to send her abroad to study. Girls are delicate, hold them close, protect them from the harsh world and invest in the son. But times have changed you tell me, arre, so often.'

Suddenly tired, both walked in silence towards the parking lot. As she opened the door of her car, her aunt looked at her and said, 'Nothing has changed,' and they both knew what she was referring to.

14

'Do not take life too seriously. You will never get out of it alive.'

– ELBERT HUBBARD

The next morning, Sammy woke up with a start. The dolphin-grey morning was misty and she could not see much. She jumped out of bed and shook herself for a second, before rushing out of her room. She almost collided with Tara who held out a cup of steaming tea.

'I will shower quickly. Have your tea first,' Tara told her. 'I have already called the hospital and Aksh is well. I have called Dad and he will join us at the hospital.'

Tara got ready and paced up and down in the lobby as she waited for Sammy. She joined her soon but only after lighting her agarbattis and saying her prayers. Today was important and her prayers were urgent and necessary.

Absent-minded and deep in thought, they negotiated their way to Aksh, brushing past patients, dodging nurses, ignoring familiar faces. To be greeted by a cheery 'Hi Mama' when they reached him. Aksh was sitting back like a serene bespectacled Pasha, propped up in the hospital bed, grinning at them, wearing crazy 3-D glasses that the hospital seemed to have given as part of a kids' play set intended for children much younger than him. The sun's fuzzy warmth filled the room and reflected their happiness at seeing him like this.

Time stopped for Sammy. She stood still and then she slowly exhaled. Her Aksh was sitting up and she wanted to hold on to the moment. She turned to Tara and tried to say something while running towards Aksh. Her words were on wings, flying but not settling as her mother's heart burst with happiness and relief.

Rishi came in soon after, laughed and complained at the same time, joined in his mock protests by Tara. 'You are blocking the way, monopolizing Aksh, move a little so that we can see your son-shine, too,' he said before enveloping Aksh in a hug while Tara kissed her brother's hand emotionally.

'I knew it; I just knew it, Aksh, that you will be fine. Didn't I tell you, Mama?' she asked, turning towards Sammy and finding her deep in prayer.

'Just as well that Mama cannot light her agarbattis because of the fire detectors, otherwise, Aksh, she would smoke the place out,' said Tara teasing Sammy with a big smile on her face, obviously thrilled to see the improvement in her brother.

And then, despite Aksh's mock protests, all three engulfed him in a family hug and laughed off his fake cries for help.

Even the nurse on morning duty was grinning. But their joy was momentary, because the resident doctor entered and rattled off a list of tests to be done and the expected outcomes as he led them out. Aksh followed, now in a wheelchair.

'Where are we going? What test? Why? What has happened to me?' he asked as they shook their heads.

'You still don't remember anything, son?' Sammy asked, holding back her tears while walking alongside him. 'I know I have asked you this repeatedly but do you remember anything at all?'

'No, Mama,' Aksh answered. And then more slowly, 'I remember the ambulance and feeling scared. It was very cold in the ambulance but I was very tired and had a bad headache. How long have I been here and what is happening? When can I go home?'

The doctor tried to explain. In a controlled voice, avoiding any eye contact with Tara and Sammy, choosing instead to address Rishi, he said, 'Aksh needs an MRI scan. But before we do that we are taking him for a routine ultrasound scan today to check for any internal bleeding. The MRI scan of the head is an imaging test that uses powerful magnets and radio waves to create pictures of the brain and surrounding nerve tissues. It is routine and we may not schedule that for today.'

Speaking directly to Aksh, he added, 'Don't be scared as I will be there. You have had an ultrasound so you know about that. We will also give you a sedative when we do the MRI scan. You will lie on a narrow table, which slides into a large tunnel-shaped scanner. The test will take about half an hour and you won't even realize when it is over! It is absolutely painless.'

Interrupting him abruptly, Sammy asked what seemed to her to be the most obvious question. 'Why? Why are we doing this test? You have done one before when he was brought in and so why this test? I half understood the explanation given yesterday, but can you tell me in really simple words?'

The doctor answered her in his detached robotic voice, almost as if she were an idiot. 'We need to understand the cause of the swelling. This happens in car or bike accidents, falls and sports injuries. Sometimes brutal physical assaults,' the doctor said. Seeing the fear in her eyes, he added, 'Luckily, your son is strong and in his teens. Things should be fine and he will likely recover quickly. It would be different if he were an adult. We would then be concerned about a hematoma.

'A hematoma can occur without any outward signs of injury. It is internal. I am simplifying it but it occurs when blood vessels in your brain, the outer layers, rupture and compress the brain tissue. An enlarging hematoma is a matter of great concern for it leads to loss of consciousness and a decline in the patient that can often not be reversed.

'So we would like to do an MRI scan to confirm that all is well. There is no need to worry. It is merely a precaution in your son's case.'

Sammy sobbed, overwhelmed by it all and her eyes told a story of their own. That of a worried mother demolished by her young son's deteriorating health, weighed down by the ifs-and-buts of life. By the overwhelming smell of antiseptic, of Dettol, of tea and coffee, swirling in the air, mixing themselves into an opaque fog of uncertainty to compound her helplessness.

She pleaded with the doctor as if he were God. 'My Aksh has to get well doctor! He is bright and young, and his life is ahead of him. This just cannot happen to him, not my son … not to me. He will fight, we have come through a lot and we will survive.'

The doctor heard her outburst with silence, a bowed head and a slight smile, and then spoke comfortingly. 'There is nothing to worry about, his vitals are good. BP is within the normal range, so is his temperature and heart rate. So just relax and let me do my work.'

'When will we get to know?' asked Rishi.

'It will take a few days,' was all that the doctor was willing to say before he disappeared to take a call, leaving Sammy to clutch a frightened Tara and disoriented Aksh.

Rishi, she could tell, was nervous because he flung his arms around to ward of an irritating fly rather than gently push it aside. His usual way of dealing with all creepy crawlies. It was a family joke that he single-handedly helped their population grow.

'In our village, they say God squashes yesterday's old moon into new stars. He will be well, he is a young boy,' they heard someone tell them encouragingly, in a voice laced with hope. Grateful, Sammy brushed back her anxious tears and smiled weakly, nodding ever so slightly at the sympathetic stranger.

Rishi lovingly stroked Aksh's head and reminded Sammy of the last time they had been in hospital with the kids. 'Remember when both the children tested positive for Swine Flu, H1N1?' Sammy nodded, holding back the tears, but they pooled in the corner of her eyes, shining bright like cut glass.

'They got better, didn't they?' he asked her.

'Yes,' she replied. 'We sat alone in that depressing hospital ward with critically ill patients. There was a stench of death all around, people walked into the ward but were carried out.'

'But the kids got better and we took them home,' Rishi reminded her. 'And remember when we asked them what they wanted most when they got home?'

'Aksh said, "McDonald's shake-shake fries", Sammy added, smiling, and remembered that Tara had wanted Domino's pizza.

'And you had craved for a long warm shower,' he teased her. 'You are the spoilt one!'

'Not at all! It's just that I love my loo, especially the one at home now with the big sink-in sinful tub with a jacuzzi, overlooking the city … sheer bliss!' she replied. Brightening up for a moment, she reminded Rishi with a crooked grin, 'Look who's talking! You ate most of the pizza when it arrived.'

15

'Isn't it nice to think that tomorrow is a new day with no mistakes in it yet?'

– L.M. MONTGOMERY

The ultrasound test did not throw up anything so the doctors were unable to draw any further information from it. They had scheduled the MRI scan for a couple of days later.

Back at the hospital the next morning, she heard an all-too-familiar voice and Sammy swirled around in its direction.

'I had to come, could not help it,' Maasi ji said, handing Sammy a packet. 'Some old photographs; you may like them. You like old things so I thought this may distract you, stop you from worrying. Let me show you,' she said, flicking the envelope open and dropping some of the photographs in the process.

Sammy bent to retrieve them while pulling a chair for her aunt. She then sat on its arm, balancing daintily like a bird.

Maasi ji handed her one of Sammy's grandfather surrounded by people. The photograph was in sepia, fading but he stood out none the less. 'Look at his ears, same as Aksh's ... a little too large, like Dr Spock in *Star Trek*,' Sammy said grinning wickedly and ducking, as Aksh reached out to tug her hair.

They looked at the photographs together. Aksh asked Maasi ji about the people, who looked quaint and from a distant land to him.

'Samaira's grandfather was a well-known and respected man. He was loved by the local people and by the British, who knighted him.'

Sammy nodded. She had heard this several times while growing up. Her grandfather would describe the earthquake that had devastated Bihar two decades before Independence. She heard the story half a century after the event had taken place but her grandfather's voice had quivered at the memory of it as he related what he had seen. Her grandfather had tears in his eyes as he described the thousands of villagers who had come to his door that he had thrown open and granaries that had been made available for his people. For that was how he viewed the people of his birthplace. His people. And they loved him as one of their own, but also that he was different.

Maasi ji's presence reminded Sammy about Santri and his wife. She was convinced that Kushal and Aksh were up to something in school and their actions had resulted in her son getting beaten up. Taking Maasi ji across the corridor to avoid speaking within Aksh's earshot, Sammy asked her aunt to describe Kushal's family.

Sammy would later on not remember Maasi ji's exact words but the picture she painted was vivid. Sinister Santri with his rotund body, a sagging belly, his unbuttoned collar, his loosened Pierre Cardin tie, his short-cropped greying hair, his coarse fat nose, his metal frames with thick glasses. Sinister Santri was not particularly tall or muscled. Not the typical henchman. The vicious, insolent expression, and his strange manner of speaking that shook his belly as he talked, reflecting his hurry to end any conversation.

'Their father reported to your grandfather,' Maasi ji said, repeating herself.

'Look, see!' She pulled out a now faded photograph to show her niece. 'There see – Dark Sadow, Black Sadow, arre Santri! In his knickers ... healthy boy. Has put on a lot of weight. He used to have a handlebar moustache, was quite nice looking and with much less attitude than his older brother. Santri was no good at studies so decided to join the air force to escape academics. But his uncle died in an air crash so Mantri ran to get him out of the academy. Poor Santri lost a year, but ask him and he claims amnesia, because they can't fail or ever be wrong. The rest of India be damned!'

Something in the conversation had made Maasi ji a bit bitter. Perhaps the lack of attention she had got from the brother. Whatever. She retorted with a little more venom on her tongue.

'Mantri or should I say Mister Mantri ji as he likes to be called considers himself to be the only brain that India has produced to date. It is true! In nearly seven decades of Independence, only one of him is enough. Look, I have some newspaper clippings, too.'

Sammy squinted and was suitably impressed with what she saw. It was from the time Mister Mantri had been a minster.

'The government's get-rich-quick man, with the magic formula,' read an article.

'Mister Minister Mantri says India has to move with the world,' read another.

Maasi ji could provide greater detail. She interrupted Sammy with her own recollections of the time. 'There was all-round optimism, great celebration, because he, Mister Mantri promised so much. He had it all planned out. Santri was by his side. They planned to be the John and Robert Kennedy of India, ruling and controlling everyone from the government to the Mafia. All they needed was your mother as their Marilyn Monroe,' she said to Sammy with a touch of bitterness.

'He went about his business with the applause orchestrated by Sinister, arre Santri. Sammy you have to get it, when I say Sinister it is the brother, okay? When I say Sadow it is same to same, brother. Not mine, silly girl. But what was the business? Ask me, ask me,' she prodded Sammy, who did indeed ask the question.

'Such business that brought ruin to his ministry and sunk India into deeper debt,' said her aunt. 'He made money, his friends made money. No one else did.'

After a pause, she continued, unstoppable in her tirade against the brothers. They were, seemingly, her favourite punching bag at the moment. The duo was a symbol of all the ills in society, the upholders of discrimination and patriarchy, of a greedy and avaricious attitude.

'Mister M Mantri and Sinister Santri were always to be found with beautiful women but reduced them to nothing, robbing them of their vitality and mental balance. One on a wheel chair and the other on a cocktail of prescription medicines that she drowns with alcohol.

'Sadow's current woman has the measure of him and controls him to some extent. Sinister Santri, I believe, plays golf now; poor man, always trying to swing ... a deal, a life and now the club. He does what is in fashion, to be in with the crowd, not just any crowd but the hip one. So golf it is now! But he swings elsewhere as well,' she said with a wink.

'Come on, Maasi ji, he hardly sounds the type,' said Sammy, getting the innuendo to sexual swinging at once. 'I have heard they are God-fearing people. My friend Monica tells me that your Shadow Santri goes to the temple every morning, driving miles to get the blessings of the gods, his special God. He has a vermillion mark on his forehead and his wife, trussed up in a sari, distributes prasad so piously,' protested Sammy.

'Arre, sundown and Sinister Santri is happy; no one can miss his slurred, somewhat incoherent, speech and rolling eyes. I am not a fool; I know everything.'

Maasi ji continued her description with the same intensity, 'And he found a tall, beautiful, athletic young woman for his wayward son from his first marriage, did Sadow. Sinister Santri's daughter-in-law beats his mistress-wife in her beauty and sexiness, even though both women are quite pretty. And the daughter-in-law is just a bit younger than his present woman.

'Sinister Santri's daughter-in-law has them attending to her every want,' Maasi ji grinned, oblivious to Aksh having slipped into a tired sleep on the bed a little distance away.

'Her husband, Sinister Santri's son from his first wife, God rest her soul, was found with his pants down, doing you know what with another woman two months after his wedding. Mister Minister Mantri and Sinister Santri hushed it up, paying for the daughter-in-law to spend three-months on a first class world cruise and she came back to a villa gifted to her in Two Tree Estate and a fashion boutique in Lado Sarai. Sweet deal for an ambitious girl! She knew what she was getting into!

'And they talk about family *izzat* and *khandaan*, about honour and respect and virtues. Did you know that Santri is truly Sinister? Took the money to pay the girl from his wife's share in her father's property? But they are the first ones to criticize others for anything, because they are the loudmouths of society, tut tut. Drag secrets into the light and they disintegrate leaving a residue of powdered ash.'

Aksh was fast asleep by now but Sammy was soaking in the gossip.

Where did Aksh fit into this complicated family, she thought.

'Stay a little longer,' she begged Maasi ji, eager to hear more and her aunt obliged, reaching for a biscuit from Aksh's bedside table.

'Get us some chai,' she told the nurse, who Sammy realized had been attentively listening to the conversation, all ears, and therefore left rather reluctantly to get the tea.

'Sinister Santri's mistress is quite something. I don't know if he has married her or not, but she is his woman now. Kushal's mother. Has the man dancing to her tunes! You see, she is beautiful, foreign, exotic and had a track record ... arre, it was well known, her dalliance with a married man even earlier. But Sadow wants her and is like a dog in heat around her, so she can do anything. And Kushal is completely spoilt by both of them. The lady liked pets, and not the animal kind, and is allowed to carry on, just so long as she is discreet!

'Nothing is as it seems. They have fooled the world with their slick talk but I know better. The reality, of life and work, is far more complicated as is this wretched family. And the truth cannot be hidden, mark my words.

'But that story is for another day, my darling. I must go now,' Maasi ji said, getting up to leave just as the nurse brought the tea, a special Christmas eve high tea for visitors to the hospital.

Warm hugs and a prolonged goodbye followed after which Sammy plonked herself near Aksh, drinking tea in pensive silence.

Many questions still remained unanswered. How had Aksh become close to Kushal and what were they up to together? What had been the relationship between Sammy's mother and this Mantri ji? Where did Sadow, Santri, fit in with what had happened to Aksh at his school?

16

'There is nothing more deceptive than an obvious fact.'
– ARTHUR CONAN DOYLE

Rishi had spent the day at Sammy's home, as he had to write a research note for an investment meeting in London and would be able to work more comfortably from her place than from the hotel. Sammy was at the hospital and Rishi had missed the entertaining and informative session with Maasi ji.

When Sammy and Tara returned home in the evening, he was hesitating to tell her something. She knew him well and wondered what he was hiding and should she be concerned about his lies. She pushed him until he blurted it out.

There was a strange phone call during the day. Rishi had picked it up. 'I think it was Maasi ji's manservant,' Rishi told Sammy as she sat back in a chair. And after taking a deep breath, he added, 'I cannot be sure, so don't get me wrong. I didn't like her, your mother, at all so I am not holding a brief for her. I must have gotten the message wrong, seems odd.'

'Get to the point, Rishi,' Sammy muttered. 'What does my mother have to do with all this?'

Undeterred, for he had spent a lifetime with Sammy and they knew each other's moods so very well, Rishi continued. 'I could not understand what he said but it was something about an old woman and that he saw her. A call about an old woman, an old woman found outside the house. Something about your mother. Your mother being possibly alive!'

Sammy stared at him. 'This is not the time for jokes,' she said reproachfully. After a lengthy pause she continued, visibly annoyed. 'She is dead and you know it!' And she added after another long silence, '…in more ways than one.'

'Well, yes, I know and that is what I told the caller before hanging up the phone. Yet, it rang again and I was told that I must pass on the message to you.'

Sammy glared angrily at Rishi. She resisted the urge to set him and the phone ablaze. Her face was a kaleidoscope of emotions, changing colour, contorting with irritation. She stood quietly digesting this information, dealing with the moment. As they stood quietly, all that could be heard was the ticking of the clock. They stared at each other, each caught in a web of life and living. Each labouring with a struggle, past and present.

'Why are you telling me this, huh? And could you not have chosen a better time? My son is in hospital and SHE is dead, so what the hell are you trying to do? Dig up a corpse, dead and buried, long forgotten?'

'I just mentioned what happened. I told you as I happened to be here when the call came,' Rishi told Sammy. 'Guess there is nothing to it. I thought it would take your mind off Aksh for a minute but bad timing.'

'It can't be!' Sammy whistled. 'It just can't be. You're both mad as hatters! You and that person who called. You know that she is dead. Dead and gone! Cremated by my brother!'

Unresolved issues and childhood memories flooded back into Sammy's mind. Anything was possible with HER. She thought to herself, 'Only SHE can come back from the dead. How is it possible? Is that even possible? She died a couple of years ago. Is she back to plague my happiness? Make me miserable yet again?'

Aloud she said, 'I remember watching Oprah Winfrey shows when cable television had just come into India. I remember finding her programmes absolutely preposterous. Especially those in which she united families, where brothers met parents after decades. I was so innocent, thought it happened only in America. It was near impossible in our culture but look at me, look at me! I could be a poster girl for Oprah's programme on dysfunctional families. The star of her show. The very same one that I had scoffed at.'

Changing tack, she went on. 'Anyway, I am not interested! But if he or anyone calls telling you that my beloved Nani is back, do let me know. For her, I will run to the phone. As the song goes, I will climb any mountain, ford any river to get to her.'

She saw clearly before her the one face she wanted to forget. There was no getting away from the thin lips curled up in a permanent sneer. Her frozen look of perpetual surprise and astonishment. She saw the prominent nose, the long strands of hair floating above her as the face looked down at her. A large mass of unsmiling meanness. Her mother. The mother from hell. Not a long-forgotten memory but a smouldering presence singeing her peace. The mother, whom Sammy was trying desperately not to emulate. To be as different from as she could be.

Growing up with a self-obsessed mother had made her tough. Once again it seemed that she had tripped, fallen into the gaps when she least expected it. That is what life does. It catches up with us when we least expect it to and sends our world crashing down around us.

She wondered … could that woman, the woman about whom the phone call had come … could that really be her mother? How was it possible? Her brother had cremated her, the brother who just wouldn't talk to her anymore and who had been obsessed by their mother.

The power equations had been different for Sammy. Why had her own mother and brother raped her? In mind, if not in kind!

17

'Everything was beautiful and nothing hurt.'
– KURT VONNEGUT

'He will be all right, Mama, he will be,' repeated a nervous Tara, as she watched Aksh being wheeled away for the MRI scan.

'Shake the fries,' said Aksh, reminding them of the family joke and now a code for getting better, as he sailed past, hurried along by the nurse, the sedative just about starting to kick in.

'Mama, remember when you used to ask Aksh to get something from the kitchen, to fetch a jug of water, he'd first stick a spoon in the sugar bowl, then into his mouth and swallow, before returning to the table. He is so wicked!'

They were filling their anxious space with anecdotes about Aksh, about his foodie habits and his time spent on the football field.

'Or how he ate granola bars that had nuts in them, somehow convinced that they were healthy and had energy. For him, this sugar ritual was a part of the football training,' Tara said softly. And then, almost in a whisper, 'He will be back on the football field soon, don't worry, Mama. I know my kid brother! He's tough!'

'Remember Aksh wanted to go to the soccer stadium while we were in Istanbul on holiday last year? And he wanted to get the team T-shirt? But I didn't take him. Tara, the stadium was closed. I didn't get it!'

'He wanted to walk on the turf, he dreamt of playing there, Aksh told me later. He wanted that T-shirt so badly but you just would not listen!'

'I wish I had,' Sammy said quietly, her voice full of regret.

Rishi meanwhile had been in a world of his own, venting his frustration at not being able to get hold of Aksh's attackers. 'And we will find out what happened, who bloody did this to him,' they heard Rishi mutter, curling his hand into a fist. 'No one, just no one can get away with this,' he said, looking towards the room that Aksh had disappeared into. 'I will hunt the bastards down even if they are in hell and make sure that they don't get out!'

Sammy felt a chill of fear for the unknown perpetrators, for she knew what Rishi could do for those he loved and the hordes that he could call upon when he needed them. He would rise like Poseidon and throw a tsunami in the direction of those responsible even before they knew what had hit them! The problem was that he had nowhere to direct his anger and this was eating him up.

'Any news from the school? Anything more about this gang? Who were the others with Kushal and Aksh?' he asked rhetorically, not really expecting a response.

Tara, quick to sense the tension and her father's mood,

changed the topic back to Aksh's antics, much to her mother's relief. Sammy wasn't ready for Rishi's interference at this stage.

'Mama, our early morning drive to school in the winters when it was still dark and the lights were just coming on in houses that we passed made the drive feel like we were watching a movie. We would pretend it was. Aksh would not say a word. We would listen to the lyrics of James Blunt, to the guitar loud and bold and watch familiar landmarks fly past. Ambi Mall, the Toll Plaza and Lands' End. We would watch flights take off and pretend that we manned them, taking them to far away countries and exotic destinations. Our take on the game, Name-Place-Animal-Thing.'

Tara continued with tears rolling down her cheeks; she loved her little brother so much! 'Do you remember how we always fought over Pizza Pizza or Fat Lulu's. I knew that he longed to say something to me those mornings on our way to school, wanting me to dissolve the fight we had had the night before, but I would pretend to be angry and sulk, and ignore him. Yet, that kid would not give up! He wanted to be a friend, an equal, so he tried and tried and would never say never. As we turned into the cul-de-sac near the school, he would take two huge bites of his sandwich, offering it to me as we finished it in four, and giggled seeing the fat principal hurry us up.'

Sammy smiled. 'You were Aksh's little rock star, and at times I was a little jealous. Even as a baby, his eyes always followed you around. In his little baby-walker, he would go as fast as his fat legs carried him to you. He would throw his rattle in excitement when you got home from school and gurgle in delight. He would blow bubbles to get your attention.

'As Aksh grew up, nothing changed. He was always watching you for signs of what was possible, how to make decisions, what to like and how to tell. He knew that you did not want your kid brother trailing you in school. So he kept a safe distance behind you so that your friends would not tease you about not being cool, but wore the same Converse All-Stars as you did, the same jeans. He was a smaller, androgynous version of you, except he was starting to like shin-guards and Ralph Lauren,' Sammy told Tara, as they swapped stories to drown their mounting anxiety.

'And remember when he wanted Jenga and kept pulling you to the Pantaloon shop?' Tara asked.

Sammy nodded. 'Yes, it was very funny because he kept saying "Pantloose" has it and it took me ages to understand what he was talking about! I think both of you thought I was a bit mad when you were small. Remember how upset Aksh was when he screamed out "Mama, I love you" almost knocking me over as he ran to hug me and I replied "I love you, too"?'

'Yes, yes! He told me later that "I love Mama hundred but she loves me only two"', Tara said, as they both grinned.

'And what about you in nursery class?' Sammy asked, smiling. 'You copied the teacher, even wrinkling your eyes, flaring your nostrils and shaking your little head, imitating her as you sang during the music exam.'

Both chuckled at the memory, and Tara protested, 'I thought the teacher would be very happy with me but for all the effort I made I got the lowest marks...'

'...sometimes your smartness trips you, my love,' Sammy said, pulling her close.

'And how Aksh was the only one who knew that the young one of a kangaroo is called joey. And we were amazed when we used the then new search engine Google and found out that he was right. He was three at that time. And how he called all fairy tales "Snow What" stories preferring to change them to action stories full of cars and bad men as he cutely referred to the villains.'

'And I tried to sneak in life lessons into his Snow What tales … which he hated. But I am a mother and just had to.'

Tara looked around pensively for a bit with a hint of a smile on her lips. Sammy could tell that her daughter was caught in her own thoughts for a moment but happy ones.

Tara at length looked at her mother and spoke seriously. 'Mama, Aksh is growing up now … he is a big boy. Handsome, a sportsman, involved with things at school. The girls at school have started noticing him in the last year. He's quite the guy! That was the remark that I heard from some of my friends from school who are in London. While he will always be my baby brother, he's not a baby any more…'

Completing her daughter's thought, Sammy said, '…and we need to find out more about who his new friends are. I am concerned about this boy Kushal. It seems that Aksh made a new circle of friends and was no longer as close to Jay and his old friends as he used to be.'

They continued to chat to kill time, to control their anxiety. It was, however, getting all too much for Rishi, who looked as if he was ready to hit someone, anyone, the first person who crossed his path.

They walked across to the kiosk down the corridor to get some coffee.

Sammy spotted Aksh coming out and ran to hug him, pouring her scalding coffee into the nearest bin as she got close to him.

'Hey Mama, I am okay. It wasn't bad at all,' he told them as Rishi and Tara caught up. 'I am fine, guys, and the doctor says

I can go home soon,' Aksh announced, grinning as sunshine filled the room, trickling in from the open window and bouncing off Sammy's heart. He extended his arm and took Tara's hot chocolate, which she gave him after putting up a little mock fight, their little game.

Sammy's little world was humming with relief, spinning on its axis, as she quickly said a prayer. Rishi, too, looked relieved, but there was an anger in the depth of his eyes that Sammy recognized and wondered just what he planned to do, because do something he would or explode from inside if he had to wait any longer.

'Mama, I want you to make me chocolate brownies for Christmas. The *New York Times* recipe with your secret ingredient,' Aksh demanded mischievously, adding, 'I will go to Two Tree Estate for tombola at the carnival next week and then football but first chocolate brownies! You have to get me some today itself, Mama,' he said, reverting back to the Aksh she knew. Impatient, demanding, happy … but not quite healthy or out of hospital yet.

So baking it was that filled Sammy and Tara's afternoon.

18

'Hope is being able to see that there is light despite all of the darkness.'

– DESMOND TUTU

The morning had been stressful and busy at the hospital. The sheer relief of seeing Aksh looking better and being cheerful after his scan had relaxed Sammy and she dozed off in the car on the way home. She slept through the incessant honking of impatient cars, the pile up of traffic on the National Highway and even missed the busload of students, singing as they sailed past on the way back from a competition.

Aksh loved chocolate brownies. As soon as they reached home, Sammy set Tara on the task of collecting the ingredients. They were going to bake a lot of brownies!

Almost a decade ago, when Tara was still home and they lived in a smaller apartment, the children had shared a room. Their space was often converted into a makeshift camp, with collapsible tents and sleeping bags adding to the excitement. The night raids, 'scrounging' for food, were naturally a large part of the fun! Sammy would have strategically prepared their favourite snacks, including the brownies, which had to be discovered and brought back to the camp in triumph. Tara and Aksh would sing 'We're Going on a Bear Hunt' all night long, till it almost drove their mother crazy! With their mini-Maglite's, in their cute pyjamas that they would be embarrassed by the memory of now, the two of them would creep up to the kitchen and into the dining room, grabbing whatever caught their fancy. The fruit and salads, left hopefully by Sammy on the table in open sight, were mostly ignored. The potato crisps, brownies, hot dogs and colas were more to the liking of the baby bears!

Tara had by now gathered the ingredients and Sammy came back to the present to focus on the task at hand.

In just about half an hour, the brownies were done. Sammy had by now sat back to enjoy the moment with a cup of tea. The smell of baking and chocolate filled the apartment, triggering endorphins in the brain, hormones that caused the pulse to speed up and gave Sammy and Tara a pleasantly high feeling.

'Rishi is missing this!' Sammy said.

'He's off "investigating" and "meeting some people"', Tara added. Sammy had encouraged him to go out so that he would be able to work off his anger and energy, but she had clearly cautioned him against going to the school. She wanted to control those discussions herself.

The brownies didn't disappoint, with a crisp, slightly glazed top, to the spongy yet firm centre. Sammy broke off an edge and exclaimed 'Yum!' as she tasted the piece. Tara had been licking the mixing bowl clean, enjoying the batter as she had done from infancy! Sammy sighed happily, content in watching her daughter's obvious delight.

Sammy left the brownies to cool on a wire rack as she pottered around, pleased with her effort. A bit later she decided to change, ready to take the treat to her son in hospital.

'Aida, please cut and pack the brownies when they have cooled down. I will smuggle them in past that irritating security guard at the hospital.' With those words, she disappeared into the bathroom, humming to herself.

Leaving a tired Tara to relax at home and wait for her father, Sammy got into the car, clutching her box of brownies. At the hospital she looked at the imposing figure of the surly guard at the gate to the ward rooms and wondered how she was going to sneak the food past him. Perhaps the people milling around could prove to be a distraction. In the end, Sammy just walked through without being challenged.

Aksh yelped with delight on seeing her and asked conspiratorially, 'How did you smuggle them in?' as he reached out for the brownies.

'I sneaked in quiet as a mouse,' Sammy said with a smile.

'Yum, absolutely divine,' he said, biting into one and letting the taste of the chocolate settle in his mouth. 'These are the bestest ever!' he exclaimed to a delighted Sammy.

'For that matter, it is a mother's love that brings out the flavour. Aksh is right, it is your special touch,' Aksh mimicked Maasi ji and they burst into peals of laughter.

Back home now. Monica was going to be with Aksh for a while, allowing Sammy to grab some 'me-time'. Wanting to do something normal after the stress of the last few days, Sammy was keen to momentarily reclaim a semblance of her old routine. Not all fun of course! The regular pattern was an aerobics class now just a few minutes away! For the first time in weeks she wanted to literally dance her blues away. It was a Bollywood Dance Class and she got there just in time.

Just in time to see her picture perfect neighbours sway to the latest songs. She watched their taut bottoms in skin-fitting track pants, the proud breasts and long hair hastily tied into ponytails with strands flowing over chiselled faces. Swinging, swaying, turning left and right following the beat of the song, their manicured hands cutting delicately through the air. She joined them and effortlessly moved to the thumping music, wondering how many of them had experienced drama in relationships. Jumping and clapping with the rest of the class, humming to the cheesy Honey Singh number, she looked away guiltily as her stares could well create the wrong impression! She admired from a distance their perfect and seemingly uncomplicated lives hoping that her life, too, could somehow be as blessed as theirs. Her heart tugged in rhythm with the beat and seemed to ask her, 'If not now, then when?'

Her face bore a smile, for smile she must, turning and clapping as her face flushed with the effort of keeping up with the song. Would they relate to Sammy's life if they knew it? Would they continue to include her in their perfect outings and luxurious spa dates?

The class broke into groups to take a much deserved water break. Sammy was happy to bury her nose in her cup of H_2O as the kids called it and ignore attempts at conversations since she was not in the mood. She tried hard to fit in; she liked to believe that she belonged with them. She hoped that her secrets would remain curled up forever like smoke, like Tara's baby rubber bands in her secret drawer. And that Aksh would be home soon, the mystery surrounding his attack solved and that nothing would disturb her little nest.

A half-hour later Sammy smiled and watched the class giggle over a cup of latte in the afterglow of burnt calories. The women reaching out for the low-fat fig and yoghurt pudding, a speciality at the club, as they gossiped about diamonds bought and millions spent. She wistfully looked over her cup of coffee and her eyes glazed as her thoughts floated to Aksh, to Tara and to her own unlived aspirations. 'If only I could change my choices, re-edit my life, re-mix it like the music in movies, some old clips with new choices, add a few years subtract many … would it make the hurt go away?' she wondered. 'Would it dull the pain and drown the noise in my head?'

Sammy smiled absent-mindedly as she hurried back to her apartment, waving to the spa receptionist, greeting the concierge while taking her mail from him and stopping for a moment as she often did to admire the elegant and contemporary lobby. The floor-to-ceiling glazed panels with cleverly placed bevelled mirrors that revealed as much as they concealed were gleaming and glistening in the morning sun. Still humming the Bollywood number from her class, she got into the lift and pressed the button to her floor.

19

'It is not in the stars to hold our destiny but in ourselves.'
— WILLIAM SHAKESPEARE

Not having spent enough time in Delhi over the last few years, Rishi felt disconnected from the city and its society. He was irritated by Sammy's insistence that he stay away from Aksh's school but he also understood that he didn't know anyone there and would just come in the way. Sammy would have to handle the school. Rishi therefore decided that he would catch up with the many friends he had in town and try and see what he could find out through parental chatter and society gossip. So he spent time on Facebook tracking down as many old pals as he could find. He sent Aksh a mental note, 'Joining this century, dude, if this is what it will take to be part of your world!' The difference between the generations was much like sifting and shifting sand, passing it through a sieve. He sighed. So much had changed.

Winter, particularly the Christmas and New Year period, was high season in Delhi society. NRIs, expats and returning Indians, mixed with the cream of Delhi society and there just weren't enough days to fill all the social engagements. So, armed with five invitations for every hour, Rishi hit the town.

Early brunch, brunch, lunch, late lunch, 'meet for coffee', art exhibition, sundowners, early cocktails, supper, dinner, reception, after party, late drinks.

Natural questions about London, catching up on years between meetings with some people, polite enquires about Maya, his second wife.

Rishi had moved permanently to London after Sammy and he had divorced and it seemed to work out for him financially. His firm took up a large office on the Great West Road, visible to commuters heading out towards the M4 or dashing to Heathrow. It helped that he had a home in Knightsbridge, within walking distance of Harrods, Hyde Park, Royal Albert Hall and the museums in South Kensington.

He met his childhood sweetheart, Maya, in London. Maya was still single, now a successful lawyer and devoted to her job. She was keen to be with Rishi but part of his heart and mind still belonged to Sammy and their children. Rishi and Maya spent a month in Romania, wandering lazily through the marshes of the Danube Delta with its nesting bird colonies, admiring the painted monasteries, following the tourists in Dracula's castle and lazing around on the Black Sea beaches in Constanta. It brought back memories of their many holidays with Maya, young and sexy in shorts and halter-tops and Rishi trying to sneak a feel when he could in the joy of youthfulness.

A month later, they were married at the Indian embassy in Bucharest, with two local aides to the Ambassador as witnesses and no family in sight.

The problems began soon after they returned to London. Maya was possessive and neurotic, flying into fits of rage seemingly without provocation. Rishi tried to please her, conscious of the need to make his second marriage work. She refused to let him be in touch with Tara and Aksh, not wanting the past to be a shadow on their fragile present.

Rishi snapped. He invented illnesses and feigned depression, trying to gain sympathy from Maya, even reaching out to Sammy in an effort to keep alive a link with the people who were most important to him. Six months later, Rishi realized he had made a big mistake. Maya and he were incompatible as a couple and it was not working.

Divorce number two followed eventually. And then Tara came to live with her Dad and Rishi found his rooting once again.

Just as there was much that had happened in Rishi's life, so had the lives of his friends in Delhi moved on. This was just one day but a day where Rishi met everyone who mattered in Delhi. Meeting old friends, making new ones … moving forward with an agenda. To find out what was happening with the children of Delhi's social circles. He was convinced the answer to Aksh's beating lay in the underbelly of the cocktail circuit and the rowdiness in schools that increasingly became apparent to him.

He air-kissed with abandon, hugged old friends, thumped others on the back with a laugh on the lips and danced with new pals. Greying, but with a dimpled smile, his British accent and clearly single with wealth status meant women always gravitated towards him. As repressed and puritanical as the Indian society was when under the spotlight, it was equally bohemian in private. Some of the women were looking for hook-ups and many of the lecherous men just wanted someone, anyone, for the night. Most of the people were unknown to Rishi but once in a while he spotted a person he knew and often his eyebrows went up.

I just don't know Delhi any more, he thought. And he was even more surprised when he ran into Sammy's sister-in-law, Lola, her brother's wife. Luckily, she didn't recognize Rishi but he saw her sitting drunk on the lap of a far younger man on a barstool, running her hands down the front of his jeans. Definitely not Sammy's brother, thought Rishi, as he went out of the door and off to another party with a pal from his school days.

For Rishi, it was all with just one purpose – to find out what was happening to the children of this segment of Delhi society.

And just as society itself was varied, he found a smorgasbord of parenting and kids. Being overly critical and angry due to what had happened to Aksh, he had begun with the stereotypical notion of neglect from parents, rowdiness and bullying by spoilt kids. Yes, that did exist as he was finding out and in more frightening ways than he could imagine. However, along with the dark side of parenting were the stories of committed single mothers like Sammy, warm and loving families, children striving to build friendships and reaching out for wonderful futures. There were far too many helicopter parents as well, he thought, far more than he encountered in London. Micro-managing their kids' lives, defining success in a narrow fashion.

Were there counsellors for kids in Delhi schools, he wondered? It seemed that there really weren't, even though someone did mention that all schools did need to have counsellors on their rolls.

Rishi's agenda was not to explore the nurturing and supportive parenting ... he was looking for the seamy and sordid stories about Delhi schools. And he heard a lot!

Alcohol, drugs, sex, bullying, discrimination, violence ... they were rampant in Delhi. In its schools and its children. The picture that started emerging was one of children who had too much money for their own good, very little responsible supervision outside school hours, protection through personal bodyguards to keep them 'safe' in the large metropolis.

He heard stories of after school parties, going away parties, coming of age parties ... parties that would have shocked Paris in the 1920s. There seemed to be small groups of children who believed they could get away with anything. Sneaking alcohol into parties wasn't required when you could carry bottles in openly. No one seemed to care that girls wore skimpy clothes, lost their innocence early and that some boys demanded and got sexual favours from their favourite girl of the moment. Drugs of all kinds were floating around ... Molly was the new favourite among high school students, milder than Ecstasy but the rage these days. 'Conti' or continuing parties in Goa were IN, while talking to parents was definitely OUT. Much that Rishi had never heard of.

Entitlement. That seemed to be the one belief among the spoilt rich kids of Delhi. They believed they were entitled to a 'good' life and they were going to grab it with both hands, while barely into adolescence themselves. Sometimes playing on the guilt of parents who were busy or themselves too stoned to care and sometimes with the active involvement of parents trying to appear liberal and 'with it'.

Delhi was in part an unholy mix of influence through its political class, new money, old relationships, power equations and a lack of respect for rules; and it was this that had crept into some children in the best schools of the city.

There were sensible kids and responsible parents in the most. Yet, even they were scared of the wild bunch and the influence of the unruly parents.

Some names came up repeatedly. Kushal's was one of them. Fortunately, Aksh was not mentioned and had managed to keep below the radar of the adults but Kushal was definitely one of the ring-leaders and Aksh was his friend. Rishi was glad that Tara had escaped this hell and turned out to be a wonderful young lady but he was worried for his son.

He asked about Santri and his lady, Kushal's mother. They were very much part of the Delhi party circuit but Rishi didn't bump into them. They were always expected everywhere but turned out not to be where he was.

Rishi came away from the day with a hangover that would hammer away at his head all of next day. He also came away with renewed respect for Sammy. She was well known and seemed to be generally liked. She was clearly not a party animal and definitely not on the wild side.

He was in control of himself as he staggered into his hotel room but collapsed at once, slipping into a deep and troubled sleep. He had seen and heard a lot in one day. Aksh was running with a dangerous crowd. Kushal was the ringleader. And somewhere, somehow, things had gone bad and Aksh had ended up in hospital. Pre-dawn blackness enveloped Rishi in its tight unrelenting grip.

20

'Some memories are realities, and are better than anything that can ever happen to one again.'
– WILLA CATHER

Sammy had spent the evening at home, drifting into thoughts of the past.

There had been great love but a lot of differences too between Sammy and Rishi. He had a strange childhood, being brought up for most of his life by his elder sister. His had been an accidental conception, more than twenty years after his sibling. Sammy's sister-in-law disliked her from the first day. She, a young bride, was an adversary from the very beginning. The differences eventually led to a separation and then inevitably to divorce. Sammy was alone, trying to fill in the gaping cavity made by an absent father for the kids. Not to mention her own relatives who, despite being in the same city, pretended to be on another continent. Her experiences of that time meant that Sammy never quite trusted anyone and rarely opened up, scared to be let down yet again. She hid her vulnerability well.

Ever since the children had been little, Sammy had tried to do everything, be everyone to them – mother-father, grandmother-grandfather. She had always spent weekends with them packed with activities be it a trip to the zoo when they were little, a visit to Dilli Haat in the blazing summer for a school project or a Disney movie. Sometimes doing girlie things with Tara and sometimes more boyish stuff with Aksh. And they had been little … Aksh barely four and Tara turning eight when Rishi and Sammy had gone their separate ways.

So it was foot painting with Tara who had been so small that drawing a butterfly on her little toe had taken ages. It made Sammy laugh as she remembered how Tara had frowned while balancing herself on the little stool to prevent herself from falling into the tub. The tub that had seemed so large in comparison, dwarfing the little girl. 'Just like her,' Tara had told the street artist, giggling as she pointed to Sammy, insisting that she wanted the foot art for both. A curly mop of hair, twinkling eyes, shy smile and a haze of pink perfection. She looked adorable with both feet in the air as she blew bubbles waiting for the paint to dry.

Aksh had, in the meanwhile, played his Pokémon game sitting quietly as they waited for Little Miss to finish.

'Can I get a transformer for my birthday, Mama?' he had asked her one afternoon and had become visibly agitated by Sammy's lack of enthusiasm.

'Really! Is that what you want, Aksh?' she had asked, quite puzzled, glancing at the voltage stabilizer attached to the air conditioner and thinking that was what her son wanted.

She hoped that he would forget about it and be happy with a football instead.

Not one to forget easily, Aksh had reminded her of the promise, counting backwards to his birthday. Ten, nine, eight…

'Mama, we have to get the transformer tomorrow because my birthday is in two days,' he had said with excitement. 'Sure, son-shine,' she had told him as they had dressed for their long drive and excursion to Khan Market to order the cake and arrange the party games.

Even today, Sammy chuckled to herself as she remembered Aksh's puzzled expression when she nudged him into Ahujasons, the electrical shop. 'There,' she said, pointing to a shining black voltage stabilizer and avoiding the shopkeeper's eye. There was no way that she was going to explain to him why she had given in to her son's strange request. 'Science experiment,' she had muttered under her breath, checking the price.

Aksh then grabbed her hand and pulled her into the toyshop next door. Pointing triumphantly at a pile of toys, he said 'Transformers!' and burst into peals of laughter.

Life had been simpler back then and how Sammy wished that she could reset the calendar and turn time back. Back to a time when her talkative son bubbled with stories and pulled her head towards him whenever he wanted her attention, clasping her face with his tiny baby hands and gurgling with joy. It was his daily routine to distract her as she tried to dress Tara for school.

Her eyes misted over as she remembered her arguments with a more grown-up Aksh. This became more apparent when Tara left as well. The fights with Aksh were becoming more frequent and worrisome. Sammy hoped these were just a passing phase and she had ignored the signs, wanting to believe that all was well. That Aksh was well and that they were all just missing Tara, each in their own way. Perhaps missing Rishi a bit, too.

Time had passed and Rishi was ensuring that his work took him back to India more and more often. He had married Maya but what a disaster that had been! Sammy and he had found that their friendship was strong, just so long as they didn't have to be in each other's lives all the time. This worked well for Tara and Aksh, though Sammy felt that Aksh missed his father when he was away.

The worst part of the arguments with Aksh was that Sammy had started feeling guilty if she reached home late. Late tonight, late the night before, late again. Too late, it always seemed, to talk about why he seemed so moody and withdrawn. She became a habitual watch-checker. It became a habit, always behind schedule, chasing life through the day.

Aksh had pleaded with her not to be constantly racing against time, not to run her life by a schedule and a Filofax. He had sat her down to watch movies like *Dances with Wolves*, urging her to throw the calendar, with its days, weeks and months, out of the window. 'Look at the eagle soaring in the sky,' he had said. 'It is never late, it is not checking its appointment book, but allows itself to enjoy the wind, the thermals and the joy of the sky. Time passes for everyone but we humans are unique; we are obsessed with time. We measure it and plan it out in excruciating detail. For we are scared, afraid that time will run out for us.'

Shit! She was guilty! Guilty of being a terrible mother. Where was the balance? It was all a bit too much. She had to juggle her job and be a single parent. There was no margin for error. No support from anyone around her.

It wasn't always about survival. Sammy was successful and wanted to be so. Financially, it meant a lot, but success was also about self-esteem and about the high that it gave her.

The world outside her immediate home was where Sammy found her refuge. The first home she grew up in and then the one she married into, had scorched her happiness. Not just the homes, the women in her family including her mother and her brother's wife, Lola, had destroyed her happiness. Rishi's sister had done the rest.

'I too have been bullied Aksh,' she thought. 'The only difference is that it was done at home under the garb of civilized behaviour. I was weak and unequal, low in the pecking order of the family and had to suffer. I was told to bear it in the name of family. My mother told me to be subservient to Lola and Rishi's sister asserted her superior position in the family. As for my mother...' Sammy shuddered just thinking about it.

Sammy never had any luck in relationships, not even with her parents, especially not with her strange mother. There had been no Prince Charming, no knight in shining armour. Not that she would have wanted one in any case! In fact, her healthiest relationship was with Rishi, whose greatest redeeming factor after all the drama had been his unstinting support for the children and her.

That was then and she had foolishly believed that the worst was over. Never again would the ugly shadow of the past eclipse her happiness in the present. 'Never!' she had told herself.

But she was wrong, so wrong.

She remembered Aksh's frustration at not being adjudged the best speaker at the Model United Nations, the new debating style that had become so very popular in India. Disappointment did hit him like it hits all of us but he had pushed it aside, dismissing it so that they could continue with their lives. Was that an act? Sammy now wondered. Looking back, it seemed too sudden a capitulation after all the work he had put in.

Unlike his friends, Aksh had appeared to be balanced, not given to chasing material happiness. Model cars, friendships, gadgets. Even as a five-year-old boy, he never stopped smiling and had taught Sammy that happiness was not a pursuit or a purchase, it was simply a way of being, an attitude. Maybe even that was just half the picture. The other half seemed to be his life as a schoolboy gang-member. Did she really know her son?

21

'It does not do well to dwell on dreams and forget to live, remember that.'

– J.K. ROWLING

Rishi had dropped into Sammy's apartment during his day out, to take stock and compare notes with her in the early evening, before he was heading for a college reunion drink. They sat together, Rishi patting Tara with one hand, while Sammy held their daughter close. They sat like this, joined in their thoughts and in prayer for Aksh.

They had made some progress. Kushal's best friend, it appeared, was another rich kid – Dadlani. Those two were always to be found together. Everyone was scared of Kushal. Even in a city like Delhi, there was something brutal and uncaring about that boy. His mother spoilt him silly but couldn't be bothered to spend time with him, so just gave him what he wanted. Sinister Santri was Kushal's big support. Rishi had heard that Santri had shown his care for Kushal, spent time with him, all with the intention of worming his way into the mother's pants. Kushal, for his part, Rishi had been told, completely understood what was happening and made full use of the situation, in a way pimping his mother for getting what he wanted from Santri.

Tara had spoken with her friends who still had younger siblings at the school and conflicting messages were coming through. Kushal was to be feared, yes. And Aksh was often seen with him. But no one was quite sure what the relationship between them was, for Aksh had often had fights with the Kushal-Dadlani pair and they just did not seem to have a natural affinity. On the other hand, some of Tara's friends had pointedly said that children in school had started staying away from Aksh because of his association with Kushal.

She had also reached out to Jay, having known him for years. He had been reluctant to speak and it had required Tara to almost blackmail him with embarrassing stories she knew about him from early childhood to get him to speak. He was scared, almost terrified of something. 'I don't want to end up like Aksh,' he told Tara. 'You must understand that this Kushal is trouble. Being around him can get you into big trouble!'

Jay didn't know or wouldn't say what had happened that day when Aksh was beaten up. He seemed to know something but even Tara couldn't get more out of him. All that she gathered was that he was terrified of Kushal.

For her part, Sammy had spoken to more parents and got the same feedback. Aksh was a nice boy, he had been growing up so well. 'But of late…' and the sentence would never be completed.

Sammy thought back about her marriage with Rishi. She had tried; she had definitely tried. But once it was broken,

Sammy had known that it could not be fixed. It was simply not fixable and yet she had tried for Rishi's sake and then for the children, for family peace. Weren't all women supposed to do this? Sacrifice personal happiness to keep the family together.

She smiled weakly. The tussle belonged to another time, a life long past, gone. A time she no longer wished to remember. The scar had faded and time had dulled the pain. She saw herself as she was then, a young bride in the early years of her marriage, timid, unsure and so eager to please. Trying to be the ideal wife, daughter and daughter-in-law. And in the process forgetting who she truly was, what mattered to her and what made her happy. Caring, giving, forgiving, sacrificing. She had been conditioned to ignore and overlook her own happiness because women came last in the pecking order.

Rishi's sister had wanted her jewellery and then her salary. 'Give it to me,' she had said, helping herself to Sammy's silk saris. Sammy had been called materialistic because she had resisted. When Sammy got a job with a big MNC, her sister-in-law chose to suddenly transform into a working woman with a career. No one dared mention that the glorious career was that of a tour guide. 'Give me your salary darling, for safe keeping,' she had drawled but Sammy had resisted with Rishi's quiet support.

However, Rishi had been unable to deal with both his wife and sister. Eventually, Sammy's life caved in when Rishi left, and her sister-in-law had shrugged her off and her little mites. 'Rishi is our primary concern,' she had said smugly, shutting the door on Sammy, Tara and Aksh.

Nervous thoughts and long forgotten scenes rushed through her mind, with words shooting through her memory and burning holes in her head. And an old conversation with Maasi ji came back to her.

'In those days, women were bound by tradition. They were expected to run the house and interfere in little else. Be seen but not heard. Your great-grandmother, Dadiji, ruled the family with an iron fist until her death and spared neither the daughters nor the daughters-in-law. She insisted that they divide their time between the kitchen and in appeasing the family deity at the temple set up by her son.

'Contrast this with the girls today,' Maasi ji had said. 'Even the blush of the bride is not virginal. Brides dresses must be hot, flaunting their bits for all to see and their bedroom scorecard is a badge of honour.'

Sammy too was repeatedly told that girls from good families kept quiet, kept the izzat and protected the family name. 'We will stuff you and your litter back, leave you at Rishi's doorstep,' her own brother had thundered. And later, more aggressively, her mother had shouted, 'What makes you think you are special? Turn a blind eye to his faults, live your own life but within the four walls of his house, your marital home. Be like me,' she had said. 'Don't throw over our lives and our reputations and the family name. Don't create a scandal; just be quiet. No noise please, I have important things to do, houses to buy and lectures to give.' Her mother's sharp tongue and filthy abuse had cut Sammy's throat without a physical stab, while her brother's brutal beatings had almost sent her to hospital.

'Life is so tough,' thought Sammy. 'And so unexpected.'

Of all the broken relationships in her life, this one had survived. Rishi and Sammy. The one she least expected. Her marriage had ended but the relationship had taken on another colour in the years that followed. Maya and Rishi went through a bitter court battle before parting ways, but he had seemed to grow stronger as a person with each passing challenge. And Sammy could not for a moment doubt his love for the kids.

Her thoughts merged into the present, seeing him hold Tara close. They had discovered that Kushal was the local hero, the person around whom much of the bullying and excesses at the school revolved. But they had still not been able to discover the reason for Aksh being beaten up.

Rishi left soon after that for his college reunion, hoping that the rest of his evening would provide him with some more information.

Aksh continued to slip in and out of depression. At times he was quite cheerful and at other moments, he would brood and stare into the distance. Lying awake at home and concerned about Aksh, for this was one evening when none of them would be with him, Sammy's mind had drifted again to the past.

People had judged Sammy and they still talked behind her back; she was made out to be the villain. At work, even years later, colleagues and team members gossiped and gave advice. 'Do not mind, but what happened?' they would ask, invading her privacy. And not getting a response would cluck sympathetically, mentally calculating her age, stage and salary. Which car? Where do you live? Which school are the children in? Even Maasi ji had repeatedly asked, 'How much money? Arre, tell me. Want to know for knowledge sake. Must know everything so that when that young thing at the beauty parlour brags I can drown her voice. After all, you are successful Samaira.'

'I wish I had not tried so hard to shield the children from the truth,' she thought for the hundredth time that hour. 'Maybe, just maybe, Aksh would have better understood what I have been through ... or would he?' Could he have, given how young he was then?

It was not something she could talk about lightly even now; it was not a bedtime story. She had to shield her children, to protect them from the harsh reality of life but not wanting them to judge their father and to find him wanting.

Motherhood had been hard, especially being a single parent in her late twenties while working. Yet, she ... they ... had survived. Their true salvation had been Aida, the nanny who had cared for Tara and Aksh for over a decade. It was her compassion and caring and excellent cooking that had truly kept them afloat. All three had missed Rishi; the children more than they would sometimes admit; Sammy more than she could bear. With time, the pain had eased and life had taken over. She had to work, she had to be there for the children and she had done just that. Sammy had done it all. Looking back, she wondered how she had managed!

Sammy wrapped her warm pashmina tightly around her drooping shoulders and closed her eyes, scared of falling asleep. Sleep too took its time coming, perhaps as scared of her as she was of it.

'Enough,' her tired mind yelled at her, as she drifted into sleep.

22

*'It is wise to direct your anger towards problems – not people;
to focus your energies on answers – not excuses.'*

– WILLIAM ARTHUR WARD

More than a week had passed since Aksh had been hospitalized. The recovery was slow but there was progress. However, there was still very little information about what had actually happened at the school. There was a gap in the narrative. Everyone agreed that Aksh had a normal school morning till close to the end of the regular school hours, the time when the sports practices began. Then came the gap. And in the end there was the moment when Aksh had been found beaten up at the basketball courts. No one could shed any light on the missing time.

The alarm woke up Sammy early in the morning. She hurriedly gulped the last few sips of her tea, reached for the newspapers, bundling them together and stuffing them into the bag she was taking with her to the hospital.

She drove to the hospital in silence. She saw the imposing façade with the heavy iron gates carrying the impressive logo, the building with its steel, glass and brick frontage, and the mini-lake with a fountain in the front quad. It seemed so familiar now, so different from the cold and uninviting lobby that she had passed through to see Aksh for the first time.

She walked slowly, past the overly cheerful lobby manager and rushed to the ward and across to Rishi who was already there ahead of her. Handing him the warm croissants she had bought, she resisted the urge to cry and hug her sleeping son. Instead she ran her hands through his uncombed hair, kissing the back of his thin boy-man neck, wrapping her arms around his shoulders. All the while trying to breathe him back to health. To smoothen his creased forehead while holding on to the picture of him as she remembered him and not as he was now, a scared and skinny gawky teen. She saw him as a little baby in his walker, as a little boy squealing with delight as he chased Tara. Dressed in his cute school uniform, hiding behind her on his first day at school, holding on to her and peeping out from around her legs as his naturally inquisitive nature started to get the better of him.

He had been such a sweet, simple and happy child! That image dissolved even as she struggled to remember him and to hold on to her memories of him. Smiling, waving, as he rode his tricycle. Full of life, which is why she called him her son-shine. So different from his listless form lying on the hospital bed now.

The pause stretched into a long silence and Sammy could hear an unmistakable change in his breathing. He was sleeping, sedated and under strong medication so that his wounded body could heal.

'Rishi,' she whispered. 'I hate seeing him like this. Fragile like a dandelion. His long skinny body looks like the thin stalk and...'

But she could not get herself to complete the sentence and bent down to kiss Aksh instead. And just then the doctor strode in with the confidence of a king; the king of his territory, the hospital ward room. His entrance was followed by a flurry of activity. Attending doctors, juniors carrying reports, nurses carrying trays and what not. Sammy understood – he was the Super Specialist. His time was money.

But he was striding across the room to a teenage girl on another bed in the corner of the ward room and not to where Aksh was at all.

Leaning forward, staring with avid interest, almost like the crowd near a road accident, she spotted the child he was attending to.

'Very sick,' the nurse whispered far too loudly to the bystanders, of whom there seemed to be far too many in the ward room. 'The child came to us with complications. What can he do? He is not God. The doctors at Children's Hospital & Research Centre in Old Delhi had suggested procedures to treat sleep apnoea, recommended tonsillectomy. The mother was worried about her child's weight. Pah, mothers these days are so concerned about weight, their weight, child's weight, your weight, my weight! And now look! *Deeaad*! What is the use, I ask, of torturing the child?'

Sammy looked with concern towards the crowd around Bed 212, while the nurse continued. 'Mother was pushy. Wanted better marks. She should have taken the exams herself if that was what she wanted! Her daughter's attention span was short. With all her ailments, surgery was advised.'

The nurse had been with Girl 212 in the recovery room and was holding forth while the Super Specialist examined the child. 'Soon after surgery, I could see her condition becoming worse. When your time comes, no one can do anything. Even the best specialists cannot save you.'

Touching her forehead and oblivious to Sammy's increasing panic, she continued her monologue. 'The doctor did his best, obviously, but two-thirds of the girl's brain had swollen. Her mother is unwilling to believe the end has come so suddenly and is hoping for a miracle.'

The mother had not left her daughter's bedside. She kept repeating that her daughter had responded to touch and was showing other signs of life. She didn't want to switch off the life support.

The nurse said in a loud whisper with some finality. 'If not today, then tomorrow, and then someone else will be on that bed. This is life.'

By now Sammy was no longer listening, her face contorted with emotion and concern for Aksh, holding on to him with one hand while flicking through old photos of him on her mobile phone. Looking, searching, yearning for those moments of joy once again, much like a junkie on an Ecstasy trip, wanting the memory to last and finding it slipping away.

The nurse first busied herself making Aksh comfortable, fluffed up his pillows, turned him on his side and then came closer to tell Sammy and Rishi the hospital gossip.

'Doctors don't have an easy life,' she said and pointed not too discreetly to an elderly hunched man shuffling along slowly, his clothes baggy as if he'd wilted and shrunk. 'His life was a living nightmare,' she continued, undeterred by the cross looks she got, filling Sammy in with the sorry, sordid details.

'Last year, he and his wife of more than four decades legally parted ways, at her instigation. She loves May-donna and dresses like her, red lipstick and powder. Just because Madam May-donna has a young *chhokra*, she too got herself one and left the doctor.'

The nurse's perfect Hindi accent had slipped for just a minute and her use of a non-Hindi word had revealed something about her. Sammy suppressed a smile and asked, 'Did you live in Mumbai?'

'Yes, in Matunga, until I got married,' replied the nurse.

Sammy squinted her eyes to catch the nurse's name on her badge, but was distracted by a flash of lightning. The nurse ran to the large glass window. 'Oh my God, there is a huge thunderstorm! Looks like it will hail.'

Walking across and standing at the window with the nurse, looking out, Sammy quietly watched the gathering storm. Even though it was mid-morning, the sky was darkening. Such winter cyclonic storms happened every odd year in Delhi. She saw trees shake and toss, branches lashing furiously in the wind. Left and right, up and down, like whips rather than parts of a tree. Sometimes they almost crashed against the windowpanes, banged against the walls with a thud, slipping down in the slick rain. Bangs of thunder followed the lightning flashes almost immediately, telling Sammy that the storm was almost directly above them. She watched, rooted to the spot, mesmerized by the force of nature in all its glory.

She took strength and courage from the storm too, safe within the hospital ward room. The trees were clearly out of their league in a straight battle with the storm, so they did not fight the winds and rain but bent submissively before their rage, almost surrendering. In supplication, they survived.

'This is how we will survive,' she thought. 'And this is what Aksh will have to learn, and I with him. I will have to accommodate, to understand and yield to my child.'

And in the slow deliberate movement of the trees, she saw hope. Her son, she knew would get better; a mother's instinct. 'I know it!' she told herself.

Standing by the window with Sammy, the nurse lowered her voice and whispered conspiratorially, continuing to gossip and not noticing the inner conversation that Sammy had just had with herself.

'And that sister, there,' the nurse said, under her breath, 'is soft on a married young boy in the accounts department but he likes the lab assistant in radiology. And the pretty one at the nursing station, she is playing the field. All the young doctors want her, but she is in love with the owner's son. Pah, such aspirations for a girl from a humble background will not augur well. You mark my words. I have seen so much drama in this hospital. Yes, this very place. And your sahib looks like a good man, why don't you ... family problem, madam, has to be forgotten. This is India; sacrifice is a woman's middle name. *Chhodo ladai jhagda*. Don't fight.'

At another time, Sammy would have told her off but not today. Getting up, she excused herself and walked away, deep in thought. She strode towards the little chapel in the hospital, past the chemist and the greeting card shop now celebrating Christmas that was just two days away. Greeting cards were a recent phenomenon in India. Previously, there had been few days other than festivals that had cards for them. Nowadays there seemed to be cards for every occasion.

She walked quickly to the chapel, drawn there by an inner voice. Once inside, she knelt in silent prayer, head bent and hands folded, pleading, begging and beseeching the gods for a breakthrough for Aksh. For his health, of course, and also in piecing together the cause for his injury, for clues to help understand his recent past.

Sensing the presence of someone, Sammy opened her eyes to see a three-year old child, drowned in a large oversized hospital gown, touching her shoulder. The girl reached out to her and giggled, placing a small toy in her hand. A Transformer.

Sammy smiled back and looked up. 'My granddaughter,' said the old woman next to them, weary with care. 'She pulled me in. She loves coming here, to talk to God. She says he must get lonely standing there.'

The child sat down next to Sammy and pretended to close her eyes, peeping through the curled fringe of her eyelashes impishly and grinning at her. Sammy smiled back and walked back to Aksh, skipping in her hurry, for in the toy that she clutched tightly in her fist, she saw hope.

Many hours went by. It was evening now. Rishi suggested that they should rest and nudged her towards the hospital exit and into the car. 'Our son is asleep, we need to pace ourselves, get some sleep,' he told her before dozing off himself in the car due to exhaustion.

Sammy, however, could not rest. Her mind replayed the conversation with Monica and Mrs Khanna. 'Why? How did it get all so mixed up?'

It would be a while before answers came. Her heart, she would discover, was resilient and was going to be broken a few times before it could be glued back together. What she did not know that day was how literal that statement was or how soon she would need attention. A few days later, her heart would be on fire.

23

'Gossip needn't be false to be evil – there's a lot of truth that shouldn't be passed around.'

– FRANK A. CLARK

Returning to the hospital the next day, Sammy found Maasi ji already there and sitting with Aksh, her aunt not having left for her vacation as yet. She was happy to see a kind face. Sammy had just received a rude email from a client and faced a resignation in her team at work, all adding to the tension. This was not what she needed at this time and she wondered whether her life was coming apart, bit by bit.

A loud exclamation from the door and looking up, Sammy saw a somewhat familiar figure clasp Maasi ji in a big hug, not letting her go for several minutes. 'Kitty!' exclaimed Maasi ji, examining the rings on her extended hand, quietly sizing up the diamonds.

'So good to see you, and that too after so many years! You haven't changed, not one bit,' exclaimed both together in a chorus.

'Who is the bigger liar,' wondered Sammy mischievously, for it was none other than her dead Nani's friend.

'I am here to see a friend. She is ...' Kitty let her voice drop, '... not so well. You can say dying. Such good *boyz*, looking after her. So devoted.'

Sammy gave the new entrant a hard look, taking in everything and enjoying the moment. Despite her age, she was pretty in a voluptuous way. One arm dripped and dipped with the load of glass bangles all the way to her elbow. Her eyes were outlined with blue kohl, her lips scarlet, a fuchsia pink handkerchief tucked into the bosom of her tight and see-through blouse and keys swung from the waist. She was a throwback to Bollywood vamp Bindu or the more sophisticated Helen. Trendy reading glasses hung casually on a pearl string that ended just before her cleavage, a visual delight as it moved with every sigh. Stuffed rather tightly into her low sari blouse revealing more than it hid.

She watched Kitty walk and was reminded of a circus performer rushing forward on stilts. Sammy spotted her outrageous six-inch Italian stilettoes, with the red painted toes delicately sneaking out from beneath the sari. Kitty was not quite five feet minus the footwear and she was never seen without her heels.

'So nice to see you! Don't ask I am *sooo* busy these days,' Kitty almost sang out before rushing forward to give Sammy an exaggerated hug and planted a wet kiss on her forehead. She then took a chair and moved across to join Maasi ji.

'Sammy was asking me about Mantri ji,' explained Maasi ji. 'His brother, Santri has got involved in a matter in some way,' she went on rather obliquely.

Kitty lowered her voice and whispered, 'Be careful if you deal with Mister Mantri ji – he has a foul temper. Don't let that soft voice and poetry fool you. He refuses to shift into the government bungalow and his supporters sing songs about it, but think, just think why? He does not want Santri, that sinister brother of his, to take over the house. After all, still waters run deep. The truth is that there is a wide rift in that family, but they show a united front. They believe they are a family in the public eye and their image has to be just right. They think people are fools and can't see through it. Sinister the Santri,' she said getting the names mixed up, 'hates being the no-count person, the brother in reflected glory. But what to do! God forgot to stuff brains in that big fat oaf.'

And then looking towards Sammy, she continued, 'It was known that Mister Mantri ji was the genius and that Sinister, that Santri, was merely the little family pumpkin, the one to be endured. The joker. But that was until Sinister Santri's ambition reared its ugly head. They managed to find jobs for him. After all Santri, they thought, he is a simple boy – give him a drink, massage his ego and he will hum happily. Mister Mantri ji propped him up and the only promise he had to make was that he would not disappear from parties. Santri cannot allow Mister Mantri ji to know that he slinks out of parties leaving his so-called wife behind, or tell him where he goes,' she rattled off, ignoring the chuckling Sammy.

'Sinister the Santri has a secret life. His secret life is a kind of locked box, full of forbidden, sinful little dalliances. Men are like pressure cookers; they need to let off steam,' she said, winking slyly. 'Pressure cooker.'

Maasi ji, not one to keep quiet for long, butted in to add her philosophy of life. 'God has made men different. They need their little distractions, their pastimes, which allow them to keep going and whistling through life. And through that they allow us women to do what we want to do! I have seen it all, so what if I did not marry? I too have had experiences!'

Suddenly, they saw the nurse adjusting Aksh's pillows and realized that he had all along been playing on his phone and was listening intently. 'I have a theory,' he told them with a wicked glint in his eye and a mischievous lop-sided grin. 'Your Mister Mantri ji should be called M&M because to me he is just that. He is sugary, sweet and colourful on the outside but without too much substance, so M&M! Get it, get it?' he asked Sammy, pleased with himself. 'And even us children are not fooled. We are smarter than all of you,' he said cheekily, pointing to Kitty while devouring yet another cookie.

There was pin-drop silence and then peals of laughter. Sammy turned to see Maasi ji in splits with tears rolling down her cheeks as she laughed convulsively. Undeterred, Kitty moved the conversation along by changing the topic abruptly. She was conscious that she had revealed more of her inner thoughts than she had intended to.

'And did you know; the brothers are trying to find a match for my cousin's daughter? Mine! The girl is quite beautiful, doe-like. I mean she is a cow – simple, sweet. And don't you laugh, Samaira. Intelligent, too, in a bookish way, but a bit stupid in worldly matters. She works in the film industry and feels that life is like those movie romances where marriages are made by dancing around trees and in heaven.'

Maasi ji was enjoying the gossip, for she knew the people involved better than Sammy did. But Sammy was all ears for very different reasons. On the one hand, she thought that she might get more information about Aksh, and Kushal seemed to be the only thread to pull at this moment. It was difficult, though, to speak openly with Aksh listening in so Sammy decided to take a different tack, one that may not appear threatening to her son.

'Maasi ji,' she said. 'Tell me more about this Mantri ji. You said that he knew my mother, didn't you?'

Kitty burst out into peals of laughter. Barely able to control her giggles, she said, 'Mantri ji knew your mother very well. He knew all of her very well!' And she burst out laughing yet again.

Aksh was looking a bit perplexed but Sammy was red in the face, regretting her decision to ask the question.

'Yes, your mother was too friendly with Mantri ji,' said Maasi ji to whom the question had been addressed. 'And for such little gain. Your mother was always willing to use herself, in every way,' she winked, 'in order to gain something. But in this case, Mantri was even smarter than her. He used her and discarded her. Your mother didn't learn and was always available for him. Why, even I have seen her coming out of Mantri's house early morning and rushing to her car!'

'And what were you doing outside Mantri's house so early in the morning?' asked Aksh mischievously.

'Never you mind!' retorted Maasi ji sharply, not wanting to go down that line of conversation. Sighing loudly, she turned away, lifting one hip to let out ... well you know what. But the moment was not lost on Aksh. He lay in bed rolling his eyes and wickedly mouthing, 'Sassy, gassy, Maasi ji.'

This wasn't working for Sammy and she wanted Maasi ji by herself. She was also tiring of the gossip that was now making her head spin. 'Maasi ji, why don't we go for a little walk outside,' she said. 'It will be good to just stretch our legs.'

She left the room, while her aunt decided to use the washroom and then join Sammy outside in a few minutes.

24

'Being a mom has made me so tired. And so happy.'
— TINA FEY

In the parking lot outside, Sammy saw a city alive with its myriad hues and people out on the streets despite it being a chilly December evening. Beggars and street vendors, parking attendants and security guards, sweepers, delivery boys, patients, families, drivers. And suddenly, she felt lonely amid the hustle-bustle of city life, exhausted and tired.

Her mobile phone rang and she jumped. It was a wrong number. Sitting by the side of the little garden outside, trying to distract herself, she flicked through the phone to read the gossip on MSN and Google.

Mobile phone apps these days, she gathered, were playing havoc; destroying lives and burning marriages. There were applications to track your current love interest, stalk your ex and search for new relationships. You download an app. The next day, your ex's new girlfriend and their sleeping habits fly across your screen. Is that the best thing to happen to you? Can you move on?

'It was the worst of human nature,' Sammy thought to herself, 'that was being exposed here.' Dragging each other down, vengeful, spiteful comments.

Gossip was no longer two elderly women sitting and drinking tea together. It was altogether different. These apps made gossip something to worry about, to think about. An ill-advised comment or a drunken confession was out there for all to see and read and comment on. And forever.

At the end of the first page of listings, Sammy looked up and spotted the lights of a lone aeroplane making its way across the sky, away from her. For Sammy, it was always a marvel when something flew and soared in the sky, broke free from the tug and pull of gravity and hung in the air like that. She yearned for its freedom, for its speed and ability to distance itself from problems. Its ability to turn its back on life's little concerns. She smiled to herself, for to it she must be a small dot with not so big problems hanging out in a garden.

She was tired and her mind wandered back through the dusty by-lanes of her memory to the past few months when life had been just right and Aksh had been just an ordinarily extraordinary teenager. Extraordinary in her eyes, her son-shine.

She saw Maasi ji slowly make her way out towards her. It was almost time for the evening meal to be brought around to Aksh but they would be able to spend some time alone before then.

Her aunt addressed her directly. 'My heart broke at first to see her, the little idiot, your mother, for making Mister Mantri her hero. I thought she was being silly and was captivated by power. She was, but there was more. I know everything. I saw that it was your mother who was trying to use Mantri, to rise in society with him. But he was the one who used her. And he already had his sadow, Dark Sadow, Santri.

'Now, your mother is no more, but that Lola is even better than her. I see everything! She is shameless, is that Lola. Openly she goes ... no shame ... no caring who sees her. And the clothes she wears. Even in winter, such clothes that she may as well wear nothing at all. Your brother ... he is not a man!' Maasi ji had pronounced her judgement.

Sammy shuddered with memories that flashed in her mind and hit her like a rock between her eyes, things she had suppressed. Her Nani had been sick, very ill. Like the rest of the family, Sammy's mother was there. Shouting to everyone that it should end, the plug should be pulled. She made wild promises that she had no intention of keeping. 'I will look after Sammy, mother dear,' she had said to Sammy's Nani. A promise made to her dying mother, a promise that had been left unfulfilled and abused. Sammy was not fooled by the machinations of the Indian family and those friends who called themselves the respectable extended family. Oh-no, not she! But she flicked away the thought before it depressed her.

Another memory. Her mother waking her up, angrily shaking her and always in a bad mood. Raking up her favourite subject, the miserable life that Sammy had and what a failure she was. She remembered Tara telling her years later, 'Aksh and I would wake up and huddle close. We would try to cover your face with our tiny hands.' And, in doing so, they had hoped that they could hide Sammy from her mother and block out the tirade. It was a pattern that her little children recognized. No sooner did their grandmother catch sight of them smiling and humming, or their mother getting ready as she took out her clothes, or noticed that they were happy and in high spirits, then her resentment would surface and she would not give in without picking a fight.

Maasi ji disturbed her thoughts. 'I leave for Singapore and then Indonesia tomorrow. I will see you soon. Look after Aksh, he will get better soon. And when I come back, we will go to Bengali Market for golguppas. Take care.'

Sammy went back to Aksh's room. She noted with satisfaction that he had eaten most of his dinner. It was a great sign of his increasing and significant improvement.

Her silent observation was disturbed by the arrival of the night nurse. Anita, the nametag said. Tall, middle-aged and statuesque, efficient but quiet. She looked almost mechanical and expressionless, like one endowed with the efficiency of a robot.

She spotted the housekeeping lady, the swish-swash of her wet mop catching her attention. They seemed to clean the hospital several times a day! Probably a good thing, Sammy thought. This cleaning lady was quite attractive and Sammy saw the men in the hospital look at her, some openly and others slyly. Some blinking myopically from over their glasses and others from below their newspapers.

With a bit of a grin on her face, she saw her little Aksh also look, attracted by the beauty of the young woman. Perhaps he wasn't so little any more, she thought!

Actually now that Sammy paused to think, there was a resemblance to her sister-in-law. Lola had been young and luscious when she married Sammy's brother. And notorious even then. It had been such a long time ago and Sammy had to strain to remember the details. What she distinctly remembered was how Lola played with men and got them to look at her by slyly showing just enough skin to keep them interested. She had obviously become more brazen since!

Seeing her own son in a different light, Sammy saw the adolescent sparkle in Aksh's eyes. He was not a child any more and his hormones were firing at the moment. A thought that pleased her at some level but also was a cause of disquiet. In his brief look, for he averted his eyes and concentrated on his food after a short while, Aksh had shown that he was becoming a young man.

Sammy herself was stunningly beautiful, but she had never paraded her body in the way her mother and Lola, her sister-in-law, routinely did. They attracted men consciously, making sure that they created situations where looks bordered on lust. Lola was thin, with big breasts on a small frame. But it was her slim waist, flowing hair and swaying hips that had men mesmerized. It muddled their senses and curdled their judgement. She teased men with her presence, even in ordinary household situations, and they giggled convulsively as she tried to edge past them, but being provocative as she did.

Aksh, she also remembered, had been fiercely protective of women, even as a little child. She remembered the incident one Holi, when Tara and Aksh had gone down to play in the central courtyard of the condominium. Holi, the festival of colours, was celebrated with fervour in North India, and the condominium was usually completely safe and decent. This year had been different and some young college boys had come with one of the residents of the colony. A friend of Tara's, a few years older than her, was sobbing in a corner when Aksh and Tara went down. She had told an unblinking Tara that one of the boys had played with the string on her salwar and had tugged so hard that it had broken as he slid his hand into her clothes, covering her face with his free arm. Too shocked to cry, she had whimpered in pain and freed herself and run away.

Despite the social conditioning and behaviour expected in a close community, these visitors had feasted their eyes and their imagination had run amok. They ogled brazenly at the girls, unhindered by etiquette or dignity. And their words were most shameful. Bets were laid, cup sizes discussed, lemons and oranges tossed in the air only to be caught and rubbed suggestively. Or cricket balls passed around, rubbed and fingered. Cricket, like repressed sex, was a national pastime in India.

Even Tara had been asked her opinion in merriment, even though she was just a chit of a girl. Her innocent answer had resulted in much merriment, jesting and joking among the boys.

It seemed that Aksh had sensed his sister's discomfort and the other girl's humiliation as she put up a brave front. The boys followed the girls, humming the popular Bollywood songs of the day, with their suggestive lyrics. Aksh didn't understand what was going on. He had stared at them, the college boys, as they had watched the girls. The boys watched like hawks, exchanging notes on figures under the wet clothes drenched with Holi colours. Instinctively, without needing to be told, Aksh had understood that their discussion was hurting the girls. On his small baby legs, he had run up to the boys and kicked one of them hard on the shins. Hard, again and again. Shouting, 'Don't trouble my sister. Don't trouble.'

It was at this moment that some of the adults had figured out what happened. The incident caused quite an uproar in the little community, and Aksh had been the hero. Sammy smiled at the memory ... her little Aksh!

But this was years later now. Years had passed and Sammy had learnt many hard life lessons. With Aksh's beating in school, she had stumbled into a vortex of unspeakable things and had been exposed to another harsh reality of life, that people are not what they seem. That people put up a front to hide behind. Her brother had been no different. What about Aksh? How much had he changed? Had he grown up to be just like those lecherous boys on that Holi afternoon?

A little tired, Sammy almost nodded off. She woke up a bit later with a start, looked around and then bent over to hold Aksh's hand as he grimaced. He too had gone to sleep and was dreaming.

25

'Nothing makes us so lonely as our secrets.'
— PAUL TOURNIER

Aksh had looked stronger the previous day and it was time, thought Sammy, to start probing even deeper into what had actually happened. The school was closed today, so they would have to begin at home and with Aksh. All three of them were back at the hospital and Sammy's heart was pounding as she wrapped her fingers tightly around the bars of the wrought iron railing and squeezed it. She was sitting drowning in worry on the first floor of the public staircase in the hospital, sitting for what seemed to be hours.

Her thoughts were broken as a cup of coffee was thrust into her face. 'Drink,' she heard Rishi tell her and she obeyed. It should have warmed her up but instead she was sinking, sliding down on to the cold, hard floor. There she sat, propping herself up in the foetal position, balled up against her knees, mouth pressed hard, shut lips pursed together, as if she were bracing herself for an emergency landing.

Rishi had been watching her and sensed her despair. To ease the pain, he muttered, 'It happens to all of us. There is a stage in life when we hide things, things that are so insignificant later on in life but so important at that point. It is not just Aksh, all teenagers go through this. They feel parents just don't get them.'

And then more softly, almost speaking to himself, he said, 'I could have been more involved. I could have done more, been hands on.'

'Wait a minute, who is beating himself up now? You have done just fine. There are parents who live in the same house but are still absent, totally uninvolved. Just look at this kid Kushal Singh for instance.'

Rishi leapt up and plonked himself next to her. 'You know something more about him? What?'

'Well, Maasi ji told me that Kushal treats Santri as his father. And Santri's strength is his brother, Mantri. It seems that Kushal's father was this huge beedi magnate and had an empire across the country. He had political ambition and was fielded as the MLA candidate in the last elections but lost. He owns land across Haryana and is in with the real estate mafia. But the biological father seems to want to have nothing to do with Kushal and feels his responsibility is limited to giving the boy money.'

'What about the mother? Do we know anything more about her?' Rishi asked.

'Not much. She's the queen of kitty parties and is never at home – Santri's home, where they all live together. Kushal has been brought up by the servants. And if it is to be believed there was an incident with a servant, about Kushal burning a cigarette on the arm of a servant. He should have been thrashed at that time!'

'Whew, how did you discover this?' Rishi asked, taking it all in.

'Simple! When all else failed I turned to Google and all the newspaper reports came up. It was hushed up but the Net can never be completely scrubbed. So you can see reports from a couple of years ago and then nothing,' Sammy added.

After a long silence, Rishi bent closer to Sammy and asked, 'Please involve me more in what is happening, Sammy. Please? For the sake of the children, maybe for me? Maybe for us?'

Taken by surprise Sammy opened Aksh's iPad to compose herself. She had brought it from home. There was another one of Aksh's poems and she distractedly read it out. Winged words darted out but did not settle … like her feelings. She thought about life's unexpected twists as she read.

Deception and distrust became common practice
Too blinded to see that demise awaited us
Unwilling to look beyond individual interests
And centuries later we know the cost.

Battles were fought and blood was shed
Father of the nation used the unconventional
Mentally and physically our heroes fought on
And decades later we have respect.

Slowly Rishi pulled her into his arms as her words wavered. The past and the present were coming together in ways that were just too much for her. He took the iPad and read instead.

> Holi colours mark the end of weary winter
> Diyas chase away the darkness of the night
> Customs are followed and festivities occur
> India is the country in constant celebration.
>
> Followers of Islam turn towards Mecca
> Temple bells sound new beginnings
> Gurudwaras and churches present in abundance
> India is the country with every religion.
>
> Madhubani and Warli art of the tribals
> Pottery and sculpture and paper craft too
> Even the graffiti symbolizes urban design
> India is the country filled with imagination.

These were the words of a sensitive child. A boy who noticed, cared for and articulated thoughts about the finer things in life. Not the thoughts of a bully or a gangster. Where and when had he changed?

Rishi had found more of Aksh's inner thoughts in his writings on the iPad. Their son was an expressive and prodigious writer; words flowed from his soul. Choosing the written word to bring out his feelings, albeit using technology rather than quill and parchment.

'I have just read Aksh's UWC application forms,' said Rishi, referring to the United World Colleges that Aksh seemed interested in. Aksh had considered changing his school, leaving the city to go to the residential environment of the UWC.

'It seems that the shift from your old place to the new apartment was not easy on him. He struggled to bring some order to his new life.'

And more wistfully, Rishi muttered under his breath, 'and it seems he did not get over our problems and my choosing to end our marriage. For so many years we felt he had been a baby and did not remember. We thought the incident had not been traumatic for him. But I was so wrong. Life trips you up when you least expect it! We can never go back on things we have done, the years I have spent trying to make it up to him, to Tara, pale in comparison. And look at him now! My heart aches for him but, unlike Tara, he is closed to me and will not speak to me about what he feels.'

Sammy looked at him, seeing the hurt and regret, and sensed his abject despair. She reached out to hold his hand while she read Aksh's essay from his application form.

All of us have a source of comfort, of security and of joy. I had found this in the home and community that I grew up in. I lived in a colony of apartments for many years and was incredibly attached to it. My childhood consisted of walking in the various parks, climbing trees and being scolded by the guards, hiding in the nooks and crannies, playing football and cricket and dancing at the colony parties. The house itself held many memories of my sister and me growing up. The marks on the wall and the paint on the furniture spoke volumes of our misbehaviour. And then she, like my father before her, also went away.

My friends there were like an extension of my family. Whether it was to watch a movie at night, to celebrate something or just to talk over a glass of iced tea, there was barely an occasion upon which they did not turn up at my house. They'd seen me at my happiest and my saddest and had been there for me through it all.

Because of the sentimental value that the house, the colony and the people had for me, it was incredibly difficult to think of ever leaving. But last year, we had to shift. I was scared of leaving my safe haven for an unfamiliar area and I was scared of losing touch with my friends. Initially I felt sad, but upon considering the situation I realized that I was overreacting.

Looking back, I'm glad we didn't change our decision because of me. My mother and I enjoy the new apartment. My old friends come over to this house too and I've made new friends here. This shift was a challenge for me as it was the first time I faced such a big change. It taught me that change is inevitable and that you must embrace it, adapt to it and make the best of it. It also taught me that starting a new chapter of your life doesn't make the previous one any less important.

But that was not all there was. It would have been simpler if there had been no more to read. Secrets were hidden on social media, embedded in Facebook.

26

'The soul becomes dyed with the colour of its thoughts.'
— MARCUS AURELIUS

Tara was tired, having spent most of the day at the hospital and was taking a well-earned nap once they were back at Sammy's place. Rishi was sipping a cup of tea while Sammy paced up and down in the drawing room, clearly restless. She sucked in a lung full of air and then they went back to the iPad and the secrets it contained.

Aksh, it seems, had been trying to visualize an alternate past while conjuring up a different present. His parents felt the silence hum as the world stood still; both felt disconnected, though for different reasons; both were lost in thought.

'I never knew that he felt this way. Aksh seemed so well adjusted, so balanced. Good grades, never a complaint about him. But that was what he wanted me to see. He hid his uncertainty, his turmoil. Why? For how long? It is my fault!

I tried too hard and maybe pushed him to do what I thought was good for him. Experience, I told him, while nudging him along. He had a few friends; his life was on the football field...' her voice trailed off as she bit her lip.

'Don't do that,' Rishi told her sharply. 'It doesn't help and makes you look like a pouty and sulking politician.'

And they quietly scrolled down to see his friends on Facebook. 'Who are these people? He has over a thousand friends?' she asked, a rhetorical question. And then, 'I thought he did not have many friends...'

'Look,' Rishi said, drawing her attention to conversations, Facebook chats, which seem strange and surreal. 'It is so different from the quiet son we think we know.'

> Milkmaid at 2 a.m. Sugar rush in the morning. Missing the sunrise, rising at noon. Day after day. Loads of coffee, lethal bouts of storytelling. LOL I was sleeping shshsh ... where are we going? People, where are we going????
> Confused. Feel terribly confused ☹
> Don't go all Buddha on me!
> I sent email bout my scene ... Two hook-ups, One cheating, sloshed and non-veg jokes
> Summary of my night. Pssssst Deepak kissed Soha Aksh message you know who ... chutiya
>Leave something for me
> Ajit kissed Shuchi – full on tongue
> BC you have your nite to describe
>Except we are more mature and our Lady is a whore
>> OMG!! I can't believe it! You're going to Bangalore! For heaven's sake!

>> Try not be yourself. I mean normal. Take care ... take good care of her. Good care! You know, care...
>> Try not to be stupid! And don't ignore Georgie. Talk so that he can understand. At least you guys won't get raped! ;)
>>> Welcome back Axeman! Did you get lucky? Congrats on winning, mate! We missed you big time. Some action here too!
>>> Anyway, Sundi has a surprise for you. Hidden in the stomach!
>>> Uff! Don't post such stuff on someone's wall, guys!!

'What is this? Shocking!' burst out Sammy, looking up at Rishi. He ignored her, deep as he was in thoughts of their son.

There was a post that said the Agarwals were getting divorced. Their son looked so distressed. 'Look at these messages,' said Sammy, pointing at the screen. 'And look at this poor child, just diagnosed with cancer. So cruel. Look at her sharing her feelings and talking about it.'

'But this is so not true,' interjected Rishi, a little behind in the conversation. 'I met the couple in London and they are expecting their third child. No question of a divorce. They are so together.'

'You can never tell,' replied Sammy. 'This child, why would their son post such lies then?'

'And now you will tell me that this girl's morbid remarks are just to get attention and sympathy. And that there is nothing to this? Huh?' Rishi ignored her but pointed to a girl who had run the marathon a couple of short weeks ago.

His voice reflected his worry. 'Why does a child need to think about death? Why, I ask you?' he said and showed her some of Aksh's posts. 'Two of them in fact. Quotes from popular songs, I think. But why is Aksh quoting from these? He seemed to be influenced by Donald Roeser. See, here he is quoting from a song called "Don't fear the reaper."

Come on baby
(Don't fear the reaper)
Baby take my hand
(Don't fear the reaper)

'And our son goes on to add comments of his own. What is the reason a child should be thinking like this?' he exclaimed and read aloud, '"Laugh out loud." "Dance, even if you're no good at it." "Be childlike." "Death is not the end of it all." "Carpe diem ... you never know when the day may be your last."'

'There's another one from Pitbull, too,' added Rishi. 'I recognize this one and it's more positive at least!'

Me not working hard?
Yeah, right! Picture that with a Kodak
Or, better yet, go to Times Square
Take a picture of me with a Kodak
Took my life from negative to positive

Flicking to another app on the iPad, he said, 'And look at the photos in his WhatsApp gallery. Look!'

Both, Sammy and Rishi stared at the screen in disbelief.

Sammy broke the spell, as she sobbed seeing photograph after photograph of Aksh. Looking cockily into the camera, with a cigarette dangling from his mouth. Another with a glass. And then she gasped as she saw one with him bare-chested cowering on the floor, scared ... the bravado replaced by fear.

Sammy and Rishi stared at each other, joined in their concern. The screen slowly loads and Sammy moaned ... there is a picture of a girl cutting her wrist and then one with Aksh's name written in blood.

'Was this his girlfriend? Did he have one?' she heard Rishi ask her, but his voice seems to be funnelled from the bottom of the sea. GIR ... L ... FRIE ... N ... D. She heard disjointed and broken syllables.

She barely made it to the bathroom in time to throw up. She shook violently as she gagged; it seemed that her guts were being thrown out along with bile.

'Why me? Why after all that I have been through?' she asked herself. Her tired mind shouted out loud, 'Will it never stop?'

And then she saw her mother's face leering at her, her long hair bellowing around her mean face, her broad forehead shining; her skin was plaster white, bleached by her sins and devoid of feelings; her lipstick creeping into wrinkles around her Botoxed lips, mouthing the words that summed up Sammy's troubled existence. 'Fucking failure!'

She felt her insides being clawed out and thrown on the floor like strips of discarded kite paper. Her pain was real, as was the despair Sammy now acutely felt.

The image of her own mother burned holes in her mind and she could not rid herself of the memory. For her mother had caused Sammy and her children endless pain. Her neglect had caused Sammy to almost die of pneumonia on one occasion. On another she had left Sammy bleeding on the floor as she impatiently applied Dettol and left for dinner with her glamorous friends. She was a miser too, leaving her daughter with just $50 in a foreign country, left to fend for herself and find her way back as her mother hopped into a limousine and disappeared to the airport. 'Will make you tough,' she had said at that time. Only a kind relative helping out with $100 had saved Sammy from living on the street. Her graduation from a prestigious college had no cheering family; instead her success was met with a grunt. The praise and accolades were for her brother. Somehow, in trying to escape her legacy, Sammy had tripped over it. Tried too hard to be different and, in the process, maybe fallen flat on her face. Literally. Sammy at that moment, as she had done so many times in the past, felt that she could rip her heart out and fling it aside. But that was not an option, for she was a single mother and had responsibilities.

'I won't be like HER,' she had told herself repeatedly over the years, trying to outrun her past. 'I will never do the same to my children. I have learnt the hard way and will protect my little mites.'

'Your children are just like you; failures! No-good bastards!' her mother had told her at their last meeting. 'Mark my words – NO GOOD!' her mother had spat at her, taunting her for being a single mother. 'You will be re-living that failure for the rest of your miserable life. The cold bed, the fact that you will be alone. You drive everyone away!' she had screamed.

Sammy had given up hope for a relationship with her self-centred mother. She had never imagined that in some well-hidden, deep dark corner of her mother's heart, bitterness for her children would have remained.

She doubted herself today, after so many lonely years. Years in which she had stepped in to cover up for all the missing relatives. But maybe she had not done enough. Maybe she should have tried harder, done more. Maybe she should have adjusted, as the world had told her. Maybe accepted everything for the sake of peace, for her children. Maybe she had made it all about herself and not enough about her children and what they needed. Sammy felt alienated and confused. And so alone.

'You were wrong and now it is too late!' her mind screamed out, as Sammy sobbed. In trying to do her best by Aksh, she had let him down.

'I am a failure,' she told herself, washing her face to hide her sadness from Rishi. 'Having let Aksh down, I cannot let Rishi see me like this,' she decided resolutely.

'We will survive, we will. And I will get to the bottom of this,' he told her, as she came out.

She had, in a candid moment, confessed to Monica, 'I still experience intense pangs of grief – *painful unpleasure*, to use Freud's exquisite phrase.'

Sammy took a sip of water, let it swirl in her mouth and exhaled deeply. 'We will survive, we will. And I will get to the bottom of this,' she told herself, her spirits bouncing back. She said a silent prayer and felt instantly better. 'We are together … the children and me, and even Rishi,' she said to herself, feeling instantly better. 'And we will make it through.'

27

*'Never cut a tree down in the wintertime. Never make a
negative decision in the low time ... Be patient. The storm
will pass. The spring will come.'*

– ROBERT H. SCHULLER

Night came. The morning followed. India was playing Australia in the Boxing Day Test Match. Sammy had a challenge of quite a different kind. She could hear Tara in the other room. She knew what her daughter must be thinking. That they had discovered a lot. Yet, they were no closer to getting answers to the two important questions. Who was Peasant P? And, what had happened that day?

Sammy was clearly unnerved. She felt vulnerable and as mother's taunts rang in her head. She closed her eyes but could see her glowering face, the memory crystal clear.

'After getting you married, I heaved a sigh of relief. Just as I thought I had time for myself, you became my responsibility again. Back like a bad, bad penny! The responsibility kills me!'

'Yeah, Mom! We know what killed you,' Sammy said to herself. 'Your lies.'

She could almost hear her mother bemoaning, 'Why does this always happen to you? Look at the world around you, look at all the smart girls. All of them handle their marriages and keep their husbands on a leash.'

Her words echoed in Sammy's mind and, with Aksh in hospital, she had begun to doubt herself. But better sense prevailed and, in the light of the morning, she saw the inherent weaknesses and contradictions in her mother's arguments. She saw her leering smile and mean eyes, and in them the ambition that had driven her ruthlessness, her greed. No compromise, no lie had held her back.

Some people like her mother were just born selfish, period. It had taken Sammy years to internalize this. There was just no rational explanation for her mother's weird behaviour. She remembered being hit again and again; she had been neglected but somehow she had lived through the nightmare. It was as if her soul had separated from her body, rising to the top like oil floating on water; like a bird flying in the sky, unfettered, light and free.

Sammy went back to her room, not wanting to be with anyone, not even with Tara at the moment. She sat back in bed and drew the covers over her as the mobile phone rang, breaking the calm that she had started to create around her. She watched it vibrate as it rang, shrill and unwelcome. Sammy did not move an inch. Enjoying the power she had over it, the power to ignore it, and she flopped back, her tired body drifting back to sleep! 'My Aksh is well and the world be damned,' she told herself, wriggling to a more comfortable position in the centre of the bed.

Aida came in and drew open the curtains letting the yellow morning sun into the room. It bounced off the cream walls, grinning with warmth as it greeted her. Stretching her limbs, Sammy reached out for her morning cup of tea and the newspapers. It was a perfect morning ... until the phone rang again. She stretched her sore limbs trying to shake off the sleep and lurched forward to grab the phone. She looked out lying in bed and watched the potted tree in her balcony sway, the branches looking as if they were floating in the breeze, their movements light and fluid.

The phone in her hand crackled to life and she heard a vaguely familiar voice breathlessly shouting into the phone, 'Madam, the *malkin* has gone to Singapore. She called to tell me that she is going to some island ... Surbhaiya she said ... for meditation. Now she is not picking up her phone. I am worried for malkin!'

'Calm down, nothing has happened,' she told the caller, placing the voice! 'Maasi ji can look after herself!' She chuckled to herself, amused that her feisty old aunt had come up with an ingenuous excuse to keep her housekeeper engaged, an unpredictable routine spiced with drama.

Bored and in a hurry to end the conversation, she told the housekeeper that he should not worry. 'I don't know where this place is but all must be well. Call me when you hear from her, when she calls you. Better still; clean the house and keep it ready for she can reappear as easily as she can disappear,' she said, picking up the newspaper and trying to disconnect at the same time, having lost interest in the conversation already.

She had spent too much time at home, she realized and rushed to the bathroom, suddenly in a hurry to get ready and go to the hospital. Sammy abandoned the newspaper, leaving it on the bed as she got into the bathtub, surrendering herself to the jets of hot water spurting from the showerhead, which was so welcome. Up and about, she gobbled some cereal before charging out of the door, shouting out for Tara and bundling her into the car.

On the way, she rang Rishi to check when he would reach the hospital and told him about her morning call, laughing at the antics of her aunt. He was already with Aksh.

'What a story!' he said, 'But are you sure she is okay?'

'You mean, you really mean that she may have decided to vanish and not inform anyone?' Sammy asked, a little concerned.

'Yes,' Rishi replied quietly, 'anything is possible. You do not know for certain. Anyway … maybe her housekeeper has it wrong. Maybe she met some people at a chanting group and decided to go to this meditation centre with them.'

'More importantly,' he said. 'I have to tell you something. Aksh has welts on his back, a cigarette burn. I saw these when the nurse came to adjust his bedding. It is not recent, quite an old burn the nurse told me, so nothing to worry about immediately. But I asked him when and how it happened. And he is refusing to speak about it … totally withdrawing into a shell, distant and uncommunicative. So unlike yesterday.'

'What?' Sammy spluttered, in shock for the second time that morning, as the pause stretched to eternity and the words hung uncomfortably in the air, suspended in silence.

Then, taking a quick decision, she said, 'I am going to the school. I will talk to his friends, run through the events of the day. Tara will be with you and she can try and speak with Aksh.'

She left Tara at the hospital and rushed off in the car, saying 'I have to get to the bottom of this; see you in a bit.'

28

'In a dark time, the eye begins to see'
— THEODORE ROETHKE

Monica had joined her at the school. Walking into school with Sammy, she had stood with her waiting for the class teacher. Both watched as they waited; the place pulsated with life. Children running to class, talking, chattering, giggling, chasing each other, cursing, swearing and calling out as they passed in the corridor. Innocent, fresh and full of life. Schools in Delhi closed late in the winter, with just a day off for Christmas and the vacations began only in early January.

Sammy shut her eyes for a brief second, blocking the image of a surly and closed Aksh lying on his bed. Her son-shine belonged here at school and at home with her. Her tired mind wanted to erase the past week and pretend it had never ever happened.

She did not want to talk to people. She noticed how the teachers scurrying past avoided making eye contact with her.

The very same teachers who used to gravitate to her just a month ago. No one wanted to talk to a mother whose child was in hospital. And certainly not about an 'innocent fall' in the playground.

But Sammy too was hiding something behind her oversized sunglasses … the guilt and the grief she so acutely felt. Because it was Sammy's fault, of course, that Aksh was in hospital. That he was injured. It was a mother's job to protect her child, even from himself. And she had failed, utterly and completely.

Sammy had thought often about killing herself in the long days and lonely nights when the children were little. Even now when yet again her world had spun off its axis. About how to do it and when; but in the end she had lacked the nerve and the will. Thinking she needed to pay for her failings, for not agreeing to adjust to society for the sake of her children, as her family had demanded of her.

An arriving elevator chimed behind her and Monica nudged her into it. 'We will find out and all will be well,' she repeated for the hundredth time lamely, not quite sure of herself, as they walked down the hallway towards the meeting room. Sammy felt her heart thumping in her ears, as the blood rushed to her head.

Aksh's class teacher had agreed to meet them. The school, while not actively helping, was not obstructing them either.

She clutched Monica as she steadied herself and let her friend pull out the chair for her to sit down. She exhaled, her shoulders sagging a bit as she leaned forward to listen to the class teacher.

Aksh's teacher complained, 'These days, the Internet is the air that children breathe and the world they see. Our opinion does not count. They pounce on us if we make half a mistake, taking vicarious pleasure in destroying us, so the pressure on teachers today is huge. Tut tut, gone are the days of Dronacharya, of teachers being gurus.

'Every boy wants the abs of Shah Rukh Khan, the brain of Einstein and Katrina Kaif for a girlfriend. Children these days are obsessed, they want to be everything all at once. They want to be macho and popular. Girlfriends, branded goods, designer clothes, expensive phones, latest gadgets. Get as many likes as possible on this wretched Facebook. Real friendships can't come as FB requests and technology is a way of staying in touch not losing touch. Attention, more attention, is the curse of this generation. They will do anything to be in the spotlight. Last week we heard of a divorce made up by this child, I won't take names, just to get his class' sympathy,' she spluttered as Sammy looked away guiltily.

'There is peer pressure to succeed like never before. Ivy League colleges … no parent wants less. So children fight to be good at academics and great at sports. We haven't seen it, the likes of this and are frankly quite shocked. Parents pay to get the perfect college application. Every child, it seems, wants to serve the poor, write a book, make an app! Everyday we hear of some new and ingenuous way to make children stand out. They brag and boast about this too, so what message does the child get? Tell me … tell me? Anything can be bought these days!'

Sammy heard her mobile ping and without thinking opened it just as the teacher ticked her off. 'Parents tell their children not to be on the phone all the time, not to constantly be on social media messaging but look you are constantly checking your phone. So teenage angst is as much your creation. You have to walk the talk. Every house, same story.'

And then, the teacher reached forward to grab her glass of water, swallowed mouthfuls in loud gulps before coming to the point and continuing.

'Ak-saha was a good boy but of late has been distracted. He used to run to help me. Always first boy to get to class, first hand up when I ask questions in class. But nowadays, sits at the back and hardly speaks up. He used to get me samosas from the canteen and refuse to take money but now doesn't even look up and meet my eye. He seems distant and aloof. Always lurking around that good for nothing girl's class. Raging hormones, I tell myself! But look where he has landed, in hospital.'

Then lowering her voice conspiratorially, 'It is the fault of that Kushal kid. Too much money, parents have no time. Brought up by servants, tut tut. And I saw with my own two eyes a growing fondness between the two. That Kushal kid is the leader of this gang. Even the teachers are scared of him, his parents descend in full force and his uncle, the Mantri ji, is on the school board, so the principal looks the other way. He pushed that boy from the EWS' – Economically Weaker Section – 'down the stairs and hurt him but no one dared to complain. Your Ak-saha is part of the gang, I see him moving around with them. And then there have been rumours about the white powder; you know what I mean, and the vodka in shampoo bottles, the electronic music. These boys in their sleeveless T-shirts strut around in dark corners after school hours. We have tried but haven't been able to catch them because he pays the staff and is known to have slapped the school peon.

'Ak-saha is a good boy but it is the company … that day there was a fight. Loud squabbling, angry insults and the noise of fisticuffs. Something happened but by the time I got there your Ak-saha was on the floor bleeding. No child has come forward to speak; it is a conspiracy of silence. We know he was beaten up, but there is no one who is saying anything.'

Sammy sat there transfixed; with a feeling that she was being suffocated that very instant. The seemingly unavoidable emotion spread, compounding her misery.

The school seemed to have changed its stance and was being more open than it had been until now. Sammy had been repeatedly calling the school, had visited twice, but this was the first time that anyone had shared the school's perception of Aksh. And it was certainly the first time that the school had admitted that there were unsavoury things happening which they knew about but were powerless, it seems, to do anything about them.

'They say that this Kushal child carries a gun; some kids have told me. He takes it from his bodyguard; the father is a wealthy politician. He has been known to wave it in the air. No, no, not in school but outside in a mall. He lost his temper when his food was served cold. Raved and ranted and his guards did the rest. Like vultures, they swooped down and broke the waiter's bones and threatened to have his carcass picked clean within hours if he did not apologize. That too at the behest of a sixteen-year-old. Terrible!'

Sammy's face froze and Monica did not bother to correct the teacher's pronunciation of Aksh's name because her words had stunned them. Teachers sometimes don't understand how hollow, how lethal, how devastating words can be. Words have power; they can destroy.

Monica had seen Aksh grow up and was amazed that the quiet and docile boy she knew was mixed up with a gang. She shook her head as Sammy sat there opening and closing her mouth like a drugged goldfish.

Finding her voice, she spluttered, 'There has to be a mistake because Aksh was always regular, did his homework and never mentioned this Kushal Singh at home, not once.'

Standing up, the teacher waved Aksh's incomplete work in Sammy's face and the red cards for unruly behaviour. 'All in the last term. See here, you have signed. Look see,' she said, triumphantly as Sammy spied a familiar scrawl ... but it was not her signature, just a clever copy. Until then she had been hoping that the teacher had the wrong boy that she had imagined it and that it was a mix up.

Excusing herself, she ran as fast as she could to the washroom and spent the next ten minutes huddled over the toilet. Nausea hit her in waves. She sat there until Monica found her. Without saying a word, Monica understood everything. Sammy had chosen the life she felt she belonged to and could deal with. And was proud of. Until now.

Sammy stumbled into the car with Monica's help. 'How can this be true? Aksh, my Aksh, a quiet, gentle child with a great sense of humour, has joined the gang of school bullies? And watches waiters in malls get beaten up, smokes and drinks and curses? Lurks around in dark corners of the school? And where did he get money for all this? His pocket money is not enough for this. And why did the school wait for so long to tell me this. Why did they not tell me earlier?'

Monica looked out of the window for a long time and then held Sammy's hand and said, 'One can never tell what is going on even in the neighbour's life. Everyone pretends, puts up a show. People party together, kiss passionately and hold hands ... and then you find out that they are fighting bitterly in court. And they over-compensate with their child. So who can say what goes on in a child's mind! Who can tell? And these years are the worst. Boys do rebel; they just don't listen. But this is bizarre. Aksh is just not the type. I am so surprised!'

The class teacher had given Monica a thin folder to hand to Sammy. There was some information they had found on the school computers. The School Web Protection software kept a track and recorded what the students logged into through the school firewall and they had managed to find some files in the cache in Aksh's account.

'And this print out,' Monica said, giving her a sheet of paper the teacher had passed across, 'is pretty harmless. I have seen worse. And are these code names, because it does not have Aksh in the conversation? Look. The teacher has got some of it mixed up. Take heart. We will get to the bottom of it. Looks like he got mixed up with the wrong crowd. It can happen to anyone.'

Sammy read the paper holding back her tears but was as confused as Monica, because the words made no sense to her. They might as well have been in Hebrew for all she cared! It was a print out of a Facebook chat session.

> Mary Mohan: Our discussion is not your business, Nosey-Parker Jugnu Sebastion! Did your mom not teach you any manners?
> Jugnu Sebastion: i didn't nd degree in manners ... nd u shudn't be talkin as d fact is dat u were gossiping with my sis ... Bitchy Mary
> Mary Mohan: Since when did facts become gossip?
> Jugnu Sebastion: u wdnt knw facts if dey hit u btween d eyes! yeah RIGHT!!!

'What is all this about, Monica?' asked Sammy but her friend also does not know any better. Her only suggestion after a long pause was, 'Check with Rishi. Maybe he sent him money. Check with the house help, the driver. Search everywhere, look in his cupboard.

'It is not too late,' she continued. 'Be cool and calm. And just because he was...'

Monica bit her lip and continued, her face reddening at the faux pas, 'I mean IS a good kid, and doesn't mean that he cannot make mistakes.'

And then, to drive home her point, she continued, 'I read on the Internet that if you expect the world to be fair with you because you are fair with them, it is like expecting a lion not to eat you because you don't eat lion.'

Those were Monica's last words as she got off in front of her house. And as she did, she handed Sammy a letter from the school. The class teacher had given this for Sammy as well. It seemed official. A letter that lay on Sammy's lap unopened. Monica's words, far from being reassuring, had upset Sammy even more.

29

'Sometimes life hits you in the head with a brick. Don't lose faith.'
— STEVE JOBS

'Where did those days go?' Sammy wondered. When Tara and Aksh had been born, they were with her forever. And now forever seemed to be coming to an end. Tara was gone to college in London already and Aksh seemed to be sucked into a black hole. Her little home, her nest, seemed to be emptying out. Aksh wanted to take wings and fly, too.

Lines from a favourite poem came back to taunt Sammy as she sat back and closed her eyes on the way back from the school. It was a poem that had helped her focus on the immediate, on life, on her children, until now. Not being able to recall the lines she Googled what she remembered; despite the slow Internet connection in the car, the browser took her to the right words. Sammy read; and as she read, she remembered Aksh running behind her shouting. And Tara clapping her hands in glee as they shouted out the chorus. 'Dust if you must, Mama, dust if you must.'

She smiled as she read the last stanza:

> Dust if you must, but bear in mind
> Old age will come and it is not kind
> And when you go – and go you must
> You, yourself will make more dust.

Her chain of thought was disturbed abruptly by the driver. 'Didi, I saw with my own eyes. There were seven children, older than Aksh, and they got out of a car and pulled this boy out of his. And then, Didi, they beat him up with hockey sticks and left him bleeding on the road. Police *ka lafda hua*, the Police Control Room van took him to hospital. Arre, Aksh is not like that at all, he would not swat a fly. There is something that the school is hiding.'

Sammy quizzed him, 'Do you recognize the boys? Any one of them? What time did it happen? When? Why did you not tell me?' In the end, she gave up because no further information was forthcoming. He could not tell her much else.

Sammy nodded, grateful for the support. Grateful that he mirrored her feelings that this incident was bizarre and out of place.

'*Yeh* song, baba listens to all the time,' he said, putting it on. Sammy listened, groping in the dark for clues to Aksh's unhappiness, his withdrawn and guarded behaviour. Anything that would help; a clue, a key to his mind.

> Please don't see just a boy caught up in dreams and fantasies
> Please see me reaching out for someone I can't see

Sammy listened mesmerized, the words haunting her. The words of Adam Levine's 'Lost Stars' talked about youth being wasted on the young, about children searching for meaning. It was a peep into Aksh's mind, his troubled state. Sammy's eyes stung with unshed tears. She felt Aksh's emotions and the words 'suffer', 'resent' and 'rage' pop up in her mind as she heard the chorus play it again and again.

> God, tell us the reason youth is wasted on the young
> It's hunting season and the lambs are on the run
> Searching for meaning

Her mobile phone vibrated, bringing her back to the moment and she reached for it, absent-mindedly flicking it open. A message. She scrolled down to read it.

> Watch it, Bitch ... don't stand so close to me. Don't get too close.

The number was hidden, protected. Only the rich and powerful were able to hide the Caller ID.

Sammy was a bit concerned, but not overly bothered, for there was not much she could do about the message. She closed her eyes; the rest of the drive was a blur.

At the hospital, Sammy remembered the letter from the school and took it out to read. Cold, impersonal. It summed up the problem in one sentence.

> The school is investigating the cause of the incident and a special committee has been set up, which will determine the findings in the matter and then appropriate action will be taken.

'Bastards,' Rishi muttered under his breath, 'trying to distance themselves.'

'The schoolteacher told me that he had money. His pocket money was limited so did you give it to him?' demanded Sammy.

She did not need an answer because Rishi's drooping shoulders told her the rest. Children often exploit situations and Rishi had toppled easily, his guilt had over ridden his good sense. But he was not the only one; she too had been blindsided by Aksh. She too had not seen the signs of withdrawal; her sense of his privacy had made her overlook a lot. Maybe, just maybe, she could have prevented the situation.

Rishi held out his arms uselessly as if he wanted to hold her, but a distance too vast to be crossed, separated them.

Sammy reacted sharply, perhaps too sharply. 'Rishi ... you should go. Leave me alone for some time. Go, just go!'

He thought of arguing but realized that she needed to be by herself, that this outburst was not really directed at him, that she didn't really believe that Aksh's condition was due to his giving some money. He didn't say a word, turned on his heel and walked out slowly.

'So what had changed, what is different?' Sammy wondered after he had left, thinking about the time when Rishi had been the big problem in her life. The monster that had betrayed her. Years had flown past and now it seemed as if that chapter belonged to another lifetime, years ago. The time would come when her closest relatives, her mother and brother, too would scar Sammy.

'How did I survive those years?' she wondered, helpless and hapless with a husband she barely knew, having agreed to an arranged marriage and a hostile unwelcoming sister-in-law. Always around to criticize and to give her opinion on even the most personal matters. 'The pill makes you fat, get a diaphragm,' she had ordered. All talk but had she lifted a finger to help? No, never.

She remembered the scene Rishi's sister had created standing in the courtyard of her prestigious college after eating at the cafeteria, all the while running it down, talking as though it was the den of vice and not a place of learning.

And as if it had not been enough to run her college down, she had even written to Rishi about how she felt, turning the knife in deeper. This was in the early years of her marriage.

> Do some introspection, it always helps. Just why do I have to prove my affection? Haven't I done enough over the past decades?
>
> Can't I also feel hurt? How much time does Samaira give me? So what if I arrived a fortnight before her university exams, after all I am her sister-in-law and that counts for something.

Rishi had suggested a meeting between his sister and Sammy to see if the two women in his life could make things work. Fat chance! Sammy's mother had decided to play mediator.

Sammy winced at the memory of the meeting that had taken place over steaming cups of tea and fried dim sums. Her mother, instead of supporting her, had run down Sammy, implying motive where there was none, calling her greedy and stupid much to the delight of Rishi's sister. And Sammy had not even heard the end of the conversation, hanging her head in shame and letting the tears run down her face, while her mother continued to demean her. The shame that even her own mother agreed with Rishi's sister. Sammy lost the thread of the conversation, engulfed by despair, the doors and windows of her old and new homes clanging shut in her mind. Both her mother and Rishi's sister united to show Sammy her place in the family, at the very bottom of the family hierarchy.

Then began the silent treatment, where her mother would cut her off completely and not speak to her for weeks in order to make her subservient to Rishi's sister. Sammy did not budge. Her mother would know deep down that Sammy was suffering, often loudly acknowledge to her son in Sammy's earshot, but would do nothing about it; she would walk away and simply ignore it.

That had been the past and Sammy knew that she was being unfair to Rishi. He had changed, had been supportive, loved the kids immensely. He did care for her deeply, too. The past could not rule her present.

But she was also human and on edge. Perhaps it would be best for Rishi to stay away for some time.

30

'We do not remember days, we remember moments.'

– CESARE PAVESE

Upset himself, but understanding Sammy's feelings, Rishi decided to use the time away from the hospital productively. He asked around, looking for particular people. He finally got access to exactly who he was trying to find.

A phone call, cautious but receptive from the other end. The caller was speaking with Rishi only because the introduction came from a friend who mattered in the political world. A school buddy who had run a village development NGO before going into politics and becoming a powerful Member of Parliament (MP). Rishi was looking to speak with the political agent of Kushal's biological father, the would-be Haryanvi politician, and the call was the outcome of his friend's intervention.

A meeting was set up near Badshahpur, on the outskirts of Gurgaon, and Rishi got an hour with the man he wanted to meet. Under the protection of his MP friend, Rishi was given the inside story about Kushal. In order to protect the father, the political agent had kept track of Kushal and his doings.

In the meantime, Tara had fought with her mother, with some straight talking and some firmness. The plain speak helped Sammy recognize that she had been unfair to Rishi, so she called him to apologize. But she couldn't get through as his phone was out of network coverage area.

Where has he gone to, she wondered. She sent him a message asking him to come home in the evening and perhaps spend a couple of days with them there. 'It will be good to have you around,' she wrote.

It wasn't turning out to be a good day at all. Sammy and Tara tried speaking with Aksh but he was being completely uncommunicative, refusing to speak. He had barely said anything since morning.

'He is worse than the bloody Sphinx!' muttered Tara.

Tired and despondent, they left Aksh to sleep in the evening and went home. Tara kicked off her shoes, curled up under a duvet and watched a romantic comedy on television to relax. Sammy sat back and closed her eyes on the sofa in the living room and slipped into an exhausted sleep.

When she did come around to noticing her surroundings, she found herself next to a very, very angry Rishi.

'This is the limit! I have been doing my own investigation. Aksh got involved with a group of crazy boys, outright bullies. It began in fun but he got sucked into it, deeper and deeper. The bullying repulsed him as well as the beating of younger kids but he went along. It was the drugs and drinking that he refused outright. And it was then that they began threatening him, abusing him and trailing him even to his tuition centre classes.

I went there and the owner told me that he watched these much older boys heckle him, provoke him. It is insane what the kid has been going through!'

'Why? Why did he not tell us? And since when?' No one could prevent the words from tumbling out. They came out with passion, tinged with fear, anger and dejection as she felt her little world sliding under.

'They threatened him into silence, those bastards! That unsavoury politician's son wielded power, subjugating and terrorizing younger children,' said a visibly tired Rishi. His skin was almost ashen grey with worry.

'It was Kushal. He is at the centre of all of this. I haven't been able to trace what happened that day but I know that Aksh was drawn into this gang and they have been threatening and beating up other kids as well.'

The spoke well in to the night. Planning, thinking of Aksh, figuring out the best way to get through to him, to tell him that they loved him.

At some point, sleep overcame both of them. Tara saw them lying on the couch and silently covered them with her duvet, smiling to herself.

31

*'There are only two ways to live your life. One is as though
nothing is a miracle. The other is as though everything
is a miracle.'*

— ALBERT EINSTEIN

Rishi's arm was under Sammy's head, buried beneath the cushion she had used to rest her head on. He had fallen asleep, watching her. It had been a long and frustrating day for both of them. She had fallen asleep, a disturbed sleep on the ottoman in the living room.

Sammy seemed aware, far too aware, of her own deep sounds of breathing. A pause that stretched into a long lull. An unmistakable change in breathing. She paid no heed, tired and frazzled as she was.

Then suddenly, she tossed and turned and woke up ... there was discomfort and a growing pain in her chest. A pain that she could not wish away or dismiss. She knew in that instant that there was something wrong.

She felt tears on her cheeks and waited for the pain to ease. But it did not. She cried harder, suddenly scared. Immobilized with fear.

The irony of life. She had yearned for sleep over the past few days and now was being visited by both; the Greek God of Sleep, Hypnos, and maybe his twin, the God of Death, Thanatos.

She lay there, breathless, trying feebly to reach out to Rishi, to wake him. 'I feel awful, help me, there is something wrong,' she groaned, all the while trying to shake him awake.

He jerked up, suddenly sure that something was wrong. In an instant, he was alert and completely awake and totally in charge.

And what a near call it turned out to be for Sammy! Rishi, a former amateur rally driver, pushed her car and his skills to the limit, rushing her to the ICU barely breathing, for he didn't want to wait for an ambulance. Good call and she was lucky to be alive!

Sammy found herself under blue lights as she spotted a grim doctor, a tearful Tara and a relieved Rishi.

'What happened?' she asked, trying to sit up. Before she could proceed any further, Tara flung herself into her arms and Rishi clutched her hand, muttering, 'Thank God, thank God, you are okay.'

Tired, exhausted, uneasy and breathless, Sammy heard nothing more. She knew that she was not well and she sensed the resident doctor's rapid-fire questions; watched Rishi's lips move in answer.

A few hours later, Sammy was still quite disoriented. Rishi explained how he had woken up to find her slumped nearby, moaning in pain, her breathing strained. 'For one brief moment, I thought the worst. It is lucky that Aksh is already in hospital; we had no problem getting you here,' he joked, but his joke fell flat as Tara glared at him.

Sammy smiled weakly. Even as she lay on the hospital bed, there was something serene and gentle about her face, her smile.

'Thank God, I was able to get you to hospital in time,' Rishi said. 'The doctors told me that if left until morning, it might have been too late. Lucky that I was there and we could rush you here. It was a heart attack. You have to take it easy on that heart of yours; it is complaining, old girl! Often, until you're headed over the edge of a waterfall you don't realize how fast and furious the current actually is.'

Sammy nodded and blinked as tears began to collect in the corner of her eyes. In the face of her own mortality, she felt humbled. Not her degrees nor her worldly success could insure her life nor protect her ailing heart. Suddenly, she was glad to be alive, glad for a second chance at life and the business of living. Acutely aware that her body, her heart, was telling her to take it easy, to worry less and live more. She heard her tired heartbeat tell her, 'It is not over until it is over! So live a little more, laugh a little more, worry less; take care of me!'

'How is Aksh?' she asked.

'We haven't told him,' Rishi said, his Adam's apple jutting out as he struggled with the right words, trying to frame an appropriate reply.

She clutched Tara, hugging her. And told her softly, 'We will go back soon and all will be well. Aksh will go abroad to study if he gets admission. You have to get on, too. I like the young man you spend hours on Skype with. Finish your studies and you must spread your wings. Against all odds I grew my wings and now it is your turn to take flight. I have made a go of my life not because of my circumstances but in spite of them. And the world stretches out for you my sweetheart Tara and for my son-shine.'

Tara immediately interrupted her. 'No, I don't want to go. I cannot leave you, Mama. I will look after you,' she told her, as Sammy reached out to stroke her face and ruffle her long hair, a familiar gesture that eased the tension in the room.

'Hush, my darling,' she said, just as the doctor walked in.

And the doctor fired questions one after the other. 'Does she smoke? Drink? Heavy, mild drinker? Is she addicted to any substance?' Rishi shook his head ... no to all the above, he thought.

A nurse looked at Rishi and asked, '*Ghana gaya kab* last?' No one answered because the question was lost on them.

The doctor butted in and continued, 'A lucky save. It was a mild heart attack but could have been worse. The echo and the ECG did show some changes but not serious. You will, of course, need to be under supervision for the next two days and then we will send your son and you back. I have spoken to his doctor and the results of the tests rule out abnormalities. So all of you will be home soon.' And then he broke into medical jargon that was lost on her.

She groaned and complained, 'Doctor you are burying me under a pile of medical details! Tell me in simple language. Is my heart broken or will it repair?'

The irony was not lost on the doctor and he quickly replied, 'You are a brave woman and are strong. We will ensure you walk out of here on your own two feet.'

And then the nurse standing quietly with a medical chart in

her hand said, '*Aap ka* blood *samble* will be taken so *ghana gane ka nahin*.' Sammy suddenly got it, the nurse was asking when she had eaten *khana*, her last meal, for a blood sample needed to be drawn on an empty stomach. She began to chuckle.

Tara repeated grinning, 'Mama, *ghana* not to be eaten! When *ghana* eaten last?' She went off to check on Aksh, laughing to herself.

The doctor had forgotten his mobile on Sammy's bed and rushed back to fetch it. He smiled and then softly said, 'But that heart wants a little time out. Be gentle on it, ma'am,' he said, before disappearing into the night.

His words, meant to soothe her, disturbed her instead as she grappled with her own mortality and fear of hospitals. She had spent hours with her beloved Nani in hospital, nursing her back to life and always happy to get away when her grandmother got better. The numerous tests, the labyrinth of endless corridors, the grim faced doctors, and the medical jargon frightened her.

Rishi knew this and patted her hand reassuringly. Tara was back with news that Aksh was fine and was asleep. Rishi and Sammy looked at her and exchanged a quiet smile as they saw her fall asleep on the armchair, and Rishi soon curled into a ball on the hospital sofa. Sammy had been, fortunately, given a private room, as she needed a calm environment that a ward would not provide.

Sammy wriggled to a more comfortable position but was unable to fall asleep immediately, in spite of the mild sedative she had been given.

She closed her eyes and just as she was about to fall asleep, she heard two voices.

Opening her eyes seemed an effort; they seem to be weighed down by lead, so she listened quietly with her eyes closed.

Voice 1 (Man): 'The Big Boss wants us to push operations. The conversion is missing the target number. They want us to fill in the executive suite, arre the re-furbished one where they herd in the Dubai patients. Not enough numbers, so he wants us to sell your client a bed tomorrow.'

Voice 2 (Woman): 'I can't do this. It was an ordinary delivery case. I felt bad, but took her in for a C-Sec. How can I keep her longer?'

Voice 1 (Man): '*Majboori hai*! Make her unwell; just up the dosage. She is anyway a hypochondriac and will willingly stay back. You will be doing her baby a service, it will arrive in style. And there is no labour pain.'

Voice 2 (Woman): 'The pain will come later when we present the bill, eh.'

Voice 1 (Man) 'Is there nothing noble about medicine? Even this has been reduced to a *dhanda*, a business.'

Voice 2 (Woman): 'Arre, one of my patients was cut up and they removed the wrong kidney. He could have lived for years without the operation but the Doctor frightened his old father into allowing it.'

Voice 1 (Man): 'Did you watch the Doctor in Allahabad being beaten up? Arre, patient died and the relatives pounced on him, they snatched his mobile phone, gold chain and broke the door. In our hospital, every day this happens. What can the doctors do? They chase fat targets and bonuses all day.'

The lady doctor's words fell like rocks in Sammy's mind, heavy and sinister. Selling hospital beds like hotel beds! The owners were religious people, she knew, running after this godman and that guru by day and counting money by night.

The doctor was speaking again.

'They don't leave the women alone; chasing skirts all the time. That new nurse, she went for orientation again tonight. Why so many orientation sessions for a nurse with the owners? It happens everywhere, we all know, but in a hospital? Disgusting!'

The man's voice responded with caution. 'Don't raise your voice or speak against these powerful people. They will throw you out and get you blacklisted as a troublemaker – they have a hold on the industry. They will even say you sleep around so your reputation will be tarnished beyond repair.'

'It was the same story,' Sammy thought, as she lay still as a marble statue, 'whether it was the hospital or any other place.' She recalled friends who had received messages from intermediaries, messages with a hint of authority. A hint of benevolence. If the woman employee played her cards right, she would be looked after. If she didn't pick up the hint or refused to sell her body for a promotion, she would be helpless, made insecure about her job and would wonder why she was being targeted. The organization would always side with the owners; they held all the power.

But this hospital seemed to be even worse than Sammy could have imagined. The whispers told her that the owners organized parties with substance abuse, prostitution and depravity for rich foreign tourists, in the garb of medical tourism and rehabilitation. This brought in the profits, the big bucks, while the perception was of a noble calling, of helping patients recover.

The lady doctor was quite worked up.

'My foot,' she said. 'He pushes them closer to the grave and counts the money as they decline, grinning all the way to the bank.'

Voice 1 (Man): 'Shshh, we have to be careful. Even walls have ears ... but this is our way of the world, little genius, make your peace with it.'

Voice 2 (Woman), obviously talking about Sammy: 'Look at that woman, Samaira. Tomorrow morning she will be told that she needs an endoscopy and we will have sold another bed ... the unsuspecting fool will never know. She will thank us profusely before leaving the hospital, grateful that we saved her life. But the truth be told, there is no problem, just an anxiety attack.'

Sammy shut her eyes tightly, barely breathing, and heard their footsteps recede into the distance. 'Oh my God!' she exclaimed to herself. 'More the fool you! One less bed sold and two patients will flee your clutches,' she said under her breath, resolutely, disgusted by the corruption, by the filth.

Tara was curled up on the sofa, though someone had covered her with a light *razai*. Rishi was not to be seen. Sammy shut her eyes, but sleep came fitfully.

32

'Being different is a revolving door in your life where secure people enter and insecure exit.'
— SHANNON L. ALDER

There had been opportunities in Sammy's life that she had not taken, not followed through on, which might have taken her far away from the futility of some of what she faced. The roads not taken. One of which had been her time in New York City, a magical, carefree and often careless time, when she had been footloose in the greatest city in the world. She remembered Italo Calvino's wonderful description of the pull of living in New York.

> New York is not exactly America … but what does it matter? It's New York, a place which is neither exactly America nor exactly Europe, which gives you a burst of extraordinary energy, which you immediately feel you know like the back of your hand, as though you had always lived here…

Sammy had once told Rishi, 'It was different, so different to anything I had experienced before, or would ever experience again. Sometimes I would sit in the dark, on the ledge of a rooftop garden, taking in the sounds and sights of the city. Looking, gazing out into the night, at the grand old buildings of the 1930s, the moon and their lights playing a delightful courtship with the buildings. They watched over me, and sometimes I did the same, waiting to see the lights blink off before sunrise.'

'I dreamt…' she had told him, sitting on her balcony in the fading light of the dying sun a few years ago, sipping a glass of wine.

Those dreams seemed so far right now as she sat in hospital on Sunday night, not quite well herself. She thought about her life yet half-lived, half-finished. Time had always been a reference to the future, a better tomorrow and a better life for her children. She had never really lived in the present, Sammy realized with a start.

'God, give me time, please,' she prayed in silence. 'I have so much to be thankful for,' she thought. Rishi must have come back into the room when she dozed off and her eyes glazed as she looked at the two of them sleeping on the couch. 'So much to attend to, to build back.' Her mind turned to Aksh, '…and so much to sort out.'

'What is the meaning of life?' she wondered, as she looked out of the window. She watched the dense sky turn translucent as the deepest part of night crept in. From where she lay, the warm golden sun seemed a million miles away, literally and metaphorically.

The thought made her smile for no good reason as did the oddly associated memory of Tara and Aksh huddling together on stormy nights. Upon hearing the thunder, they would bury deeper into the quilt, muttering to themselves, 'Big fight today. Mrs God is in a bad mood; she is throwing the furniture down from heaven. Poor Mr God,' they would say cheekily, making Sammy giggle.

'There is no home where Mr God gets more sympathy,' she would tell them, drawing her children closer, always closer, always holding them in a tight hug as they struggled to get free in mock protest, enjoying every minute with her.

Sammy decided that she was not going to spend her life in the shadows of what could have been versus what was today her reality and the life she had struggled to create.

Yet the finality of death continued to bother her. She saw the futility of seeking control. She saw her mother's addiction, her urgent need to be in the spotlight all the time. And the ugly consequence of her insecurity on her family, on her husband and her son, but most of all on her daughter, Sammy. Even the grandparents had not been spared.

She remembered her Nana, old and hunched in front of the television set, waiting, waiting for someone to pass by, his daughter to drop in. Lonely and alone, waiting for his time to run out. And when it did, he had gone suddenly.

And it was his daughter, her mother, who had rushed to grab his wealth, playing with the emotions of a lonely old man. Visiting him at odd hours, often when the household was asleep. Always straight from a party, bewitchingly beautiful, she would arrive to bemoan her fate and get his sympathy.

'What will I do when you are gone?' she told him. Feeding on her old father's affection, she had got him to change his will in her favour.

The thoughts jumbled up in her mind and Sammy fell fast asleep, calm and at peace. The drug-induced sleep soon took over but as she slept, she saw the quiet streets of her childhood, lined with Gulmohar. She saw the flowers in full bloom, *mirchi* red and tantalizing. She saw a dust storm and the flowers going mental in the wind but she was not scared. She passed them by, touching their trunks as if to leave an impression of herself, wanting them not to forget her as the swirling darkness descended. She heard the wind blow around the house, scattering the dry leaves and bursting through the windows as the doors rattled. She saw mountains in the distance, their peaks turning blue-grey. In her dream, her street connected with the mountains. It was long and winding ... complicated ... and she was chasing someone ... two children running away from her.

33

'The thing is – fear can't hurt you any more than a dream.'
– WILLIAM GOLDING

She woke up the next morning with sounds of normal hospital activity around her. Rishi and Tara had gone off somewhere, the razai was casually tossed on the couch. Someone had left the newspaper on the locker at the side of her bed and Sammy picked it up, though she wasn't particularly interested in what was happening in the world.

She squinted to read the headlines and gasped. The paper screamed out at her in large bold type. Air Asia flight QZ8501 had disappeared! Stunned, she lay back against her pillow, shocked by the news. Out on the road, a truck roared by as the metropolis began to stir. She sat quietly, much disturbed.

She called Rishi on his mobile phone and he confirmed that he had also just seen the news. He was with Aksh in the ward room.

'There is a flight that has disappeared. It is an Air Asia flight on the route Surabaya to Singapore. The plane seems to have vanished without a trace. The Indonesians have set up an investigation team and the FAA has sent across some experts as well. According to the TV news, there were no messages of anything untoward from the crew or from the automatic systems of the aircraft. They didn't relay a distress signal, no indications of bad weather or technical problems before the aircraft vanished. While they haven't ruled out terrorism, I think they really don't have much of an idea about anything at the moment.'

He went on to add some technical details and finished with, 'The plane was a relatively new Airbus A320-216, a very safe aircraft. I often take this type of plane when I come to India from the Middle East.'

She reached for the TV remote and switched it on at a low volume, flicked to CNN where Richard Quest was anchoring the only news that mattered at the moment – the missing airplane and she heard personal accounts of the horrific incident. For horrific it was; CNN quoted experts who said that the aeroplane had most likely crashed. The deadliest aviation disaster involving an Airbus A320.

Some people had failed to board the flight! 'Karma,' Sammy thought.

Sammy watched in shock. She heard the machines around her hum. She felt her heart race, all the time wondering if her Maasiji had been on the flight. The frantic call from the housekeeper didn't appear that odd any more. Did Maasi ji go down with the plane? But hadn't Maasi ji first gone to Singapore? She wasn't quite sure. What were her thoughts as the flight made its descent? What does one think about? The futility of life, maybe? Does one give up hope, or wish for a miracle? Does one think positive and happy thoughts, even as you speed to chaos and certain destruction?

And then she remembered that Maasi ji hated two things most – water and darkness.

But surely, Maasi ji could not have been on flight 8501, Sammy tried to convince herself, for hadn't she gone to Singapore and was then going out to Indonesia?

Sammy realized in that instant that one could try as hard as possible to imagine someone else's tragedy ... or grief. Drowning in icy waters, living in a city split by a wall or a war, rejected by loved ones. But nothing truly hurts until it happens to you.

Her thoughts of Maasi ji were broken by a cheerful voice, 'And how are we today?' as if she had been part of a conversation with this the latest query. Rubbing her eyes, she saw a large man looking at her through thick glasses. 'I have the reports with me and there seems to be a slight problem, a little concern. We may need to keep you a bit longer,' the doctor said.

'Nope, not me,' Sammy said resolutely. 'I will come back if need be but I will not stay a day longer than necessary.'

'But your blood tests show some changes. We need to investigate and an angiography cannot be ruled out. You have been saved by getting here in time; now we have to do what we have to so that you live a long healthy life,' he said with a glint in his eye.

She crinkled her nose, a mannerism that Rishi had always found extremely cute, smiled and nodded.

34

*'Life's under no obligation to give us what we expect. We take
what we get and are thankful it's no worse than it is.'*

– MARGARET MITCHELL

'We found him depressed and miserable when we came in, sitting on the toilet, crouching and then he slumped in a heap!' Rishi said when he came to her a short while later.

Sammy was alarmed and she covered her mouth as she exclaimed meaninglessly, 'Oh my God! Tell me it isn't our Aksh?'

Rishi shook his head, realizing what Sammy's fear was. Fear that Aksh had committed suicide!

Hugging her, he quietly assured her that her son, her Aksh was well. 'No, nothing like that,' he told Sammy. 'It is just that Aksh is very subdued. He keeps rushing to the bathroom and when he took too long, I opened the door and found him trembling. Don't worry ... Tara is with him right now and will be coming here shortly.'

'There is something that he is not telling us, something that scares him. From his actions, I think he feels safer in the hospital than at home. The nurse says that she saw Aksh visibly shrink when a ward boy gave him a card that had been left for him in the lobby. And she says, she has seen this one chap walk past a couple of times today and each time Aksh covers his head with his bed sheet. Aksh does not seem to know why he is scared, but something about this person is bringing out a deep fear in him.'

Clearing his throat, Rishi continued, 'This place is like a jungle, anything can happen here. They bleed patients for money. There is no security, people come and go at will, but they tell the world outside that it is a fortress. And these bloody blue passes for entry and exit are a sham, I tell you. We have to arrange our own security!'

A ping on the mobile made Rishi stop. He read the email and quietly handed his phone to Sammy. It was the school, telling them in no uncertain terms that since the incident had taken place technically after school hours and outside the school gates, they were not responsible. Also, their internal enquiry had cleared Kushal Singh and his cronies. Aksh, they said, had been caught cheating in the Physics exam and that Kushal, the 'good boy' as they referred to him, had reported the matter to the authorities. Maybe Aksh had hurt himself wanting to put the blame elsewhere, maybe he was being vindictive.

The school really didn't care!

A final word; perhaps even a threat. They, Aksh's parents, were advised to drop the matter in the interest of all, especially that of their son.

'This is absurd. Money speaks and money walks,' Rishi said, exploding with rage. 'These rascals have to be taken to task.

We will get them; throw the book at them! They deserve to rot in hell. Jail is the only answer for them.'

It was especially cruel on Rishi and Sammy, given how they had banked on the support of the school, in spite of the obvious hostility from the beginning. Hoping, believing in the system. Yet, all their hopes and expectation had come crashing down.

Cheating in a physics examination! That was clearly absurd as Aksh was the class genius when it came to Physics. Sammy wanted to blame someone and the school was her primary target. The school was trying to cover up for their inadequate supervision, for having an inherently dangerous environment for school children.

Sammy caught Rishi's distraught expression. 'Maybe he was pushed, maybe roughed up. But why would anyone want to hurt him this way? Someone even contemplating this is unbelievable, unreal! And he hurting himself is out of the question. They are nuts, the school authorities. It is as unbelievable as my wanting to hurt myself! Why would they say something like this? It is mad … really absurd.'

Rishi had spoken with some teachers at the school the previous day, who reluctantly gave him some information when he called them. Apparently the school had conducted an investigation, some searching. They had gone through Aksh's school desk and talked to the teachers and the students in his class. They had opened his locker, gone through the contents of his bag, left behind at school when he had been rushed to the hospital. They had looked for signs of something that could explain what had happened. They even went as far as looking for something that he could have tripped on and hurt himself but had come up with nothing.

'My guess is that those bullies are hiding something and the school is under tremendous pressure to shield the guilty, so it is trying desperately to get out of it. What else can explain the absurdity of their so-called fact-finding mission?' said Rishi bitterly.

'It has been such a long time, well over a week and this is all that we have got? An unsupported allegation, perhaps something like an apology and a take-your-troubles-elsewhere email! This cannot be all there is. There must be more. Why? Why, I ask, is Aksh so scared? Of whom? Why is he so unlike himself?' Sammy lashed out in anger and frustration.

'They have taken so much time and now we are told that our son, the child who has been full of life and dreams, who is my confidante, the child I have looked after and loved, is someone quite different. Someone I don't know. That my child is filled with anger and sadness so great that it has overtaken his life. That I, his mother, missed it all and I didn't even pick up any hint? Saw nothing. And that Tara did not see it coming and neither did you? How, just tell me how, is it possible?'

Rishi was equally angry and his eyes burnt red. 'They say he may have tried jumping in front of a car. Impulsive suicide. It does happen quite often, according to the school psychologist. She's just a clever bitch, selectively quoting research. Children and even adults decide and then go for it within hours, she said, and often there are no tell-tale signs. They don't write elaborate notes; don't give away their prized possessions – nothing. Well, tell me how many such cases has she seen or actually heard of? This is rubbish!'

However, there was more, as Rishi continued with what the teachers at the school had told him in confidence. 'They are squarely blaming his home environment. They are saying the problem was at home and not with the school. Aksh, it seems, told friends that you were too strict, that he felt there were too many rules. Maybe it was just the stress of being a teenager.'

Tara came in, a bit shaken and obviously disturbed. She said that Aksh was much better now and the doctor had given him a mild sedative and he was sleeping.

As they stared at each other, Sammy could feel Tara's watchful eyes on them, looking from Sammy to Rishi and then back again. Sammy knew without having to look that Tara's face was wrinkled with worry.

Sammy's mobile rang once, breaking the silence and vibrated, rattling loudly on the hospital tray. A message. She extended her hand to grab it, but could not reach it. Tara walked across, retrieved it for her and quietly handed it to her mother. Sammy looked at it absent-mindedly.

Curiosity killed the cat. You know it and I know it.

She clamped a hand on her mouth to suppress her scream and tried not to cry. It was getting too much for her to bear.

'Whoa, what's the matter?' Rishi asked roughly, taking the phone from her. His face darkened. She could see little beads of perspiration on his forehead. His face tightened as he asked, 'Who sent this?'

Getting the message was bad enough. But Rishi standing there with Tara, staring at Sammy, glowering with anger, was more than she could bear. She felt like a maimed animal, a failed mother.

'I have absolutely no idea,' she said softly, fighting back her tears. 'I got another one a couple of days ago. Someone's sick sense of humour.'

'That doesn't make any sense,' Rishi said angrily, handing her the phone in her outstretched hand to look for the other message. She asked, 'Do you think it is a prank? Do you think there is more to this?'

'This is not something to take lightly. Show me the other message,' Rishi told her, standing over her as she searched through her Inbox.

'I can't find it,' Sammy told him in a small voice, as Rishi shook his head in despair. And then, as if to excuse her carelessness, she added, 'It was that day, the day I fell sick,' she explained. 'I assumed that it was not meant for me or that it was just someone harassing me. But I really don't know. Nothing makes any sense.'

'It is a blocked number,' Rishi said. 'At the bare minimum we need to find out the source of these messages. I don't think it is as simple as a prank.'

He typed out a message on his phone, explaining, 'I am going to ask a techie friend to take a look. I have asked him to pop by on his way home and that it will take him only a few minutes to get here. Tara, please take mama's phone to the reception.'

'Good idea,' said Tara, grabbing the phone from her mother and she marched purposefully down the corridor, glad to be part of a positive action. 'Blocked number, my ass,' she muttered, sailing past her parents.

'I am tired; all this has been too much for me,' Sammy said, lying down. Rishi nodded, tapping away on the iPad.

The evening sunlight coming in through the glass window made him look older than his years, the day-old stubble and hunched shoulders adding to the vulnerability. Sammy's heart went out to him. He was aching and wanted to strike back at those threatening Aksh but was frustrated, because he didn't know for sure who was responsible. The rumours and stories about Kushal Singh were too vague to act upon.

35

'The most important thing in communication is hearing what isn't being said. The art of reading between the lines is a lifelong quest of the wise.'

– SHANNON L. ALDER

Shaken by both Sammy and Aksh being in hospital, Rishi decided to take the 'Kushal issue', as he called it, head on. Perhaps it was time to meet Santri ji, for meeting the mother seemed to be useless.

Another call to his MP friend, but regrets this time. He didn't know Santri well enough to set up the meeting. 'But I can get you to meet his brother, Mantri, if you would like.'

'Tell me a bit about him,' said Rishi. 'Would meeting him be useful?'

'Yes,' replied his friend. 'Particularly if you have been getting threatening messages. That is Mantri's work for sure. But remember that he has an ego the size of a mountain! The man is so self-obsessed and so self-righteous that anyone who doesn't play yes-man to him remains in serious danger of incurring his wrath sooner than later. Being educated does not necessarily mean that you are good or wise. Mister Mantri doesn't like water to flow unless he tells it to go downhill, but India has changed today. We are professionals, you and I, and have some izzat, but Mantri cares for no one. He is no longer a minister and nor an MP, but he feels superior to everyone around him. He barely even recognizes or acknowledges me! And he is supposed to be the epitome of good manners, of humility.

'Humility!' his friend went on. 'Mister Mantri made news when he walked to the aircraft as minister. Who informed the cameramen from the TV news? And why was the regular public delayed by fifteen minutes as the tarmac was put on security shutdown because the minister wanted to walk? This was VIP behaviour and a cleverly constructed image. He is a very clever man and manipulates people, does Mantri ji!

'Giving perfect sound bites does not make you a good man, a Samaritan. Doing the right thing when everyone is watching is not the mark of a real man. It is doing the right thing when no one is around that differentiates people. But they feel they can get away with it every time. This family ... is the pits! After Partition, like many others, they moved to India. The whole clan, kith and caboodle. One of Mantri ji's own uncles, father's brother, died leaving behind a young widow and many children. When she asked for her husband's share they threw her out. Called her greedy and cut her off completely. She was left to fend for herself and her children. These are his lofty values. He watched but did not intervene. Both Santri and Mantri could have helped their aunt but looked the other way and they talk about izzat. After all, I have seen people, the rich and the famous. This family turns victims into criminals. They aim guns at people who can't shoot back.

'His cousin, a young girl, liked the neighbour's son. Mister Mantri, with his Sinister brother and father in tow, burst into Volga, the hip place in the rocking sixties in Connaught Circus. He threatened to kill her, calling her a slut and roughed up the chap. All in the name of family honour. And today, they turn a blind eye to Sinister Santri's son and overlook his affairs; many in number I tell you. Even his daughter-in-law is no *sati-savitri*, I say.

'I am telling you this, Rishi, because you must know who you are dealing with. It's not about the meeting … I will set that up. It's about what will happen afterwards. Are you ready for that?'

Rishi wasn't sure he was ready for anything but it seemed like the only way to get to the bottom of this. 'Just set up the meeting please,' he asked.

'I will do that,' his friend assured him. 'This is who he is, Mister Minister Mantri ji. Often when you least expect it, the mask dissolves into the face. Tut tut, and all the lectures he gives on TV. Change the channel, but you cannot escape him, he's always there.'

The man was not quite done! 'And that bloody Sinister Santri! No words to describe his hypocrisy. He climbed up the corporate ladder holding on to his brother's coat tails and then had the audacity to loudly proclaim otherwise. All their machinations did not get him the top job at the chocolate factory. He sulked for years and then the next opportunity came. Not on a conveyor belt as they would want us to believe but with his brother's help. The bastard is known to have said, "I don't take calls from friends and family because they are always so needy, want a job for someone all the time. I run a business not a charity."'

By now Rishi had a good measure of both men, Mantri and Santri. Time to go and bell the cat.

The meeting was set up for the afternoon. Rishi reached the office, set in a residential block in South Delhi. Down a flight of stairs into a basement. A brief interrogation and then Rishi was led to a waiting room.

A few minutes later a young girl came out adjusting her sweater, took a long look at Rishi and asked him who he was waiting for. Before Rishi could reply, there was an agitated voice heard from the inner room ... it was none other than Mister Minister Mantri ji.

The girl made a pretence of patting her hair as if readying herself to go in for the first time.

Rishi was asked to go in, the girl followed and sat down in a corner discreetly. The big man was sitting behind a desk, with a pile of books on one side and a mug, South Indian freshly brewed coffee, in front of him. Something seemed odd in the room and then Rishi figured it out. There were a set of photographer's lights mounted on the walls. Mantri saw him look at the lights and remarked, 'For my television appearances.'

Silence for a bit. 'So,' Mantri ji said, 'Rishi, is it?'

'Powerful name. Not sure if you live up to it. Heard of the Sanskrit Institute at Kottayam?' he asked rhetorically. And then, without waiting for an answer, Mantri continued, 'The director is my friend, dear friend and so is Dr Nair, you know the big guy himself. He gets me whatever information I need. I never ask; all information comes to me ... But mind you, all secrets reach me. Trade secrets, state secrets, government – public affairs.

You know ... who sleeps with whom, who makes how much, and politician's pet peeves and worst fears. I know all secrets!

'So why have you come to me?' he asked Rishi. 'Be quick please as I am a very busy man.'

Rishi felt that someone who knows all secrets wouldn't need to ask why his visitor had come. However, in the interest of moving things along, he gave a polite and watered down version of what was happening at the school and wondering whether Mantri ji might be able to ask Kushal about the events of the day Aksh was beaten up.

But then came a half hour period during which Rishi didn't know whether to laugh or cry at the absurdity of what he heard. Mantri ji was in a rage, the kind he wouldn't want his critics to hear or write about.

'They don't call me Mantri for nothing! The Intelligence Bureau is nothing! I am a bulldog! When I get after someone, I get them! I then put my brother Santri on the job and we follow them to their grave, watch them burn on the pyre. Do you want us to stand and watch you burn on your pyre, you irritating wretch?'

Faustus would have leapt and twirled in this dance of the deadly sins, thought Rishi, and clapped his hands at the display of wrath from Mantri ji.

Feeling appropriately bludgeoned and cut to size but not at all cowered down by the shouting, Rishi began to speak. 'Sir, sorry, I did not mean to be disrespectful but...'

Only to be rudely interrupted. 'I can smell the aroma of the basmati, but the proof that it has cooked is when I eat it, you scoundrel! *Tussi toh* yesterday *ko* born *hue ho* ... born yesterday, what do you know about life? You NRIs are all the same … where is the proof that Kushal did anything? I need to taste it … I mean see it…'

But Rishi had never accused Kushal of doing anything. In defending Santri's step-son of sorts, Mantri ji had already confirmed what Rishi knew. That Kushal was the cause of Aksh's beating. Why he did not know, but that too would soon come out, he thought.

The office boy, unfortunately for him, walked in to hand Mantri a letter. And Mantri ji then proceeded to humiliate the peon ever so sweetly in his infamous, way. He used the power of language and his position to belittle the man. Mantri, to the girl's obvious horror and Rishi's disgust, corrected the hapless man's English.

Rishi had heard that he did this to people, but to see him in action was quite another matter. Mister Mantri puffed out his chest, dropped his voice, and in a soft dulcet voice, tried to demolish the man in front of him. He had heard rumours, whispered gently when people from his college had met, about how Mantri did the same with bureaucrats who worked with him. He reduced them to tears and one had resigned from the administrative service, a nervous wreck after dealing with the great man. Official notes put up to the minister were read with a red pen in hand; the English corrected first, glasses perched on his head and an Urdu couplet on his lips. The notes were then handed back, a stenographer brought in and the notes written from scratch in such tedious prose and style that the reader lost the argument before reaching the end. But try and meet the minster without a note ready for him to read and the result would be even worse. Working with Mister Mantri ji, he recalled one of his friends telling him, was like a road accident waiting to happen. You could see it occurring, watch the cars head towards a collision, but all you could do was wait for the crash. And like all road accidents in India, there would be the usual highway drama and curiosity, with people interested in the unfolding drama and glad that somebody else was today's road-kill. Nothing had changed and yet, it wasn't the same any more.

He then dismissed the peon and directly threatened Rishi. 'Give it up, trying to find out what happened. Give it up. If you don't, I won't be responsible for what might happen to Samaira and you.'

And then, with a menacing tone, he said, 'I hear you have a beautiful daughter. Tara, isn't it…'

At which point, Rishi got up and looked the former minister in the eyes. He continued to stare at him quietly until Mantri ji looked away and then he stood up dismissing him. The meeting was over and he ordered Rishi out.

The man did have his supporters. The girl had been in the room with Rishi, standing close to the door so that she could gaze in awe at Mantri, her hero. She seemed to be in love with his power, but was a bit shaken by Rishi having stared Mantri ji down, the threat palpably having made the former minister uncomfortable. She walked Rishi out and said to him, trying to cover up, 'You know, sir, he was such a selfless minister. Never mind that some people said he made bad decisions. He was so good, sir, we need people like him. He looks after me so well,' blushing and giggling as she said it for she knew that Rishi understood their relationship. 'He never does things in a small way and I don't know why he is not in favour any more. If he says that you should not do something, please listen to him. He means business and he does not care about people. So do what he says, for your own sake.'

Then softly, she added, 'He is best man. All of them make money, so what if he does? If you want something from him, you should not have made him so angry!'

And that seemed to be the defining verdict on the man!

36

'I have noticed even people who claim everything is predestined, and that we can do nothing to change it, look before they cross the road.'

– STEPHEN HAWKING

Sammy was resting on her hospital bed when the red-faced doctor came to her room. He was doing his rounds but seemed to be in a gossipy mood, talking about a patient in the next room. 'His father's brother, bade Papaji...'

Unable to control herself, Sammy laughed and said, 'Papaji as in Daddy, like Puff Daddy, the rapper?' visibly amused.

The doctor explained unnecessarily, 'Punjabi for elder brother, papaji.' And then he paused, unsure whether he should be talking so openly to a patient.

'I knew the man, was his neighbour,' he said and stopped again.

Why was he gossiping with her, Sammy wondered? Pressure of work? In any case, he seemed to want to talk so Sammy let him. This papaji had obviously meant something to the doctor.

'The old man had the trademark square face, fat nose, lazy eye and was balding, large forehead. He would slowly slurp his masala chai spiced with crushed ginger, blowing gustily into the cup to cool it. After that he would pop a small cardamom into his mouth; this was his little ritual. Otherwise he was harmless and spent his free time, which he had plenty of, watching traffic, hanging on his gate! I cannot forget him; dressed in an old worn-out kurta-pyjama. His aged face with the grey stubble, his narrow eyes hidden behind thick reading glasses and his scared toothless smile are etched in my memory.'

'Scared smile?' Sammy asked.

'Yes, after his only son was found dead in a not-so-nice lodge in the city, he was scared. He was ridiculed and heckled at by his family, even by his young grandson, the local thug. Now the grandson opens and shuts down businesses with such speed that it is difficult to keep count. And the women, pah, flock there, batting their eyes at him. He does have a way with them; started young. Ran away with a schoolgirl in true Hindi film-*ishtyle*.

'But coming back to the old man; there was drama every day. And then he died; sudden heart attack the neighbours were told but I am a medical doctor and not a quack. Things did not add up. The family's hurry to cremate him, their reluctance to let me near him. All it would have taken was holding a harmless pillow down with force.'

The nurse came in and he stopped abruptly, cleared his phlegmy throat, adjusted his glasses and asked for the reports he already held in his hands. Transforming from a gossip to a professional in a flash. And just like that, he turned with a cursory nod of his head, dismissing the conversation and her peep into his world, and was gone. The curtain fell suddenly, the Act was over and the Scene had changed. Just one of life's unexpected moments.

'Doctors do gossip; no secret is a secret,' mused Sammy as she watched his receding backside disappear out of the room and down a corridor.

Her reverie was broken by Tara as she bounded into her open arms. Showered, changed and fresh, her elfin bone structure and dark, straight, long hair made Sammy catch her breath. It was a full minute before she spoke. 'You are gorgeous, my little girl,' she said, holding her in a big hug.

'Mother and daughter up to mischief?' they heard Rishi ask and both looked up and grinned at him.

'Good to see you up and about,' Rishi said to Sammy.

'Where were you? You left me alone in this state?' she asked in mock annoyance.

'You were well taken care of and were busy,' Rishi replied. 'I left Tara with Aksh and then went off to do some stuff.'

He paused for a moment, knowing that his words were going to be dramatic and enjoying the moment. 'I went to meet that pompous oaf Mantri. He began to shout and threaten me but I got what I wanted. I now *know* that Kushal is behind Aksh's beating.'

'What!' exclaimed Sammy and Tara together.

'When I popped my head in, you were engrossed in a

conversation with the doctor,' continued Rishi. 'So I left you to it and made a call to confirm that the police station had registered the FIR and sent me a copy by email.'

'FIR!' Sammy and Tara repeated together.

37

*'You may not control all the events that happen to you, but
you can decide not to be reduced by them.'*

– MAYA ANGELOU

'FIR! You filed a first information report with the police! What happened?' Sammy asked, the smile leaving her face, the happiness draining from her. Concern replaced the bonhomie of the moment.

'I spoke with Jay. He looked terrified but when I reassured him that his mother would not find out, he opened up. Apparently this Kushal Singh went to Aksh's group tuition centre and threatened him, told him that if he ever spoke up he would be thrashed. Not Mrs Khanna – the other one. And they beat up another kid, their common friend, who tried to intervene to drive home the message.'

And then, after a gulp of water from the bottle on the bedside, Rishi exhaled deeply and continued. 'We do not know what these kids hold over Aksh but there is something that he is just not telling us. But I have pieced some of it together and am working at nailing the bastards. They stalked Aksh in school, following him, tripping him, laying booby traps so that he got hurt. Stealing his notebooks just before exams and he had to literally beg to get them back. They are known to have stapled the skin of smaller children. And the bloody school refuses to do anything!

'This was the limit. So, after meeting Mantri, I drove across to the group tuition centre these kids went to and spoke to the teacher there. She confirmed the harassment and showed me the glass door that shattered when they pushed another child through it. Luckily he got away with a few stitches. And then, emboldened, they shoved Aksh around. This was a couple of days before the attack in school.

'They mocked him and gave compelling reasons for him being absent, thereby making sure that he did not show up. See, see ... Jay told me about something on social media so I asked him to forward it to me and I took a print out just now,' he said, placing an A4 sheet in her outstretched hands.

Opening it, Sammy and Tara read the words again and again ... the exhilaration at finding something mixed with dread, the curse of Facebook and cyber bullying.

> Tuti is pregnant. Her boyfriend dumped her, so she is aborting. She's anyways screwed and her studies are a mess. Her parents are getting a divorce. Both mom and dad like the same girl it seems! What a fucked up family!
> Sharma sir is having an affair with our tuition teacher. He must be fucking blind! Moti has the hots for him and is far sexier

> Our school is haunted, guys. Years ago this place was a graveyard
> Or some girl was strangled here and this place is now haunted *Ugh*
> That girl who got pregnant is a slut. She sleeps with every guy in town. New guy every night. Why should her boyfriend support her? Not his child he told me
> Physics sir asked Tuti to do it with him
> He should have asked Aksh … Hee hee, anything for extra marks. Aksh will do what we tell him
> Aksh the romantic bastard asked this girl out and she rejected him. He's going through some sick depression man!
> Physics sir is a drunkard. Every morning you can smell it when he comes to class
> Coz his wife is a fat bitch and his students are so terrible. Alcohol is his only friend
> Aksh only did well coz he ass-licked all the teachers
> Or he got Tuti to do some jhol and got all the question papers a night before
> Man, if he got the papers and didn't give me, I'll kill him!
> That girl is also a druggie. Will she share?
> Share what? Herself or the drugs?
> Both man! Either … whatever!
> She needs to diet
> So do you man
> Yeah, coz you know what exercise and diet is
> Don't eat at the school canteen. Someone found a lizard tail in the rice. Ashwin and Aksh must have fallen in Ha Ha Ha
> Aksh is so full of shit

> He was bunking school coz he must have been having sex with Tuti
> Like he couldn't have been sick or gone on vacation or what?
> Hey guys. Late on the chat. You are so messed up. Tuti and Aksh. You gotta be joking!
> Coz u know or what?

There was pin-drop silence as Sammy stared, her eyes rooted to a spot on the wall opposite her. Horrified, totally speechless. Everything has a life of its own and nothing ever disappears in the digital world, Sammy realized. This generation has lost the right to forget, she thought, suddenly sad because she knew that this would follow Aksh even years from now.

'I must say, this tuition teacher was very supportive and helped me piece it together,' said Rishi. 'She even agreed to the filing of the FIR and came with me after I agreed to compensate her for her time. The police refused, dismissing it as a childish prank but she produced photographs from the hidden camera installed in her premises. And made a few calls. Her late husband, it seems, was a civil servant before he died. So she has clout. The police commissioner is his batchmate and thus a personal friend.

'Can you believe it? We had to use clout to file an FIR! The SHO and beat constable made it really difficult, reading out the Juvenile Act and cautioning us that we were taking on deadly people, with wealth and political connections. And that they are mixed up with the underworld, the drug mafia and what not. They tried to explain it to me as a friend, thinking that I am an idiot because I live in London!

'We were firm and said it has been done. I have personally added the principal's name to the FIR. It is done ... with the commissioner's help, the police have stated in the FIR that a criminal offence under Section 506 of the Indian Penal Code has been made out against person or persons unknown.'

'But Papa, the tuition teacher doesn't have to go back to school, Aksh does,' said Tara with concern, absorbing the implication of what had been done. 'They will thrash him, cut him to bits, Kushal and his friends!'

She thought for a few minutes. Tara knew her father very well. And then, after a minute and apparently having made up her mind, she said, 'Papa, you must do as you are planning. I'm sorry, I just got scared for Aksh.'

'Mama,' she said. 'I know this is the only way to sort out the matter.'

'Hush little baby!' Sammy exclaimed. 'You don't need to tell me ... I understand. We have to get this sorted out.' And turning to Rishi, she said, 'Just be careful...'

A hard and determined look came on to Rishi's face; his defiant eyes had a look that Sammy knew well. There was no turning back for him. The burst of emotion that followed was unexpected but the resolve in his voice was expected; he doted on the children. Tara and Aksh were his life, period. He could not see beyond them. And that Aksh had been attacked had enraged him beyond belief.

Every muscle in his face twitched with emotion as he resolutely said, 'This is exactly what I want to fight, the criminalization of education. The bullying and intimidation of children. Do you even know that the trauma faced by a child when he is ragged runs deep? Just last week, a young child lost his life due to what they call "hazing". Did he not deserve to live? Did he not deserve a future? Just because he came from a modest background, the sons of these rich so-and-so parents thought it was their birth right to ridicule him, to make fun of him, to torture him for his not-so-sophisticated accent, his broken English! The very definition of the word includes compelling or forcing a student, whether by way of a practical joke or otherwise, to do anything that goes against his grain, robs him of his identity, reduces his dignity as a person. So what these bastards were doing ... intimidating, wrongfully restraining, confining and injuring children by using criminal force and threatening these children ... is a dastardly act of cowardice and they have to be held accountable. There is a law in the country, it isn't some banana republic!'

Sammy had been listening quietly till now but broke in. 'Are you sure, Rishi, that this will not lead to more violence?' she asked softly. 'Will they turn even more on Aksh? Instead of a deterrent, will it encourage them?'

Rishi had thought it through and it was not an impulsive reaction from him. As he spoke, Sammy's resolve grew and she knew that he would bring all the forces at his disposal to support Aksh and her in this fight. For a fight it was now going to be.

'To remain silent in the face of evil, Sammy, is itself a form of evil. I read it in one of your books, the one by Sue Monk Kidd, lying on your table. I flicked it open and the words struck me as so true. Why did you stand up for yourself? You too faced adversity, risked your life ... for what? To win back your dignity so that you could hold your head high in society. You did not buckle down despite the attacks against you. You were brave and it was worse for you because the attacker was your family, the rarest of the rare situations. Your mother lead the ugly pack, your mother wanted to claw you and leave you bleeding for the vultures to complete what she had started. You, and only you, could have taken her on.

'You stood up to injustice and the threats, while the children and I watched. What else could we do? We spent a lot of mornings submerged in worry. We held our breath but did not hold you back. Do you know that those days I could not even taste food? Deprived of all five senses – deprived of taste, scent, sound, and most of sight. I could not watch TV, not even the World Cup,' he said. And repeated, 'Not even the World Cup.' Sammy knew Rishi. She knew that he would not have missed the World Cup for anything.

'I have also spoken with some friends,' he said quietly. 'There is nothing for us to worry about. It is time now for those bastards to worry!'

And just like that, in that instant, the decision to stand up for what was right was taken by them in a hospital room.

38

*'Every human walks around with a certain kind of sadness.
They may not wear it on their sleeves, but it's there if you
look deep.'*

— TARAJI P. HENSON

Sammy had been thinking about her stay in the hospital when she heard a familiar voice. She had been wondering when it would be okay for them to move Aksh and her away from this hospital, now that they knew the over-prescription and almost mercenary attitude of some of the doctors.

'*Bachche*, what happened? Sammy, you were looking after your son but you have landed in hospital instead. It is all the stress; life hasn't been easy for you.'

The tinkling glass bangles gave it away and she looked up. It was Kitty making her way and jingling quickly across the width of the room, rushing towards her as if on stilts. She had the precarious gait of a Japanese geisha with bandaged feet, shuffling, leaning forward, as she hurried to the bed on her high heels.

'Oh no, bachche. This is bad, too bad. So much strain and no one to take care of you,' she said, shaking her head as she spoke, her words rushing out. She was reminding Sammy of her position in life, her unfortunate situation. Treated like a leper by her own family, abandoned and rejected.

It was then that Sammy noticed a man standing behind her. He looked smart in an indigo blue shirt with a showy necktie and elegant imported shoes, sun glasses tucked into his shirt pocket.

'This is my cardiologist *frand*,' Kitty said, her accent slipping. 'He keeps my heart in shape, and myself young.'

'Myself Dr Bhalla from Jullundur city,' the smart man told Sammy.

It was difficult for Sammy to keep a straight face. 'I got him to come and escort me. These days you can't be too careful, na bachche,' she added.

She saw Kitty's '*frand*', as she had called him, escorted to the coffee shop by a nurse. Kitty pulled a chair and sat down uninvited, wiping imaginary sweat from Sammy's brow to show her concern. 'You know, *frand* is very important. You must get one. It is good for you,' and she winked.

'I have many,' Sammy told her without thinking and was surprised to see Kitty blush and exclaim, 'Hai tauba! Many!'

And then Sammy suddenly realized that they were talking at cross-purposes, with the lady referring to sharing of beds rather than cups of coffee. 'No, no! Not like that! Just the Monica variety,' she told her, colouring visibly and a little annoyed at being tripped.

'Nothing wrong with other types as well! You have always

been a prude. Be like your mother in these things. Look at her score,' Kitty said, her voice dripping with genuine admiration. Then, after a pause she added, 'There was no Minister or Opposition Leader who was not in her pocket. She showed me her contact list and it had everybody on it ... I mean every important body.'

And then, bending over conspiratorially, she shared her secret, her secret for life and vitality with Sammy.

'Bachche, I told you when Rishi and you divorced that there was no need to cry. Remember what fun it was getting facials at Kuku's Parlour? How I wished I had opened one. Now with free electricity, free water in Delhi it would have been a money machine. You would have all the men you wanted!'

Sammy blinked and was transported back to those summer afternoons when she would sneak out for a couple of hours at the salon, her 'me' time. Lying there in the darkened room, with the powerful air-conditioning, she felt as though she had gone into hiding from daily life. Reclining on the pristine white treatment bed, she loved the creams being slathered on her face. It was sheer bliss. It was a luxury she indulged in, the citrus smells and the gentle hands kneading her face, uplifting her soul.

And the therapist always had something nice to say. 'Mark my words, life will change, this will be behind you. You are pretty and there will be a life ahead but keep him dangling.' 'Him' being Rishi of course. Lifting her little finger, the therapist would tell Sammy, 'Keep him hanging and be smart. Don't sign the divorce; let him stew. That way, your children will inherit and he will have to pay for play. Playing with your emotions, feelings.'

Sammy did not want to disillusion her and so never got around to telling her that there was not much in the kitty from Rishi's side.

'Poor you, suffering like this.'

And that would be enough to make Sammy turn her face. She would look away because she did not want sympathy. She did not want to morph into a *bechari*, a poor sympathy-seeking victim of circumstances. She just did not want any of that.

Earlier that morning, Sammy had been taken by wheelchair to Aksh's room, seen him sleeping and returned after a brief loo stop to give the sample for further tests, not quite certain whether all these tests were required or not. On her return, she had found Tara perched precariously on the sofa, busy on a Skype call for an upcoming college test.

'Technology has really shrunk the world,' she observed. Gone were the days of letters and telegrams. Her children would never know the anticipation of receiving one, the satisfaction in ripping it open. Alas, much gained and a little lost.

On her way back to her floor and hospital bed, she had remembered Kitty walking into the beauty parlour many moons ago and loudly proclaiming to the world, 'Men are like aeroplanes, who knows when there is one on the horizon. Bachche, take heart,' she had told Sammy loudly, adjusting the rose in her bun. Sammy's ears had burned with embarrassment.

An odd coincidence then that Kitty had turned up at the hospital after lunch, with a similar conversation about men, and was now sitting on the sofa that Tara had vacated. Tara had little patience with Kitty and would scurry off on spotting her. Fast as a rabbit, she would disappear, with her hair flying everywhere, as she took to her heels almost running, escaping.

Sammy grimaced as other memories came back to her. Her mother never took her out anywhere, claiming that her presence was an embarrassment or was inauspicious. Kitty had once taken her to a surly tailor's shop. She remembered squirming as he felt her up, ostensibly taking measurements for her clothes. She had gone to the tailor in the hope that her luck would change and she would have places to go. The clothes had piled up at the back of her cupboard with each garment taunting her for the missed parties and New Year's Eve celebrations, weddings that Sammy never went for.

This brought back memories that Sammy didn't quite want to remember. She remembered that horrible Holi when she was back in her parent's house, drowning in misery. But just then Sammy's sister-in-law had arrived. Not Rishi's bitch of a sister, but her own brother's wife, Lola. Perfect Lola had been on a mission, with her idiot husband, Sammy's brother Pratik, trotting at her heels.

'First Holi with second husband and twentieth bed mate, including Doctor Pushkar, her brother's school captain. And then the perfect swap. Lola married my brother while her brother's girlfriend had wickedly landed in the doctor's bed,' flashed through Sammy's mind at the time.

'Cow, slutty cow,' Sammy had thought but had kept her comment to herself.

She had looked up to see her mother beam, smug that the Almighty had acknowledged her oh-so hard life by compensating her with a daughter-in-law straight from heaven.

'Loser,' she had told herself, hugging her idiotically perfect and smugly happy sister-in-law instead of running away. She would only look at her once beloved brother and wonder how marriage could have transformed him in weeks to a weak, ingratiating excuse for a man. Or Ratprick as Maasi ji had always called him!

Meanwhile, Kitty had been going on and on about something or the other and Sammy hadn't been paying the slightest attention. And then, the story over, Kitty got up to look for her *frand*, and Sammy spotted the nurses giggling in the corner of the room.

39

'Death is not the greatest loss in life. The greatest loss is what dies inside us while we live.'

– NORMAN COUSINS

'What are you thinking about?' asked Kitty. 'He will take time, the good *frand* that he is. Good doctor is doing full examination. Was top of his class in Jullundur.'

'Any news about the lost aeroplane?' Sammy asked suddenly, but got blank looks from the nurse. She reached for the TV remote control to change the channel to the news.

'Bachche, big tragedy. A flight crashing like that and all passengers dead! Even your Maasi ji … that's what her servant told me!'

'She is not dead … and she is in Singapore and was going to Indonesia later,' Sammy said in a determined voice, wiping a tear and pointing to the screen.

Both watched the ticker, as the news anchor was busy interviewing the fashion designer whose public relations company had bought time on the show. Who cared about a little thing when TV time had to be sold in slots of ten seconds?

Nothing had been found as yet of the actual aircraft ... no trace at all!

'God is great, don't lose heart, bachche,' said Kitty. 'I know you are fond of your Maasi ji, but let me tell you, she was wild when young, totally out of control.'

Maasi ji was quite something, Sammy knew. She had been known to be manipulative and greedy. In the evenings, she would dress in her very best and go to the homes of relatives she wanted to encounter, seemingly by chance. In the extended joint family, everyone lived close by and there were many opportunities and reasons for someone to just happen to pass by. She even went to where Sammy's father always had his evening tea and showed great amazement at finding him there. In such situations, she would invite herself to sit down and, if alone with the object of her attention, mercilessly gossip about a relative or a close friend.

'She was my friend,' said Kitty, 'But I know that she would stand there and run down your mother in front of your father. She would make jokes about the cheap gifts sent by his in-laws, saying that they must have been bought at discount stores, never at full price.'

Her father had always held this against her mother, thought Sammy. He had never forgotten the girls from rich families who had been brought to his door and how his family had turned them down.

Having planted a seed of doubt in her object's mind, Maasi ji would smugly retreat, holding her sari way above her ankles as though wading a river. 'A fight always followed Maasi ji's passing by, if I remember correctly,' thought Sammy. 'Much like what is said about Narad Muni!' Maasi ji thrived on creating conflict and rifts between people!

'I am the longest living witness, I belong to that generation and have seen it all,' said Kitty, admitting her age for a change. 'We came after Partition. There were only a few good families in Delhi, and we all knew each other. I know the history of every family and every square inch of their house. After all, we were all well acquainted.'

The cream of Delhi society these days was once a refugee in the city. They had crossed over the border in panic, in large numbers, some lucky and others not so. Many perished along the way. Resettlement properties, given as shelter to those who had lost nearly everything, had appreciated in value till they became the heart of the new city. And their owners cultivated the airs of the aristocracy, almost pretending to be related to the British King George VI or his soon to be crowned daughter, the next monarch Queen Elizabeth II.

But those were also beautiful times. It was a different age. Lahore was like a European city, it was said. It was clean and smart and the people were well mannered. But cities too have lifelines. They are built and then destroyed. Sometimes physically and sometimes their soul just withers and dies.

Maasi ji, Kitty and people like them had spent most of their lives going in and out of the houses of the so-called elite of Delhi. They had lived their best days in this city. And they had stories, many stories, about the politics of that generation.

'Your Maasi ji was notorious,' said Kitty. 'She would punctuate every sentence with your grandfather's name, using it to drive fear in the extended joint family. Her high-pitched voice would turn into a long squeak when she wanted something, especially if it belonged to your mother.

'She did not spare your foolish father either. Everyone could tell that there was great love between the siblings; he doted on her! You know this already, but she would play him. She would whisk his emotions to such a high that the poor man would leap up and rush to get the wretched object of her desire. Placing whatever she wanted into her hands as if making an offering to a deity, he would sigh with relief and then sink into his comfy chair. The day would end as she had wanted it to; victory was hers. She would then send a servant to eavesdrop and report the ensuing fight between the irritated couple and report the colourful bits to your grandfather, clucking at your mother's foul temper and bad language.

'She would accompany your grandfather on his evening walk, always a few steps behind him, clutching a black doctor's bag. Pah, all drama! She would fill his ears as he stopped to examine a crack in the floor here, a shrub there. They would stop and examine a flower solemnly; he would talk knowledgeably but God knows what clever titbits she had to add, for she often looked so pleased that one would have thought she had chanced on the discovery of Penicillin, maybe even invented it.'

Her grandfather had been deeply suspicious of all women, with his special watchful eye being on the daughters-in-law, who always remained outsiders to the family. Sammy recalled that family gossip talked about a turning point. Things changed when Maasi ji took a shine to her sister's daughter-in-law, Rina Babi.

They dressed in the same clothes, spoke the same way, even giggled at private jokes, making fun of the other female members of the household and followed each other around.

There was peace in paradise until a new daughter-in-law arrived, younger and prettier, displacing the older one in the family hierarchy and in Maasij i's affections. Rina Babi pouted, bit her lower lip and cursed, tried to use her charms more obviously, while she smiled bewitchingly to avoid an open confrontation.

But Maasi ji and her ageing father had a new rock star. A young girl, with flowing, shiny, jet black hair. Usually covered but often with wisps peeping out from the sides of her scarf. Her eyes were captivating; they drew you into their depths. The lips luscious and sensual. Her voice ... even Sammy remembered it ... was a whisper, enchanting and full of promise, which made the loud giggles in the house seem out of place. Almost old fashioned, you could say. The sexy, young granddaughter-in-law was plied with gifts. Only the best for her.

But then, just like that, one day he was gone. He was like the orange sun setting below the horizon. His life, like his memory, lost its shine, its edge. It was as if the night sky had dyed his mind black. Like ink dissolves slowly and colours water, it happened like that. Sammy had watched the much acclaimed movie *Still Alice* with much interest because it portrayed the early onset of Alzheimer's, a disease she was familiar with, for she had watched her grandfather decline as his mind turned to fudge and he lost his identity.

She remembered the days before his passing were dark and without texture. For God's ways are strange. The man who loved his food was reduced to stealing morsels. He spent his last years in penury, without control of his faculties and hence his bank account, while his daughters and the house full of daughters-in-law looked away. He was a grand old man, who had once commanded the attention of all who encountered him. Reduced to hob-knobbing with the servants, idling his time running after them, chasing dogs because he hated them. Even dementia did not dull his phobia. His smart Nehru jackets, ironed just so, 'on the crease' he was known to insist, were replaced by dirty soiled dhotis with rubber *chappals*.

'For a memory cannot be bought. "True that!" in Aksh's lingo,' she thought and smiled to herself. Money can turn on you, making you vulnerable and abandoned. It reminded her of Papaji's tragic end, money had hurried his death.

She had heard these stories often. Sammy swallowed hard, a lump forming in her throat because she remembered him ravaged by old age. She remembered the pale and wrinkled skin, the white fuzzy dotted hair on his chest and the speckled liver spots, as he ran shirtless, grinning foolishly at the passing postman.

It was just as well that he remembered nothing and no one remembered him as he sank deeper and deeper into his nether world. A pathetic Lear, reduced and diminished, his wealth of no use and unavailable to him. A cockroach left to rot and die in the sewer by the very relatives who had feared him when he was in his prime.

But with him dead, all the love stories came to their logical end, no matter how strange the relationships had been. The catfights took a spectacular turn; it was about who kept what. The women bitched, fought over the big things and the small things.

'Maybe the family fights will stop now that she is gone,' said Kitty. 'Even your Maasi ji could not take her bounty with her. All that is left behind are pungent associations and a stale smell. But bachche, may she rest in peace. Peace forever.'

Sammy had listened quietly. She didn't like Kitty assuming that Maasi ji had been on the Air Asia flight that crashed. As for the rest of the story, how much had been from her memory and how much Kitty had just related she would never be able to say.

This was what memories were all about. Simple things could trigger them. A sight, a smell, anything familiar. Memories didn't play themselves out sequentially like movies. They were like burrs on a blanket, attaching themselves through proximity, closeness to whatever triggered them. The pattern, or usually lack of one, in the random triggers set up a similar random pattern of memories. Bursting out in fits and starts, at any and all times. Unexpectedly. Sometimes with astonishing results.

The words hung in the air, strung on a clothesline of broken emotion and both of them looked away. To break the tension, Sammy brushed away her tears and made a completely out of context remark. 'Isn't it amazing that tortoises are unaware of their longevity?'

This elicited a half-smile from Kitty. She wasn't as stupid as she made herself out to be. 'I think, and this is my personal theory, that your mother suffered from a complex. She did what she did to you, but you must move on bachche. Her power and her powerful friends intoxicated her. She believed she walked six feet above the ground, her feet never needing to touch the dirty earth. She believed that she was a woman that even the winds and currents had to obey; even nature had to yield to her whims.

'When I saw her treat you badly,' said Kitty, 'I once asked her whether the rich industrialists she went out with would stand by her bedside when she was on her death bed? But she thought she was immortal and laughed at me. And look, even she is no more. Bachche, God has his ways.'

Kitty got up suddenly, patted the folds of her sari and let the *palloo* drop off her cleavage seductively. She had noticed that her '*frand*' was walking over.

A cursory nod to Sammy from the *frand* and they were gone.

Sammy's thoughts chased one another and then seemed to turn on her. She brushed her tears and picked up her mobile to call the airline office. Finding the number busy, she put it on speed dial as she looked out of the window. Days were short in winter. She saw the full moon frame the window, the new moon concealed by the visible plump side much like the truth. What we see is not what we always get.

40

'You cannot open a book without learning something.'
– CONFUCIUS

A hospital is always full of activity. Yet, even in its frantic pace, those working there look for moments of calm, stealing normalcy in slivers from the depressing life-stories they see around them.

'How are you today?' asked Dr Shefali, walking in to sit with Sammy. She, the young resident psychologist at the hospital, had taken to Sammy, even though she had refused to examine Aksh until he was stronger. 'I have just read a research piece on the psychology behind one of the worst cases of bullying in the US. You may be interested in it. It seems that there were three teenagers, all students of the same high school in the US. Two of them were children of bankers and one of a doctor. It seems, despite coming from good professional families, they were on drugs and beat a classmate almost to death with a crowbar over stolen marijuana. Daniel, Jessica and Rosy were arrested for attempted murder. Their victim is still in coma, so for now they have escaped the charge of murder. What intrigues me is that they came from rich and privileged backgrounds. They suspected that the fourth of their gang was stealing marijuana from their common stock and they hatched a plot to murder him.

'And they were so brazen about it ... beating their classmate with a crowbar in his own driveway, where they could easily have been seen or captured on camera.'

'What scares me,' interjected Sammy, 'is that this has come to India as well, this attitude of privileged kids getting away almost literarily with murder. Take the case of Aksh...'

'I haven't spoken with Aksh,' said Shefali, 'So I don't know the details of the matter. But I do know that Aksh was the one beaten up. It would be classic but for the fact that Aksh is not the classic victim. Bullies can't exist without victims, and they don't pick on just anyone. Those singled out to be victims usually lack assertiveness and radiate fear long before they ever encounter a bully. No one likes a bully but no one likes a victim either.'

'Aksh is not like that,' she mused. 'He does not lack assertiveness and doesn't appear to be fearful either.'

'So what is it then Shefali?' asked Sammy. 'Why do the bad guys always seem to win?'

The doctor thought for a moment, choosing her words carefully. 'There are specific psychological reasons why bad people are able to exploit others to their advantage, and part of the problem is our tolerance for bad behaviour. There's also an unwillingness to intervene when we see bullying around us. There is more that we can do to stop the bad behaviour and promote the good. But we don't do so and this encourages bullies.

'It takes a special person to stand up alone to bullies,' said Shefali. 'Bullying is cruel and has lifelong impact on the victims. But bullies also feed on their own behaviour and their success. So, it is extremely difficult for peers to stand up to bullies … they seem to get their way. Particularly when the adults around them are weak or scared to intervene.'

'What about Kushal?' asked Sammy. 'I have told you what I know about him. Is he a classic bully?'

'The people in a bully's life have an important effect on their behaviour,' agreed Shefali. 'Kushal is a classic case …. on the one hand, he has a family that does not care about his behaviour and on the other, from what you tell me, Santri may even encourage it because he is the same way towards people. Kushal's mother may also be fearful of him and therefore be afraid to stand up to him, leave alone correct him. As I said, this is a classic pattern. If the parents are scared of disciplining the bully, then the child learns that they can get away with their behaviour.'

'What I have understood,' said Sammy, 'is that if Santri and his bitch of a girlfriend are in a good mood, then Kushal gets away with bad behaviour. And if the parents are stressed, then he may be shouted at or not, but he gets away with anything just the same!'

'Yes,' agreed Shefali. 'Kushal is a classic bully. But I repeat … Aksh is not the classic victim.'

'What about me?' thought Sammy suddenly. 'Am I the classic victim? I too have been bullied, haven't I?'

Out aloud, she didn't say anything about herself to Shefali. Instead, she narrated the story of a book she was reading, where the mother had been the bitch from hell. What did Shefali think of the wicked mother figure in literature? Were they realistic?

Shefali laughed. 'I know the book,' she said. 'But it is the daughter that would have driven Freud and Jung crazy! Steve Biko, the South African activist, has said that "the most potent weapon of the oppressor is the mind of the oppressed" and it was the mind, the spirit of the little girl that the mother could not get to. She survived, untouched, and her story in book is but the first triumph of her unfettered enlightened spirit.'

'What is it that makes the protagonist's mother behave in such a strange manner?' persisted Sammy. 'I know movies have been made from stories where mothers killed their own kids, but this woman has been sketched out as pure evil!'

Shefali smiled at her. She could see that the answer meant a lot to Sammy, so she didn't make the quip that immediately came to her mind, 'The mother's just a bitch!' Instead, she sat back to give a serious answer to the question.

'You know, of course, the story of Narcissus from Greek mythology? No? Well, he was a hunter so beautiful and so proud that he fell in love with his own image in a pool of water. Unable to resist his attraction for himself, he jumped into the pool to hug his reflection and drowned.'

'Seriously?' said Sammy, laughing.

'Yes, seriously! That's the origin of the term "narcissism". The lady in the book is a narcissistic mother.'

Sammy listened intently as she continued. 'This type of mother lives in a dream world where she is in love with her own image. But be warned ... there is Free Choice! And she knew what she was doing. These people are extremely clever and manipulative.

'Narcissistic mothers take their insecurity out on one or more of their children.'

There was a pause during which Sammy felt the first stirrings of a deep question within her. Something that she could not as yet articulate.

'What would the child of such a mother face?' she asked.

'A feeling of never being good enough,' answered Shefali immediately. 'The mother's expectations can never be met.'

'But could such a mother love one child and reject another? How does that add up?'

'That's an excellent question, Sammy. My, you're really interested in this! I must get you something to read about this disorder.'

'No, no ... just tell me for now,' said Sammy, tiring a little bit, but definitely interested.

'Yes,' said Shefali. 'There are usually neglected children and those that are worshipped by narcissistic mothers. So she loves her son, spoils him, but the love is motivated by self-preservation just as his affection is dyed in greed.'

'Wow!' said Sammy, but a little too quietly. Shefali, not knowing her well enough, didn't pick that something was wrong and that she was deeply disturbed by this conversation.

And then she paused. She was, after all, a psychologist. She looked at Sammy, looked down and then spoke in a soft voice. 'Close to home, Sammy? I'm so sorry…'

'No,' said Sammy, fighting back her tears. 'You have described the protagonist and her story so beautifully that it all becomes clear to me.'

There was more but Shefali wisely decided not to press Sammy at the moment. Taking her leave, she started to go off on her evening rounds.

'Stay, Shefali, please,' she heard Sammy say. 'There is something you should know, and perhaps it will help me to tell you about it. There was a mother … she could take something innocuous, twist it in ways you would not recognize and turn the truth to suit herself. As the years passed, her daughter no longer recognized herself. Regarded as the representation of evil itself by her mother, she hated herself for never being good enough. She was always making excuses, for unjustified allegations were constantly hurled at her. So much so, that of the mother could not find something, her instinctive reaction was to accuse the girl of stealing, pilfering. And when this was found to be untrue, there was never an apology. When the girl reached out to other family members, all hell broke loose.'

Shefali had come back to sit at the edge of the bed and held Sammy's hand in her own. 'Don't say any more, Sammy, I understand…' whispered Shefali gently and caringly. 'You are so well put together and so in control of your life…'

'That's just a veneer of control, Shefali. Thank you for giving me an explanation that makes sense. I have spent my entire life trying to win her attention and approval. But as you just said, there was nothing I could do that was right. And now she is gone and I might finally be able to get some closure! As the rock band, The Maine, puts it, I had a tongue full of tomorrows because I wanted to escape into the future, a better life.'

'Read the book, *People of the Lie*, by M. Scott Peck,' said Shefali. 'I'll give you my copy if you can't find one. He says that you can break a child much as you break a horse, without any visible sign or without harming a hair on her head. Also, Susan Forward's *Mothers Who Can't Love* is good.

'And,' she added carefully, 'they appear utterly normal, even hugely successful to the superficial eye. It is often a facade. They seek and hold on to power, wealth and influence, and certain sections of society applaud them for this success.

'You are not alone, Sammy,' she said. 'Not even in this hospital! Reach out ... sometimes, in helping others, you can help yourself.

'You must understand that narcissists are bullies, Sammy. Their lives are a fantasy, a house of cards that will come tumbling down with the slightest touch. That is why they are so intolerant of opposing views, of dissent. It threatens their very existence.'

'It is abuse, isn't it?' asked Sammy. 'Emotional abuse, to make someone feel worthless, to use the wall of silence to isolate them, to starve them of love?'

'Yes it is,' agreed the psychologist. 'It is degrading, it is mental and psychological abuse.'

Shefali added pensively, gently patting her hand, 'I have seen a lot. In my field you come across many things. So much about mental health is taboo in our country and therefore people go undetected.'

Shefali had to leave for her rounds and could not stay any longer. 'Be strong, Sammy. You cannot be the victim ... you must forgive her, your mother. And Aksh is definitely not a classic victim, so try and understand what happened with him.'

People were always telling Sammy this. Yet, they had not gone through what she had. Their words always sounded hollow. They seemed useless and did not help. The advice never soothed, it only stung. Sammy knew the psychologist had been helpful. Yet, her pent-up anger needed an outlet and she yelled out loud, much to the surprise of the nurse passing by outside her door, 'And she is dead! Dead! Gone!'

41

'I've learned that people will forget what you said, people will forget what you did, but people will never forget how you made them feel.'

– MAYA ANGELOU

Tara walked up to her mother the next morning, visibly upset about something. 'Have you seen this?' she asked, her voice full of disgust. 'In India, he will be let off. He will use money, power and clout. What chance does that poor girl have? So blatant, can't happen in London,' she said a bit too smugly.

'So the life of a daughter counts for less than that of a measly insect, a mosquito here. What if you had not wanted me, mama?' she asked as Sammy hugged her holding her in a tight embrace.

Tara told Sammy about an article she had read about a family that had killed a new-born girl. The mother had broken the story to the media. 'I will talk today,' she had said. 'I am now speaking up. I live the lie every day, I want to give them rat poison for what they have done, and then drown them in milk, just like they have done to my girl!'

Sammy nodded in empathy but there were no words that could describe what she felt, the revulsion, and absolute horror.

India was changing, particularly in some areas and in some sections of society. Not necessarily those from educated, rich or wealthy families though! There had been a sensational sexual assault case against a prominent politician that banished him from the public arena.

'A great takeaway, however, is that some men do get caught and end up paying a heavy price. But many get away,' explained a surprisingly grown-up Tara to her parents. She went on to give her opinion of what was behind the two cases. There was some commonality, she felt.

'And this happens in England and America too, my darling baby,' Sammy told Tara, not wanting her daughter to feel that isolated cases defined modern India.

'So I agree with Rishi that we need to stand up to bullies,' said Sammy, noticing the grin on his face, as that was exactly the reaction he had hoped for. 'How is Aksh?' Sammy asked Rishi the next day as he came in with Tara. 'When can we leave? Wasn't our discharge supposed to be today? I don't want to bring in the New Year from the hospital!'

'Later today I hope but latest by tomorrow, on the eve of the new year. But only once I get an all clear on you. There seem to be some concerns; some cobalt test is not clear. They have called in the specialist to find out if you need an angiography or even a pacemaker.'

'I need nothing, I am well,' Sammy exclaimed angrily, telling Rishi and Tara about the conversation she had overheard the day before.

'It is a scam, even life is no longer sacred. They herd people in and bleed them dry. It is about targets, about making money. And this place is the pits!'

Painful and conflicting emotions made her nervous. Fear and panic jostled with hope and relief that Aksh and she were going to be home soon.

'They are cowards, opportunists and hypocrites, each one of them!' she stuttered as she spoke, her voice defensive, accusatory, desperate.

And to prove her point, she pushed the daily newspaper towards Rishi, directing his attention to a particular article. 'Get treatment for what you need, not what the doctors want.'

'See, see I told you,' Sammy said smugly, taking the newspaper from him and reading out what she found to be the juiciest bit. 'India's private healthcare sector treats patients as revenue generators by prescribing expensive drugs and advising unnecessary tests and surgeries, getting kickbacks for referrals.'

'It is a trap!' Sammy said, oddly jubilant. 'It is the spider and the fly syndrome. Once caught in the spider's parlour, the medical web of deceit, the fly cannot escape. There is this massage bed in the spa here for expectant mothers. The doctor showed off and took me to it when he led me on a tour but I told him off that I won't be needing it anytime soon!' Sammy looked at Rishi with a wicked grin as she said that.

'Perhaps I should have taken it as a compliment that he tried to cover up his embarrassment by saying that he took me to be in my late-twenties, but he was merely glib,' continued Sammy. 'Not being able to sell me a maternity spa treatment, he brought out brochures of the gym, with pictures of unreal and svelte women surrounded by a couple of beef-cake men.

'I knew then that there was something not quite right, Rishi. We have to run from here. These are sophisticated thieves, all of them are just C-O-N-MEN,' she spluttered, spelling the word 'con' to emphasize her point. 'You find among them skilled workers and professionals, young people and old, all united by their greed.'

'I am going home tomorrow with Aksh at the latest, and that's that,' she said with finality.

Rishi felt a hand on his shoulder, placed in a clearly threatening way. It was the Medical Director of the hospital, who had overheard them talk. 'Listen, sonny boy. This hospital is for respectable folk. We don't want any trouble here,' and with that he disappeared as suddenly as he had appeared, vanishing behind the screen.

'Lucky for him,' thought Sammy, because he had been a moment away from ending up on the floor after Rishi would have smacked him. She couldn't remember the last time someone had called Rishi 'sonny boy' and continued to be on his feet!

She laughed aloud and then turned to watch a young woman run frantically from one part of the long corridor to the other, clearly on a mission. Seeing her like this Sammy was reminded of herself. 'A younger me!' she thought.

'A penny for your thoughts,' said Rishi, as the nurse brought in a tray of food for Sammy.

'Leave it there,' Sammy told her, suddenly exhausted as another nurse arrived to take her vitals. 'I think I will lie down for a bit,' she told them once her blood pressure had been checked, falling asleep almost before she had turned on to her side.

She must have been sedated as part of her medication, for it was the middle of the night when she woke up. Rishi and

Tara had gone. A note on her pillowcase from Rishi said that she and Aksh would be discharged the following day.

Sammy heard noises, commotion, in the area outside her room. Through the frame of the open door, she saw nurses rushing along with doctors, machines being wheeled here and there and an oxygen tank being dragged across the corridor. Everything told a story ... there was an emergency obviously.

Sammy soaked in the scene and noticed the doctors speaking to a man, the patient. Something was odd and the night nurse muttered while giving her the medicine. 'Swami of Kalimath, emergency procedure,' she explained.

She nodded to herself, now awake, wondering what stress could there have been in his life to bring about the emergency. Holy men and God's cousins get mortal ailments? She smiled to herself. And then sobering down immediately, she thought about her father. Wasn't that what everyone said about him too? That he lived in a bubble, isolated from the real world, with no responsibility to shoulder? And then, one day, he was gone. A big heart attack, the first and last. It was, as she realized later, the very non-existence of pressure that had weighed him down, worn him out and aged him.

Sammy fell asleep at some point, fatigue numbing her senses and she was unaware of the drama that had unfolded in the ICU and the operation theatre. But when she woke up again and rubbed her eyes, she spied a pile of grey bed sheets, reminding her of dark clouds, in the corridor and asked aloud, 'Who?'

42

'Just keep on going and keep believing in your own original vision, no matter what odds you have to overcome.'

– ANGELINA MACCARONE

A sound behind Rishi and they both looked, thinking that it might be Tara returning from the coffee shop, where she had gone.

They heard a familiar voice before they saw the person emerge through the doorway. 'Hello, how are you?' It was Monica.

'How did you find out?' Rishi asked her.

'Not rocket science, my dear! Called her … when Sammy did not answer or respond after a day, I called her home and spoke with Aida.'

'And here I am!' Sammy looked carefully and saw Monica holding a bunch of flowers behind her back. Yellow roses, her favourite! Before she could say a word, the woman engulfed her in a long hug.

And Tara returned just then, causing Monica to reach out and grab her. 'Gosh, so good to see you,' exclaimed Tara, rushing into her open arms.

Pulling up a chair and sitting next to Sammy, Monica said, 'I came an hour ago and spent time talking to Aksh. First of all, I have to tell you that he will be okay. He has got a rude shock and initially was reluctant to speak, so I sat in silence. He played football games on his iPad, while I watched the news. I broke the ice because there was a discussion regarding the airplane crash. They are now looking for debris. A bit weird if you ask me! Aksh and I discussed bizarre theories and it was quite a lot of fun. He feels it is the Americans. They have shot it down and are sitting quietly directing the drama. Telling first the Chinese and now the Thais to look harder. The inclement weather and the high tide have added to the woes of the search parties. The British are keeping a stiff upper lip but there is more to it. International espionage, your son says. There was something or someone they wanted to eliminate ... according to him.

'So I asked him would they bring down a whole flight just to eliminate one person? Huh? That is ridiculous. More like a new Bermuda Triangle, if you ask me.'

She looked at Sammy and asked the one question that Sammy had no answer for.

'No news of Maasi ji. I feel that she could not have been on that flight. She was in Singapore and the Air Asia flight was headed towards Changi Airport. I really don't know what to do except call her home. I have no other numbers for her. She lived in the old home after her father's death but moved out recently. I called the chanting group she is a member of, but they have no clue. Everything changed after she moved from the old house,' said Sammy.

'I know, it was quite something and so were the inmates of the house. Never a dull moment. It really was the "Zoo at Number Two". I remember visiting you there so clearly,' Monica said. And, as an afterthought, she added, 'And Aksh is on Bed Two; two is your lucky number so all will be well, Sammy.

'You mark my words,' Monica said, reassuringly.

'So what did Aksh tell you?' Sammy asked her.

'Keep calm and listen! He was initially reluctant to speak, but once he began the words rushed out. He has been bullied at school. It began last summer, when he was in the ninth grade. Although he hoped it would go away, it did not. In fact, it became worse as the class was shuffled and he found himself in the same section as this Kushal kid and his friends. Initially, all was well. He gradually became friendly with them but it was short-lived, as they began making demands of him.'

'What demands?' asked Rishi who had been quietly standing near the window all the while. 'What demands?' he asked again, his voice full of the urgency and the sadness that both Sammy and he felt.

'Demands to meet them after school, to hang out with them at the group tuition centre. Harmless in the beginning but then they began to take him along and he witnessed gang wars over silly things, an ego here and a girl there. Aksh became increasingly wary of them but was unable to break free. They threatened him, beat him up when he said he would go to the principal to complain. One guy held him down while the other pressed a burning cigarette on to his back.'

'Oh my God, my poor Aksh,' said Sammy, trying to climb out of the hospital bed. Rishi rushed across the room and held her back, steadying her as she slipped in her hurry to run to Aksh. He gently made her lie back against her pillow.

'There's not much else. He simply refused to tell me what they held over him and there is much that he does not remember. This much is clear; that the past year has been hell for him and it also explains his falling grades. I, too, would fail if I felt intimidated by someone in my class,' Monica told them, holding Sammy's hand.

'I know it is difficult, very difficult for you. You have done a great job and don't blame yourself, there is nothing more that you could have done,' she told Sammy. 'He fell into bad company; it happens, and it does not make him a bad boy. There is hope yet, because the situation can be salvaged. Find out the facts, give him time and then decide what you are going to do about it.'

'Punishing those kids cannot be the first step,' were her words to Rishi. 'First attend to Aksh, reassure him, and find out what happened. And then act.'

She stood up to leave, giving Sammy a hug. 'Have to get home, the driver is needed,' she said, moving towards the door. 'Will see you at home now, since both of you are getting discharged.'

43

*'I used to think the worst thing in life is to end up all alone.
It's not. The worst thing in life is to end up with people who
make you feel all alone.'*

– ROBIN WILLIAMS

Sammy turned her attention to Tara. 'Did you know about this?'

Tara shook her head and said, 'No.'

'Were you ragged in school? Ever, I mean ever?' Monica asked her, having paused at the door on her way out.

Sammy interjected with a 'No, never, not Tara,' but stopped mid-sentence, as she heard Tara say a quiet, 'Yes.'

She felt the room spin around her as she gingerly got off the bed and rushed as quickly as she could to the bathroom, nauseous.

On her return, she overheard Tara explain to a patiently waiting Monica, 'I was in junior school and the other children would tease me because my parents were separated. They would chase me around in class shouting, "Tara has no father ... where did her papa go?" I used to be in tears but they would continue teasing me; and the ringleader was that Puss-Reacher. She hated me and turned everyone against me. They would drop hate notes on my desk as I sat in a corner.'

Sammy felt her heart break as she pulled Tara closer. 'Why did you not tell me, my little love? My little girl. Why?' she asked Tara, wiping away her tears.

After a long pause, Tara looked up and quietly told her, 'You already had enough going on. You looked so worried all the time and then your mother would call and shout and you would cry. I did not want to add to the problems, Mama, and it wasn't as though I couldn't deal with it. So I did not tell you.'

Sammy held her daughter as they both smiled at each other through their tears.

'Just as well, because I would have put a gun to their heads,' Sammy said ferociously, as Tara laughed, touched by how protective Sammy was of her. And she wouldn't put anything past her mother!

Turning to Monica, Tara explained, 'Those were tough times. Papa was not with us and Mama had to do everything alone. Thinking about my grandmother only makes me cry. Always shouting and blaming us for her misery.

'Can you believe it, she brought us up all alone. We did not have the affection and support of relatives, so the other children showed off their perfect families to us and made us feel bad. Akki was the worst; always talking about her cousins and boasting about their achievements, looking down on us and telling us about the wonderful gifts her grandmother bought her. The only thing that bothered her was that my grandmother, Mama's mother, was quite attractive, so she made hers go to the beauty parlour. But once she discovered my grandmother's poisonous nature she never complained again, preferring hers to mine. No one wanted the diva!' Tara said, giggling convulsively.

It really was time for Monica to leave and she had already overstayed. She moved towards the door, her exit coinciding with the nurse carrying the lunch tray.

'Take Tara home for a while,' she told Rishi, who for once agreed readily, quite exhausted by now. It had, after all, been a long morning and many days of tiredness for all of them.

'I will look up Aksh on my way down and will be back in the evening. So be up and ready to go home,' he told Sammy, kissing her on her upturned face.

'Tell Aida, to turn my geyser on and ask her to change the sheets,' was far as Sammy got, before Tara nudged her father out, waving to her as they got into the lift and Sammy watched them disappear. She was still looking when the lift door closed and they were gone.

Seeing them leave, the doors closing behind them had a strange effect on Sammy. She started crying, crying copious tears that would not stop. These were the tears she had not shed for years, the tears for what her son and daughter had to go through. What other children had to go through.

The nurse came over and sat by the side of Sammy's bed, holding her hand and comforting her but soon realized that these were neither tears of pain nor of emotional suffering. Sammy was crying for the uselessness and hypocrisy of life, of opportunities lost due to selfish relationships.

As if reading her mind, the nurse said, 'We see all kinds of people in the hospital and it is the worst side of humanity that we sometimes get to witness,' she said pointing heavenwards.

'Some people have such depraved behaviour and they cover up their vices through bullying and subjugating their family.'

Seeing Sammy's puzzled expression, she filled in the details for her benefit.

'The man who passed away last night ... take his example. His wife brought him here straight from the airport. He was on a holiday with his friend in Bangkok. Two middle-aged, potbellied men ... what do you think they were doing in Bangkok? Well, his heart could not take the excitement and ... you can guess the rest. Pah, the audacity of his friend to call the wife to come and fetch him, lying half-dead in a foreign country. So the poor thing reached there to discover the horrible truth. The shame of it all. She felt utterly betrayed, she told me when she came here.'

Dropping her voice, the nurse added that the lady had cried, humiliated, when her brother-in-law had no shame in front of her, describing the women of Bangkok in agonizing detail, licking his lips as he talked.

'It was his eyes that had alarmed the prostitute,' the wife had told the nurse. It seems that her husband had a wild look and the prostitute soon realized that it was an ecstasy of a different kind that had claimed her client, not her sexual charms.

'And children are not the only ones who suffer from lack of neglect. Take the man who was going for a walk in the corridor half an hour ago ... the man who waved to you. No one comes to see him except his daughter. Tonight, when he was writhing in pain, and I called his wife, she came to visit.' The nurse made a face and continued, 'Came, pah, straight from a party and dressed to kill. Dressed in all white, like Snow White. She must have fallen into a rose bush; we could smell her a few minutes before she arrived. The cloying smell lingers even now,' she said disparagingly. 'She made such a show of tending to the patient but her eyes were only on her watch. A bow here, a wave there and she was gone.

'Her daughter speaks to me,' the nurse continued. 'She is in college and is having boy trouble, finding it difficult to keep up with her studies, is worried about her future. And her father is in hospital. The only person she can reach out to is her mother ... and the mother is never there for her. Her daughter is being bullied and she doesn't know and doesn't care. The stress will inevitably get to the poor girl...'

'So how does the girl manage?' Sammy asked, quite concerned.

'Just like everyone else,' said the nurse. 'With tears and silence. And one day she will develop a thick skin and survive or she will collapse and the world will forget about her.'

Sammy was shocked but the nurse was not being callous, merely realistic. This is what did happen in the real world. The pressures on teenagers and young adults were tremendous and parents were often not around. Some children had no one, absolutely no one, with whom they could speak, confide in, or vent their feelings. And sometimes, such children did indeed just collapse ... and yes, the world did forget them and move on.

The nurse cleared her throat as if she wanted to say something more, but then decided against it.

Tucking the blanket around Sammy, she reached into her bosom and took out a piece of paper from between her breasts. 'I heard that sir, your husband, is in education. My daughter's son, good child. Please tell sir to get admission. I have worked hard to bring her up.'

Sammy nodded and took the photograph and paper from her hand, not wanting to explain that Rishi invested in education and did not run institutions. She saw a sweet Bengali woman with a middle-parting and large deep-set eyes peering into the camera, shyly holding on to a little boy. She looked up to see the nurse's face light up.

'Yes, I will,' she sighed, turning over to make herself more comfortable and making a mental note to ask Rishi to do something.

'And you people with big houses have no problems, very good karma, I tell my daughter...' said the nurse.

But Sammy was lost in thought, thinking of her Aksh and not wanting him to be lost and for the world to forget about him, and smiled at her absent-mindedly.

44

'The shadow proves the sunshine.'

– SWITCHFOOT

Rishi and Tara returned early evening and were lost in a blur of activity. They ran around at the hospital to complete the discharge formalities for Sammy and Aksh as the two waited holding each other's hands. A signature here, a paper there. Payments to be made. Reports to collect. Slips to deposit.

And then they were done. They would be home on New Year's Eve! By now, Rishi had checked out of the hotel ... for the moment, he was also home.

'We are going home, Mama! And you will stay well, promise?' said Aksh, extracting a promise from his mother.

'And you too, son,' she said to him, putting her arm around his bony shoulders. 'And everything will work out. I promise. I am there with you,' she told him, looking into his eyes.

'Remember when we were little, we would chase you shouting promise-breaker.'

Before Aksh could complete the sentence, Sammy grinned and said, 'A promise-breaker is a shoemaker.'

Both giggled as Rishi walked up to them with two ward boys and two wheelchairs. It seemed that they had to leave the hospital in this manner – something to do with the insurance policy of the hospital and the risk of patients hurting themselves if they were to walk out by themselves.

Rishi hurried them to the waiting car, now with a ferocious looking man riding shotgun. Pleased at leaving the hospital, Sammy and Aksh had walked to the car without a backward glance, but now they gazed quizzically at Rishi. 'Ex-commando. My school friend Major Vivek arranged it,' was all he said.

Sitting between her two children on her way home, Sammy felt safe and happy. She had seen a firmness in Rishi's jaw that she had missed … and perhaps she thought he had lost it along the way. Having had a successful career and been a single mother to her kids, she was glad that Rishi was in his present frame of mind.

Tara was speaking non-stop, chattering away even more than she usually did, which was saying something! She paused just long enough to whip open her iPad and show her mother a poem she had written.

Let the Bridges I Burn Light My Way

There's a flaw embedded in the human race;
Vulnerability, love, attachment it is said.
It may be our spirit; the way we leave our trace;
But it eats our souls, leaves parts of us dead.

Not always is our love reciprocated;
No one has a reason, even the interrogated.
Caring so much, giving it our all;
For those who leave us broken and small.

We're bound by our choices, good or bad;
Yet we choose to live in misery for others' sake.
Our own lives are put on hold; it drives us mad;
In an era of transparency, our feelings aren't opaque.

Let the bridges I burn light my way;
And guide in my journey to live each day.
Not wasting time depressed or grieving;
There'll be others entering for each person leaving.

'You taught me to live, Mama,' said Tara suddenly. In that moment, with tears in her eyes, Sammy realized that her little daughter had grown up. She would be fine now ... she had such a good head on her shoulders!

But Tara was still a little baby, too. She laughed, and showed her mother a picture, a photo of an innocuous looking dress. 'What colour is it?' she asked, giggling.

'Blue and brown,' Sammy replied nonchalantly.

Aksh completed the description, with a slight difference, 'Indigo blue and jet black.'

After a pause, both turned to look at Tara because she was in peals of laughter. 'Aksh is right. Mama, you are kind of right, not completely. And all I can see is a dress in white and gold!'

'What!' exclaimed Sammy. She passed the iPad to Rishi and asked him what he could see.

'White and gold,' he said, unhelpfully.

Tara took back the iPad with a grin and said that half the world could not tell that it was actually black and blue. It had been a social media craze a while ago ... the dress that divided the world!

Sammy chuckled and hugged both her kids until they began to wriggle. And then she nuzzled Tara's neck with Aksh pulling her head until there was chaos in the car and Rishi had to calm them down. Each felt the heady freedom of being let out of a cage. Sammy literally blinked in the warm afternoon sun of Delhi's winter, glad to be out, glad to be alive. But more importantly, super happy that Aksh was well and smiling beside her.

They entered the gates of the condominium and cheered up instantly. They passed the fountain; saw the dancing water and the kaleidoscope of colours it threw up. The buildings were lit up with fairy lights to usher in the new year. It was all very pretty and familiar, more so than on other days.

The concierge ran forward to help them with their bags. Sammy lingered to admire the winter flowers as she watched Rishi vanish into the lift with the children. Very quickly, the concierge brought her up to date with the condominium gossip.

A neighbour dead. Leaving behind three small children and a grieving husband. Another neighbour ran away in his vintage car with his secretary. Yet another rushed off to Singapore where she discovered her husband was having an affair with the Filipino maid.

At night, Sammy happily presided over dinner, letting Rishi and Tara fuss over them. 'Feels good to be spoilt, Aksh?' she asked him, reaching out for the salt.

'Not so much salt, you have to cut down,' both children told her, taking the salt cellar from her outstretched hand.

'Ufff, just a little bit, the food at the hospital was ghastly,' she reminded them, grinning.

Dinner over; they sat around the cheerful fireplace. Leaving the three of them chatting in the drawing room, Sammy went in for a bath and luxuriated in the tub, losing track of time.

Soaking in the warm water and bath salts, Sammy was reminded of Maasi ji, the one who had introduced Sammy to some of her homemade beauty recipes.

Maasi ji had played with Sammy when she was a little girl, spending hours with her. It was she who had talked to her, explaining the unwritten rules of love and marriage, or bondage as Maasi ji called it, heaving with emotion. This was the family tradition. Marriages were arranged and there was no possibility of what was quaintly called a 'love marriage'.

'What is that?' Sammy would ask shyly, too young at ten to understand. Only to be hugged tightly as Maasi ji sang, ignoring the question. Sammy often crawled up to her quietly as she sat lost in thought and watched her mutter, wave her hand coyly across her face and then giggle.

'What you say, Maasi ji?' she would ask, stringing her words together in her baby voice as she clambered on to her lap. But Maasi ji always shook her head. It was much later that Sammy realized she was repeating romantic dialogues from Rajesh Khanna movies and it was then that Sammy understood her dislike for light-skinned heroines. It was on her lap at the age of five that Sammy learnt to distinguish skin colour and hope from hopelessness, and she saw envy raise its ugly head every time the hero danced with the heroine.

Sammy bit her lip because she remembered that nothing was known of the passenger list of the crashed plane and there was no information about her aunt. She didn't know whom to call. Her own family had been dysfunctional and she had lost all contact with them. They had brushed her off, almost murdering her in their neglect, and leaving her at the mercy of anyone who wanted to have a go at her. So much for close family ties, she often thought.

'Conspiracy theories be damned,' she muttered, walking into her bedroom to turn on the TV. Quickly scanning through the news channels, she noted with disappointment that there were no updates about the missing flight.

Wrapped in a towel, she lingered in front of her cupboard for a moment, before pulling out something comfortable to wear. She was suddenly aware that her world was whole again with Aksh back and Tara home. She was happy. The crisis, at least in part, had passed.

45

'It's how you handle adversity, not how it affects you. The main thing is never quit, never quit, never quit.'
— WILLIAM J. CLINTON

She hummed as she dressed and walked into the drawing room, to find Aksh sitting alone.

Sammy patted his head and sat down beside him, looking out of the window at the lights in the distance, glowing in the night. Something was not quite right; she felt his tension. 'What is it son?' she asked. He did not say a word but she felt his alienation and mental confusion.

They sat there for a long while. The colour was bleaching out from Sammy's world yet again, recasting the landscape into bleak shades of sepia, in which black and white stood out. And she suddenly felt the cold, even though the internal heating was on full power. Sammy hesitated, suddenly unable to recall anything that had happened over the past few days.

Aksh looked odd and out of place. Like a bat in daylight as he struggled to speak, instinctively hiding in the dark shadows cast by the fire. Concealed in darkness and damp, she heard him find words to his thoughts.

Leaning forward, she listened carefully as he spoke in fits and starts.

'Mama, it is not my fault.

'It all began last summer when my section changed. That Kushal and his friend Dadlani were quite good to begin with. I began to hang out with them, even played football. They would call me out of class and it all began with dares.

'Dare to jump over the ditch, slap bets and then it began to deteriorate, the dares got worse. Each time I refused, they would threaten me.

'In the beginning, I enjoyed the freedom but then it became scary. They hit Harsh so hard that it broke his jaw. They laid bets on the goals I scored in school matches, roughed me up along with that small kid Rahul if we disobeyed and gradually it became worse. I hated going to school, dreaded seeing them.

'And then, one day, they beat me up because I protested,' he said, holding his head in his hands. 'I saw them force Rahul. They forced him to take his clothes off and Kushal was so aroused by the sight of his smooth body that he cried out with pleasure, while the kid sobbed in pain.

'I could not take it so jumped up to save him but they pushed me against the wall, kicked me and beat me up. They left me writhing in pain and dragged me to the school boundary wall, to the secluded spot hidden from the authorities. But if that was not torture enough, three boys held me down while Dadlani kissed me,' he said, balking at the memory in tears.

'He, he kissed me on the lips, then looked into my eyes and said, "I did that because I love you. If you love me, don't tell anyone what happened. If you tell them, they'll beat you and throw me out but I will destroy your sister, your mother and then you." To ease the pain, they forced alcohol down my throat.

'I have no idea how long I lay there but finally I made my way home. I am no one to anyone in school. Everyone now hates me, they laugh at me,' he said, barely audible, tortured by the memory.

Their treatment of Aksh was deliberate, intended to drive him berserk, to break his resolve, Sammy realized. And they had succeeded; for Aksh had lost his will to fight them.

'Why, oh why, are bullies taken to be the coolest kids? And why was I, as their victim, made to be the outcast? I don't understand, Mama!

'After that it was daily torture. I could not concentrate. I stole money from Papa's wallet when he came visiting and I lied to you because I was so ashamed. Kushal and Dadlani made me give them protection money so that the others did not attack me, so that I was left alone.

'I hated school. I had no friends. And then, one day Rahul ran to me quivering in fear. He told me that they had pounced on Jay, that he was the next casualty. I could not take it, I saw them attack him viciously, stuff powder down his throat. I saw him gag as he lost consciousness. My mind told me to fight back and I did but they held me and beat me up. Jay was found with his pants down, lying face down in his own vomit on the far end of the field. I let him down, I couldn't protect my friend!'

Aksh narrated the acts of rejection, of his failure to protect his friend, in a way that made Sammy's cheeks burn. It was sharp and swift like a slap.

And she truly did understand. A conversation with Dr Shefali came to her mind. Shefali had explained, 'A serious issue for the victims of bullying is that the friends that they do have turn their back on the victim because they are afraid of being the outcast or the target. This further alienates the victim from their normal world.' How true!

But Aksh had more to say. 'As far as that day is concerned, the day when I was beaten up and ended up in hospital ... some vague memories are coming back. Neither have Jay or Rahul been able to tell me anything. No one else seems to know what happened.

'Mama, I'm scared ... what did I do? I am starting to remember something though. I remember fighting and that Kushal was there ... and Dadlani. I don't remember much else.'

'Listen, it may not be the right time to ask ... actually it definitely isn't. But all this is too much for me to come to grips with,' said Sammy. 'So tell me, who sent the SMS messages to me and why? Do you know anything about that?'

Aksh hung his head and softly said, 'I am sorry I have been a disappointment, my grades are not good but I will work hard now. I will not be scared. Kushal came to the hospital and he shook his fist at me and ogled at Tara to warn me off. But Mama, I will not take this anymore. I will stand up; you are with me, aren't you, Mama?'

'God, I am so stupid,' Sammy said, taking time to let it all sink in. 'I never questioned it when the low grades came in the first time, I was so worried about you. But now with all this, maybe it's time to take a closer look. Rishi is right.

'Yes, my son. Yes, yes, yes. Now and always. We will work through this. You rest now,' she told him, turning to place pillows under his head.

Having told her what he remembered and what was on his

mind, Aksh was asleep in minutes. His face looked relaxed as if a huge weight had been lifted off his shoulders.

Sammy was stunned with all that she had heard. She sat there, rooted to the spot for hours. Her life hurtling to chaos. Rishi found her there much after darkness had inked the night black. They spoke well into the night, moving into another room away from the sleeping children. At some stage in their conversation, the day and year changed.

'So it wasn't our broken marriage that toppled Aksh into this?' she asked Rishi.

'Despite what the world said and the bias you have faced as a single mother; this is not about you, Sammy. So stop blaming yourself,' he told her. 'It is so easy for you to take the blame for everything that goes wrong because of your bloody upbringing and your mother's hateful mind games. Speaking of which, that housekeeper called again and he insisted that you call him back.'

And then gulping down his drink, he added, 'Maybe news about Maasi ji after all. Do call him; he left his number. He was muttering about seeing some woman, some beggar. But I could not understand, was too tired.'

Sammy nodded, blinking, wiping her tears, as Rishi held her in a tight embrace, for they were joined in their concern for Aksh. Sammy was shaken by her son's misery, Rishi seething with rage.

She smiled sadly. 'I think maybe I have been afraid this whole time to question Aksh. I did not want him to clam up. I thought he was passing through a phase, adolescence, teenage problems that it would blow over. Maybe I was afraid of what I may find out. Aksh is a good kid; maybe I did not support him enough,' she said, sobbing into his shoulder.

46

'Jump, and you will find out how to unfold your wings as you fall.'

– RAY BRADBURY

The first day of a new year. It was time to take the issue of bullying head on, to confront the demons and hold the school and those responsible accountable.

'Being victimized by school bullies is a frightening experience for any child,' said Sammy the next morning, 'and I can't let Aksh be in this frame of mind, where he is left distraught and depressed.

'And,' she added, 'it is frustrating for me as a mother. I thought that Aksh's problems were my fault ... then I thought these were due to our divorce. But these are not of his or our creation. We have to sort this out!'

'Ignoring a bully is never the answer,' agreed Rishi. 'I have been gathering the troops for just this moment. The faster one acts, the better the chances of controlling the fallout and the behaviour of these scoundrels.'

They agreed on a broad plan of action over morning coffee. Sammy would visit the school; meet the principal and teachers, and also parents on the support association of the school. Rishi, on the other hand, would meet his friends in the government and lawyers to see what pressure they could bring to bear on the school. After the elections the previous year, government offices had fewer holidays, working even on 1st January.

Tara would stay with Aksh, who was glad to have the support of his sister. He was still low, unable to deal with the lack of resolve, uncertain about the missing bits of his memory.

The last bothered him a lot. 'What did I do that day? Is my mind blanking it out for some reason?' he thought, and nothing that Tara did or said to him seemed to comfort him.

Looking at him in this state, shrunken and almost mentally beaten, gave Sammy resolve to tackle the issue and finally get closure. She would ensure that her son was able to stand tall again.

Visiting the school was a nightmare! Sammy was made to wait at the gate and then again at the reception but she had the patience of Job and the wisdom of Solomon that morning. She knew that the FIR was a Damocles sword hanging over the head of the school and they would have to deal with her.

And deal with her they eventually did, in their own good time, over two hours later.

'What can I do for you?' asked the principal, flanked by his personal assistant, the school counsellor and Slickly Suave Parent. He did not seem to have the courage to face her alone and, in that moment, Sammy knew that she would win.

'To begin with,' she looked directly into his eyes and

answered, 'there are a few important and grave issues with this incident that you have not taken seriously, but rather casually.

'I request that you set up a formal investigation. This incident took place at the school and between students of your school. Corrective action is your responsibility,' she said.

The principal seemed to have anticipated this. Sneaking a glance at Slickly Suave Parent and exchanging a smile, he condescendingly addressed her, in a voice reserved for students who were supposed to grovel and cower before him.

'A majority of the incidents you have described happened outside the school. You, Madam, are responsible and not us.' He waved his hands around like an emperor, ruler of all he surveyed. 'Also, Madam, I would like to inform you that this conversation is being recorded and my assistant will also take notes.'

'Perfect!' thought Sammy. There were many things that she would have liked to say to him. 'You worm, you significant blown-up balloon … one little needle and all your bluster will deflate! Wait till I get started on you.' All of this was said in her head while maintaining a beatifically calm smile on her lips. Rishi and she had a plan and part of that was to make the school commit to what extent they were willing to proceed in the investigation.

So, she merely argued on the most significant aspect. 'But sir, even one incident at your school should be enough. You are aware that Aksh was badly beaten up at school during school hours. Isn't that enough for you? In fact, apart from action in this case against the perpetrators, I was hoping for a thorough investigation to ensure that such things are not happening to other students.'

'Do you run the school or do I do?' asked the principal rhetorically and threateningly, while the supposed parent representative smirked and grinned in his chair.

She would have liked to pull his tie tight and throttle him with it but maintained her composure, answering with a simple, 'You do, of course.'

'Not for long though if I have my way...' she thought to herself!

To keep the conversation focused on the issue at hand and not take it into the speculative realm of who actually ran the school, she tried to get the principal to be reasonable.

'Could I ask you, sir, what would you define as bullying?'

'I know it when I see it ... that's all that matters. And, in any case, Madam, there is none in my school, so I don't need to worry about it,' he answered with a self-satisfied smile.

'Let us examine what happened with Aksh, for a moment,' Sammy countered. 'There was clearly someone's intent, desire, to hurt him and deeply aggressive and hurtful action is evident. An unjustified use of power.'

'We don't know that,' interjected Slickly Suave Parent.

'I wasn't addressing you!' said Sammy sharply, but with a smile. The parent backed off quickly, a bit thoughtful all of a sudden, for he didn't like what he saw in her eyes.

'We know this has been repeated,' she said and hastily added, 'even if you think it is outside the school and therefore not your responsibility. And there was evident enjoyment by the aggressor.' In a softer voice, she finished, 'and there definitely is a depression, a sense of being oppressed that Aksh feels.'

'So who says that is bullying?' asked the principal, without thinking, as he was distracted by a noise of the door opening, as Rishi was escorted in.

'Ken Rigby, for one!' exclaimed Rishi, sitting down and nodding to Sammy. 'And the principles enshrined in the UN

Charter, the Washington Accord and the regulations on safety of children in schools as per Indian law.'

The nod was enough for Sammy. She knew that their plan had worked and that Rishi had the support of the government's education administration and of lawyers.

'Do you, my good sir,' said Rishi, speaking firmly to the principal, 'know of the UN's Declaration of the Rights of the Child, especially Principles 2 and 9?'

And continuing without listening to the muddled 'Yes … No … Yes' from the principal, he read out part of a letter that he then handed over to the head of school.

'This, sir, is a letter that you will also receive later today from the Directorate of Education of the National Capital Territory of Delhi. It says, if you note, that they are invoking a 2007 circular and have launched an investigation against the school under the District Level Safeguard Committee for Protection of Child Rights. The Special Committee has the power to enquire into all cases of sexual exploitation, corporal punishment, child abuse of any kind such as incidents of physical torture and all such acts leading to insult, humiliation, physical and mental injury to children. Along with the FIR show cause notice that you still need to respond to, I would suggest you see a lawyer. I can suggest mine if you like,' he ended cheekily.

This was Sammy's cue to play the good cop in the routine. 'We know it's not your fault,' she said quietly. 'The school can play a positive role here, show that it has zero tolerance towards bullying and such behaviour. The worst reaction of a school is when it knows of the harassment and is deliberately indifferent to it. This happens sometimes, I know, due to a feudal mindset, particularly where the bully's parents are influential or powerful members of the community.'

Slickly Suave Parent was now looking very uncomfortable. 'He knows something!' thought Sammy, quickly grasping the reason for his discomfort. As she looked at him, she saw him do a quick calculation in his head, realized that he was about to be caught between a rock and a hard place and he excused himself rapidly and left.

'Use this incident, sir,' she continued once the parent had left, 'to clean up the school. I know that these are powerful people but you have a responsibility to all the children at the school.'

Having made their point, delivered the letter to the school, Sammy and Rishi took their leave, ready now to fight the matter out using the government, the police and the legal system. That was their plan.

Events, however, were to progress in a different direction as happens so often in life.

The school counsellor followed them out. She had seemed visibly moved, or perhaps scared, by the intensity with which Sammy and Rishi had spoken with the principal.

'There is someone I would like you to meet,' she told Sammy. 'Could you please come with me, alone? We can go in my car…'

A nod of agreement from Rishi and Sammy was off. To where and in what danger, she didn't quite know, but it seemed important.

47

'It matters not what someone is born, but what they grow up to be.'

– J.K. ROWLING

They couldn't have driven for more than ten minutes before Sammy found herself in front of a garage in one of the many colonies in Delhi set up to house government officials. It was a beautiful part of the city, with Gulmohar trees shedding their leaves in winter and well-maintained roads.

'So different from Gurgaon,' she thought. The suburb that she lived in was where much of the new residential and commercial development had taken place. But behind walls. Walls that separated opulent construction and elaborate finishes from the almost complete absence of civic infrastructure. Delhi, particularly the areas where the government officials themselves lived, was from a different planet!

Their destination wasn't the old, white bungalow, with its neatly manicured lawns and the well-tended rows of flowers. It was the garage itself. A little more than a tin shed just outside and adjacent to the hedge separating it from the compound of the main house, the garage was intended, of course, to be the place where the official car was parked. Instead, there were people living in it, as Sammy knew. Many government officers would illegally sub-let their garage to working families, in order to minimally supplement their official income.

The door, a large steel shutter, was open and covered with a cloth that had once been a bedcover, now discarded and hanging as a curtain to let some air and light into the garage and also to provide a semblance of privacy.

The school counsellor pushed the curtain aside, beckoning Sammy to follow. The inside was clean, neat and well ordered. A small but dignified home for a family, of whom two were present inside. One, the mother, and the other an astonishingly beautiful girl, her daughter. A look of surprise and then of recognition followed. The two obviously knew the counsellor.

'This is Samaira,' the counsellor said. 'She is Aksh's mother.'

Nothing more, it seemed, needed to be said. There was an instant transformation in the expressions of the two women. The girl immediately radiant, the mother somewhat in awe but also a glimpse of fear in her eyes. The older woman fell at Sammy's feet while her daughter came close, held Sammy's hand with tears streaming down her cheeks.

'*Aksh neh meri beti ki* izzat *bachai hai.* Your son saved my daughter. Thank you … thank you … thank you…'

Sammy didn't know what to make of it and allowed herself to be led to a stool, and a glass of water was placed in her hand.

While the mother and daughter busied themselves making tea for their visitors, Sammy allowed herself a look around.

There was dignity and care, beauty almost, in the modest home that she was sitting in. A gas stove and sink marked out the kitchen area and there was a television set in a corner. But pride of place was taken by a desk and bookshelf where the girl had been studying before being interrupted by the visit. With a start, Sammy noticed the neatly folded school uniforms and the pile of books. It could have been Tara's corner in their much more luxurious home. The same school uniform, the same books.

Tea was brought in glasses, neatly arranged on a tray, along with a plate of biscuits. Offered first to Sammy as the guest of honour. She still had no idea of why she was being treated like royalty, but she was beginning to get the first glimmerings of what might have happened.

The story, when it was at last told over the steaming glasses of tea, was sordid, grim and beautiful all at once.

Priya, for that was the girl's name, was in Aksh's class but they didn't know each other very well. Aksh looked beyond the social, class and economic differences without even thinking about it but that was not the case with his friends.

'You brought him up well,' said Priya. 'He never noticed or cared that I was part of the Right to Education quota for the economically weaker section, that I was a scholarship student. He was the only one who spoke to me in the class but that too stopped when the other children teased him about it. And I stayed away ... I only went to the school to get a good education and go to college and get a job so that I can take my mother away from all this,' she said, indicating their home with a sweep of her hand. 'Away from working from morning to night at the homes of rude and demanding sahibs and memsahibs who look down on her and make her work so hard for so little money.'

Her father, it appeared, was a guard at a warehouse in another part of town but kept losing his job because he was an alcoholic. There was always someone else ready to take on any job vacancy owing to the sheer number of jobless immigrants trying to get a foothold in the city.

'Where is he?' asked the counsellor.

The mother answered as Priya looked down. 'He took the money and left. He hasn't been back for a week, ever since they came.' The knowing look that passed between the three of them indicated to Sammy that this comment too was part of the story she was to hear.

Finally the truth of what happened that fateful day emerged. It came out in bits and spurts, hesitatingly told, with fear and shame mixed with the inability often to find the right words.

It had begun as a normal school day. Priya walked the twenty minutes it took to get to school. She was happy that she was at the school, as it gave her access to a good education. But she was always a bit scared. Scared of what someone might say to her, a bitter comment, a joke at her expense. Words that she would have to listen to but could not respond to. The iron curtain of power and wealth separated her tormentors from her.

As she told Sammy, 'I saw an advertisement in an old magazine once. It said that children walk to school and skip home happily heading back home. How true!'

It was to be anything but a normal school day!

The zonal football matches were round the corner, so many boys were staying late at the school. Priya had to meet the Computer Science teacher for an extra hour in the IT Lab, since she could not do the work at home and was allowed the special access once a week. Often the teacher left with the buses, as on that day, leaving Priya alone and the maids and housekeepers to lock up as usual after they had done their cleaning round of the school.

After completing her work, Priya had switched off the computer and headed to the toilets near the basketball court to have a quick wash before heading home.

And that was when it had happened. In the most isolated place in the school, away from the football field and away from the main school building. Cornered by Kushal and Dadlani, Priya had turned around, heading towards the gate and changing her mind about using the toilet.

'What! Is our company not good enough for you, you bitch, you whore!' shouted Kushal.

Before she realized what was happening, Priya's hands had been grabbed from behind, a firm hand covered her mouth and she was forced against the wall. Her schoolbag had fallen and one shoe had come off in the struggle, as she fought the groping hands and tried to ward off the slaps.

Kushal, Dadlani and others had been rude to her and abused her often, but it had never come to this. Priya could hardly believe what was taking place and her mind was shutting down. All she could think about was fighting … fighting back … running away! But her feet were off the ground, her legs were weak, her arms were pinned behind her.

And then it got worse. A hand popped the buttons on her kameez and a hand slipped to cup her teenaged breasts. Another hand was roaming across her body. She could, with horror and disgust, feel someone begin to untie her salwar. She wanted to scream … to shout … to draw attention. But she could not. She was helpless!

And then they paused for a moment. She heard Kushal say, 'Shh! Someone is coming ... wait!'

Then she heard and felt their tension relax as one of them exclaimed, 'It's only Aksh! Don't worry ... he won't forget what we did to Jay.'

The other added, 'Ask him to join in! She's pretty!'

Kushal spoke to Aksh, who seemed to be quite close by now. 'Hey Aksh! Come on! It's Priya, Peasant P! You can join in after I have her!!'

Then a rough hand was put on her shoulder and she was pulled away from the wall and she stumbled, fell in the dust, and cut her lip on a stone on the ground. With blood on her lips, dust in her eyes and hair dishevelled, she looked up and saw that the situation had changed.

Before the other boys had realized what had happened, Aksh had grabbed her, releasing their grip on her, and had put himself between the girl and the predatory boys.

'Not today!' she heard him say, in a voice full of determination and grit. 'Not now, not ever!'

They came at him, first Dadlani who swung at Aksh. She saw Aksh easily step under the blow and punch out at Dadlani, catching him in the midriff and knocking the breath out of him.

Kushal and Dadlani tried to reason with Aksh and also to frighten him. 'She's not worth it, you bastard! Step aside if you don't want to do it. We always knew you were gay!'

Aksh was silent for a moment and then whispered to Priya, 'Get yourself together. You may have to run for it. Escape and go home when I tell you to.'

She tied her salwar surreptitiously and reached out for her shoe, slipping her foot into it and wrapped a hand around her school bag. She was still disoriented and not sure if she could stand up, let alone run.

Kushal had taken out his mobile phone and called someone. He then turned to Aksh and said, 'We will have her, even if we have to kill you! And then we will go after your sexy mom! And when your sister comes for your funeral, I will personally rape her.'

With that he advanced on Aksh from one side and Dadlani, carrying a hockey stick now, from the other. They hit him once, twice ... but he fought back bravely, with all the tricks that Rishi and his Israeli friend Harel had once taught him.

'He fought back with anger, with passion,' said Priya. 'Why for someone he hardly knew?'

Sammy understood even though Priya did not.

'He was protecting you,' she said with pride, 'but he was fighting something else. He was fighting his own demons, at having let down Jay, at having been bullied and not having stood up.'

She was quiet for a moment and then added, 'He was also imagining his sister Tara in that position. He was fighting and protecting all of us, too!'

But there was more to come. Words that tore at Sammy's heart when she heard what had happened to her little baby boy.

'They tried to beat him up, but he was possessed,' said Priya, 'and they didn't stand a chance. He was thrashing them ... alone, but more than a match for them.

'And then these two big men came with large iron rods. They were Kushal's driver and bodyguard. Before Aksh even noticed them, one of them hit him on the head, while the other grabbed his arms.

'Aksh yelled, "Run! Go Priya!" and I ran ... I ran all the way home, not stopping, not looking back,' she said. 'I could hear his screams as they beat him ... and then nothing...'

Sammy was in tears, weeping for her son's brave heart, weeping for the beating he had taken, weeping for all that he had seen and faced. All alone.

Priya's mother held her hand and gave her a big hug. 'He saved our daughter, your son. We said nothing and did nothing because we were scared.

'The evening of the incident, this Kushal's mother came with someone she called Santri-darling. His brother had been a minister and was very well connected. They threatened us and told us that we would be taken away and jailed somewhere ... and that Priya would lose her place at the school and that she would be sent to a *kotha* to become a prostitute.

'We are not proud of it but we kept quiet out of fear. But Priya could not keep this entirely to herself. As she had stopped going to school for a few days, Counsellor Madam came to visit us. Priya told her what had happened.'

The counsellor added, 'I told the principal but he didn't want to hear anything about it. It has been gnawing away at me and today I just had to let you know what really happened. The truth! You should be proud of your son and how you have brought him up, the values you have given him!'

Priya's mother added the final chapter to the story. 'Soon after this, a week ago, a man came and spoke to my husband and gave him a bag of money. This was money for us to keep quiet. With it came the threats. My husband left with the money and I know I will never see him again. And we are left with the threats.'

'I need you to record your statement,' Sammy said, looking directly at Priya. 'We can't let these bastards get away with it!'

The mother at once went into a blue funk, scared of what would happen to all of them. But Priya's voice came through clearly, cutting through any objections. 'Yes, it is right. I will do it.'

Sammy called Rishi, who had been hanging around outside the school and quickly briefed him on what had happened. He had become quite friendly with some of the policemen at the local station, but he also knew which ones could be influenced and which ones would not be.

Within the hour, Rishi's lawyer friend in attendance, Priya had recorded her statement before a magistrate; a fresh FIR was filed against four persons, with the school mentioned in the report.

It should have ended there. But more was to come, for power and influence stretch a long way in India. Priya's statement was inviolate. Recent changes to the law and the manner in which her words had been recorded, meant that no one could ignore her allegation. But would it be enough? Would it be enough particularly since Priya, at the insistence of her mother, had not named Kushal and Dadlani, so the four attackers were 'persons unknown'.

48

*'Happiness can be found even in the darkest of times, if only
one remembers to turn on the light.'*

– J.K. ROWLING

There was another eyewitness. Aksh. But there was a problem, for he had limited recollection of the events of the day. His memory was coming back, but too slowly. The silver lining to this dark cloud was that Kushal's family and their minions left Aksh alone … for the moment anyway. The bodyguard arranged by Major Vivek was always with them, as Rishi didn't want to take any chances.

Dr Shefali, the young psychologist who had made friends with Sammy, had an idea. Research showed that memories came back more easily if the 'subject' were placed in the surroundings that might trigger recollection. In simple words, Aksh needed to go back to the school, to the basketball court.

With care and forethought, Sammy took her friend's help in setting up the stimulus to Aksh's brain. The school was being thoroughly cooperative; they had no pressure from Kushal but the forces that Rishi had unleashed on them were threatening to shut them down.

An ordinary day ... mid-afternoon ... Aksh walked slowly with Sammy to the basketball court at the school. He turned the corner and saw a young girl, a fellow student at the school, held against the wall by a boy in school uniform. The girl turned her face towards him ... Priya.

Aksh stiffened. Muscle memory leads to instinctive responses and Aksh's body was telling him that he was heading into danger. His nerve cells were tingling and his brain was working overtime, processing the scene in front of him.

The boy turned his face towards Aksh ... it was Jay!

'Stop,' yelled Aksh and ran towards Jay, jerking him away from Priya. 'Stop!'

And then, all of a sudden, he stopped ... paused ... understood.

'No,' said Aksh slowly, clasping his friend Jay by the shoulder gently. 'No, it wasn't Jay. It was Kushal. And Dadlani. I remember it all now! Priya ... Peasant P ... that's what they called her! They even had customized football shoes with 'STAMPP' with a double P printed on it. It was a secret code between them; it was an affirmation of intent that they wanted to stamp P ... Priya ... and run her into the ground. I have seen her cower as they played football. I think she guessed because they would chant as they passed her in school.'

Major Vivek's man took over immediately. Bundling the family into the car and riding in the front passenger seat, he took them immediately to Sammy's apartment, to a place where he could keep them safe. For the stakes now were very high and the threat to Aksh had become real.

Sammy and Aksh sat out on the balcony all night, mother and son sharing a special bond and a closeness that excluded even Tara and Rishi. Early the next morning, they woke up the other two and announced their decision.

'Aksh is going to testify,' said Sammy. 'Only then will he be complete. We have to see that this happens.'

Rishi had many friends in India, especially in Delhi and Haryana. He had many flaws but letting go of old friendships was not one of them. He had a steady stream of visitors in London and was the local guardian for the 'Next Gen' as he called the offspring of his friends. So he casually announced that he had been in touch with his friends in the administration and the police and the matter had become complicated.

There was a threat ... a real threat, very melodramatic if it weren't so real. Word was filtering out that an underworld hit had been ordered to prevent Aksh from testifying. The police were also playing a dangerous game. While the many police officers and the public prosecutor were being supportive, offering personal security officers and escort vehicles, the Investigating Officer was insisting that Aksh's statement would be recorded only at the Vasant Vihar Police Station at a given time on a given day. No amount of cajoling, explanations, persuasions were working on him, making Rishi wonder out loud as to whose pocket he was in.

And Rishi had reason to be concerned. The ringmaster was Sinister Santri. With Santri would come the self-righteous Mister Minister Mantri, using all his connections in a vicious and vindictive manner to aid his brother and the girlfriend, Kushal's mother. 'Such a complicated web!' thought Sammy.

Looking at Sammy and Aksh, Rishi marvelled at their strength, the courage and the support they gave each other. They drew from some inner core, the essence of their being showing itself in this time of crisis. He was so proud of both of them!

Leaving home for a couple of days, Rishi stayed at the army camp in Manesar with Major Vivek; plotting, planning, strategizing. Then they came to Sammy's apartment and she spotted the flaw in their plan straight away.

'You need a decoy,' she said. 'You need Kushal's family to believe that Aksh is going in another car, while you spirit him to the police station undetected.'

It was just as Major Vivek had said ... they would need a decoy. And Rishi had vetoed the idea because he knew exactly who would have to be in the decoy car for the plan to work.

But now there could be no argument, for she was right and Rishi knew it. Only if she were in the decoy car, and visibly so, would anyone believe that Aksh was in it. Tara insisted that she would play the part of Aksh and nothing that Rishi could say or do was going to convince them otherwise.

With his heart breaking from the sheer bravery and courage of it, he hugged Sammy for being the mother that she was. However, he insisted that Major Vivek's man would be with them at all times. And the good army man had another trick up his sleeve that he would soon reveal.

So, Sammy's SUV would have cloth covering the windows and would take MG Road towards the Vasant Vihar Police Station. Sammy would be in it, as would Tara, dressed like Aksh and with her head covered, ostensibly to avoid the media and cameras, who had the story by now and were crowded around Sammy's apartment. There would be police escorts all the way ... to crowd them in for an attack or to protect them was not certain. Rishi, in the meanwhile, would use the Gurgaon Expressway to take Aksh to Vasant Vihar in a borrowed BMW 5 series; unmarked, unescorted and, hopefully, unnoticed.

The deception would not last for long and Rishi didn't want to expose Sammy and Tara for a lengthy period in any case, so he would need to drive very fast. That was not a problem. The issue was the traffic in Delhi that needed to be dealt with. The plotters had, however, come up with a possible plan for that in their two-day session.

The crucial day came. News channels had been covering the issue since dawn, as the case had caught public imagination and there was little else of note or excitement going on these days. Morning led to lunch. Lunch to mid-afternoon. The time had been carefully chosen to allow the arrangements to be made and to have as little traffic on the road as possible.

The time to leave came. The four of them gave each other hugs and parted, with Tara and Aksh almost looking like twins in the way they were dressed.

With elaborate care and taking all possible precautions, Sammy and Tara got into their car. The escort vehicles rolled into place and, sirens blaring, the convoy made its way out of the condominium complex, out on its way to MG Road and the Gurgaon-Delhi border.

Unnoticed by the media, a black BMW slipped out of the colony and turned on the link road towards Sector 40. Racing to the corner on its broad radials, down the dodgy left near Huda City Centre on low revolutions, right on the sector road and bouncing on the underpass. Rishi made a quick turn right, up the access road and he was on the Expressway. The big German V8 engine thumped under the hood as Rishi used racing changes on the transmission to build up the power as he swept past taxis and commuters, buses and casual drivers. Up the flyovers and bouncing through the now defunct Toll Plaza, screaming past the airport and swinging left to the service lane for the Mahipalpur turn, downshifting on the manual override as he drove the BMW hard.

Time for the first intervention. Harel and a biker friend from Gurgaon had been waiting near Samalkha on their classic Royal Enfield Bullets, two kilometres out, and they zipped past a deliberately slowing Rishi, and turned right on the Mahipalpur crossing, just at the intersection of the main Delhi-Gurgaon Expressway and the side road they would have to go down. And stopped. In the middle of the road. Blocking the through traffic from Delhi under the flyover. No one was quite sure what Harel did for the Office, but stopping Delhi traffic for a minute was child's play for him. For that one minute, no one was going to block the intersection.

Out roared the BMW from behind them with Rishi gunning the engine for all he was worth, on to the Vasant Kunj road, driving far too fast for the potholed tarmac. On and on, to the junction with Nelson Mandela Marg. Which was closed. A board and picket across the junction proclaimed road works – 'Road Closed'! Signs that mysteriously disappeared moments before Rishi came by, taking the left turn at high speed, burning rubber, downshifting just before the turn and then accelerating through it.

Then they were through. A straight run to the Vasant Vihar Police Station ... no one was going to stop them now!

As they turned into the police station, Aksh called Sammy and Major Vivek on their mobile phones, with a short message, 'We're there!'

Before anyone could gather what happened, Sammy and Tara were whisked away from their SUV to sit in the middle of an army Shaktiman three-tonner that just happened to be passing by. They were safe! No one was going to mess with a platoon of fierce-looking jawans, armed to the teeth, with Major Vivek sitting at the end of the truck and grinning at Sammy and Tara. Not that the army could carry live firearms in a civilian area, let alone use them. But who was going to take a chance? No, the two ladies were safe.

There was not much else left to do after that. A delighted public prosecutor got his statement from Aksh. The Investigating Officer was left gnashing his teeth. His role and that of some other officers would be exposed later by an enterprising young TV reporter, fresh out of journalism school.

That was for later, as were the debates on whether the two young delinquents should be tried in a normal court or under the Juvenile Justice Act. They would definitely be incarcerated and a strong signal would be sent out, almost making an example of the two boys, Kushal and Dadlani. Priya's name was kept out of the media. The next scandal would break and Aksh's role too would be forgotten.

This time the truth could not be subverted by the rich and powerful. Not just Aksh but many children came forward to talk openly about harassment with the support of their parents. Signature campaigns and photographs on the Internet went viral. A movement was born to curtail violence of any kind on education campuses. Even Delhi University was forced to up its vigilance.

The sound of happy hands clapping as Aksh walked up to receive the award for Devotion to Duty resounded in the school auditorium.

Coming over to Sammy, Aksh whispered lines that were now his mantra, 'Maybe it's not my weekend, but it's gonna be my year,' as she held him in a tight embrace and whispered, 'Weightless! I listen to your music now Aksh and quite like it!'

It was over and Aksh had been vindicated. Never again would he come under the spell of others or be bullied. Sammy was vindicated. She had shown that single mothers too could be good mothers.

49

'If you want a happy ending, that depends, of course, on where you stop your story.'

– ORSON WELLES

Three weeks of worry and care ended one morning with a pleasant surprise, just as a long night dissolved in one magical moment.

Rishi walked out on to the balcony, approached her and placed a printout in her hands, as Sammy looked at the jumbled cityscape spread below her. He saw Sammy leaning against the railing, pensive, lost in thought, worried about Aksh and his future.

Without a word, he looked on as Sammy read the simple words of the letter in her hand.

She read through it without a word, almost not being able to believe what she was seeing. Then she looked up, broke into yelps of joy, jumping in excitement and ran to light her agarbattis and to say a prayer. Before settling down on the sofa to read it again. She traced her finger over every word as she read. Her Aksh was going to be just fine!

30806515

UWC Committee Selection

Dear Aksh,

On behalf of the UWC Committee of India and our other national committees around the globe, I am happy to inform you that you have been selected as a United World College Scholar.

As a UWC Scholarship recipient, we will cover 100% of tuition and living costs for the first choice UWC you indicated in your application. You will only be responsible for covering your airfare, pocket money and emergency insurance coverage.

Congratulations on getting through the selection process run by the UWC Committee. Well done, this is a tremendous achievement!

You are cordially invited to attend a twenty-four-hour orientation and counselling camp. The orientation experience will be informative, challenging and fun.

You are in Group B on Day 2.

During the orientation and counselling camp, you will have the chance to learn about the UWC schools and colleges around the world. You will have the chance to meet current and former students, faculty and other scholars like yourself. You will be in a group of about ten students.

Your parents are invited to come with you to the college but they will have a separate programme after the welcome address. They will leave later in the evening and you will stay at the college overnight.

We have been looking for individuals with open minds, the capacity to learn and the ability to contribute to the learning experience of others, selected in a similar way, from around the world. We are always looking for individuals who want to do something worthwhile with their lives. There is no typical UWC student so you will be able, at the UWC, to be yourself and have fun! You have done very well to get selected for the scholarship. We look forward to welcoming you to your first UWC experience.

We would be grateful to receive your confirmation of this invitation at the earliest.

Please send your acceptance to the United World Colleges Committee by email, expressing clearly your preferred choice of UWC from our colleges around the world. As a UWC Scholar, you will automatically be granted admission to your first choice UWC.

Regards,
UWC Committee

'Woweeee,' she screamed, running to Aksh's room. Tara joined in the fun, grabbing the letter from Sammy and all of them hugged Aksh euphorically.

'We are so proud of you, son! You have done this without help; and, look life sucked you into a tunnel of problems but you are now out of it. So proud of you. You don't have to remain at your stupid school any longer! This Aksh is on point, ten on,' Sammy told him with a big smile as Aksh began to giggle because his mother was using his lingo.

But Aksh interrupted her. 'I can't go, Mom; I cannot leave you alone and my school is not stupid anymore. Tara is already living away, in London with Papa. I am now responsible for you. And this letter means that they will give me my first choice, which is the UWC of the American West, in USA! I don't know what I was thinking about when I applied! I no longer want to go, Mama,' he said, clearly upset and almost in tears.

And then softly he added, 'And school is not that bad now.'

'Son-shine mine, let us not decide today. Everything will happen when it is meant to be. Let us fill the forms, complete the process and see how we feel. Nothing is over. It is just a continuation of our lives, happy lives. Just enjoy your success and let's take each day as it comes. One day at a time.'

'Are you sure? Not even if Sammy goes along with you? To be in the US for an absolutely fantastic, super course?' Rishi asked Aksh, waving another paper around triumphantly.

He went on, saying jubilantly, 'No one is getting left behind. Oh-no, not this time. Sammy,' he said, looking directly at her. 'I know your dreams. I revived your application to Wharton.'

Turning to face all of them, he said to Aksh, 'And you are not the only one who has admission. Look, see,' he said, giving Aksh yet another printout. 'All done! Mama and you are both going to USA.

'And thanks for the concern; I can feel the love,' he told mother and son, pretending to be offended but grinning as he spoke. 'I have work in the US that I have been neglecting and can pick up. In any case, with the miles I have on British Airways and on my AmEx card, Tara and I will be in and out of the US till you're sick of us!'

The children grabbed the letter and both read it out aloud, with exaggerated gestures and with heightened drama to make Sammy laugh.

And laugh she did with undiluted happiness.

Dear Samaira,

On behalf of the Selection Committee of The Wharton School at the University of Pennsylvania, it is my great pleasure to inform you that you have been accepted for admission to the Fellowship Program as a Joseph Wharton Fellow.

Given a particularly strong applicant pool this year, the Committee was impressed with your excellent academic qualifications and work experience. We believe you and others admitted to the program possess the ability, skills, and resources to come to Wharton, experience the Program with your complete attention, and then be fully prepared to pursue your personal and professional goals with confidence.

We hope you will accept a place in next year's class, which will begin on 1st June and end with Commencement on 4th June, the following year.

If you choose to accept our offer of admission, please sign and date the enclosed copy of this letter where indicated and scan and return it to us by 9th February. In the space provided please indicate your preferred email address, which we will use to correspond with you between now and the start of the Program.

Shortly after receiving your acceptance and deposit, we will send further details about April Orientation week, visas for international students, housing and additional information to help you prepare for the Program.

Please accept our personal congratulations to you on your admission! We look forward to hearing from you soon!

Sincerely yours,
Dean, The Wharton School

Coffee and pizzas were ordered, as they talked all day. The four of them happy together in a way that they had not been for years. Neither together, nor happy ... until now.

At some point the day melted into a starry night and they slept on the drawing room ottoman, arms entwined and bodies huddled under a big razai.

50

*'For me, a happy ending is ... coming to a place where a
person has a clear vision of his or her own life in a way that
enables them to kind of throw down their crutches and walk.'*
— JILL MCCORKLE

There was little time to be lost. Days flew past with the speed of sound; there was so much activity. Visa applications were filled, school forms, papers, report cards submitted, and so much more. Although no decision had been taken, Rishi had insisted that the paperwork be completed on time. 'Keep all options open,' he said.

There had been mounting pressure on them to withdraw the formal complaint against the school and its name from the FIR. Apparently Kushal and Dadlani had been expelled from the school. No other school in the city wanted them so boarding school was the answer, it seemed. That was often seen as a way to wrench troubled kids from their comfortable environment to make them self-sufficient and responsible. However, the law would take its own course now, and the two offenders were most likely headed for Juvenile Home rather than to boarding school in Rishi's opinion.

'This is no longer our problem,' Rishi told Sammy quietly after a meeting with the School Board. 'Apparently ragging is a big issue at the school and needs to be weeded out. There is substance abuse, too. I don't want to go into details but the principal refused to acknowledge it even now. He denied it blatantly. I hate the bugger, he said he had never seen a child smoke in school, let alone smoke weed. I told him that the joke in school is that its flag and emblem contains not laurel leaves but weed.'

'I will not withdraw the complaint just because Aksh is leaving the place,' he said. 'Someone has to stand up.'

'But what if they trouble us?' Sammy had asked, her concern quite apparent.

'They cannot hold us back. There is a law in the country and the school is a bit scared of us now!' Rishi had said to her.

The next few weeks were the happiest in a long time. There was much discussion, heated arguments, heartburn, anxiety, disappointment and even tears as farewell plans were made.

No one can stop the passage of time … and definitely not when life is good. And it was time. The end of January and Tara had to go back to her college in London.

At the airport, they hugged Tara and waved happily as she disappeared into the crowd, secure in the knowledge that Rishi would be joining her soon. Sammy and Aksh had the option of following soon after, stopping over in London on their way to their new institutions in the US.

Sammy, on her part, had welcomed a new team member into the fold at work, letting go some of her old insecurities.

Certain that whatever decision was taken, she would be happy with it. She decided not to dismantle or rent out her home until the decision was finally taken. For either way, since her course was for a year, a short duration, it made sense to hold on to the house. There would be enough time for her to settle Aksh in but not long enough for her to take root. Grateful for the break from her routine, she was happy not to plan further.

'One day at a time, one small step at a time,' she told herself, humming breathlessly as she updated her list of chores to be done and projects to be wrapped up before their departure.

She was still humming happily to herself when Aksh ran in the front door. His face was flushed and for just a moment Sammy wondered if the past was revisiting them. But the colour was from his having run up the stairs, beating the elevator in the mad dash home.

He carried a postcard and a letter, flashing these above his head. He stopped next to Sammy and said just the single word, 'Maasi ji!'

And so it was ... a simple postcard with the clichéd words, 'Wish You Were Here!' sent from Langkawi three days ago.

And the letter with a similar postmark, also from Maasi ji. Two photographs ... both with her happily sitting under a sun umbrella grinning stupidly at an elderly man in a sun hat. They were obviously together!

'Oh Maasi ji!' was all that Sammy could say. She held the photographs in her hand, looked out of the plate-glass windows of her apartment and smiled at the sky outside.

51

'I choose to love you in loneliness...
For in loneliness no one owns you but me.'

– RUMI

It was a couple of weeks after Tara had left for London. Sammy rushed to her car. She had one more stop to make before she was done for the day. She had spoken to Maasi ji's housekeeper about the cryptic messages he had left with Rishi and there was somewhere she needed to be.

The wind blew hard as the sun hid behind clouds. Slowing down, Sammy's SUV pulled up outside an old colonial house on a deserted street. The house stood erect and proud amid the newer apartment buildings that dotted the landscape. It was different and aloof, having witnessed history as the decades flipped past its iron gates and generations were born and died, while it alone withstood time. The house seemed to watch as the car slowed down and it saw Sammy, once the little granddaughter of the house, drive up. The house sighed in relief and its old walls creaked sympathetically. The sound of the wind filled it, rattling the windows as it whistled through its long corridors.

Sammy looked out of the window, directing the driver to the third of the many gates that led to the imposing house. She took a deep breath and exhaled slowly, very slowly, taking it all in as a series of images flashed before her eyes.

She wished that Tara were still in town. She would have liked to have her daughter with her, giving her a hug and holding her hand in her own.

Sammy walked towards the majestic iron gates, unhurriedly and with confidence, noticing with pride that the house covered the span of the street. This house had been a landmark when her family had lived in it. Letters posted without an address but with just her grandfather's name would be delivered by the postman with a reverent salaam. It was better than an email. Just his name, no @ and no address!

No one seemed to be around. 'Strange,' thought Sammy. 'It hasn't been that long...'

Not one to be discouraged, Sammy stood on her heels to peer over the red brick boundary wall. 'Bhaiya, bhaiya,' she shouted to an old man sleeping on a broken chair propped up against a tree.

As if on cue, the old man stirred and slowly rose to his feet and shuffled to the gate, limping as he walked. He then stood on a chair strategically placed near the gate and looked at her over the wall and proclaimed, 'No one allowed inside! No one here, all gone and my malkin is gone away.'

Sammy frowned for a second and then quickly said as recognition dawned, 'It is me, Samaira! You have been calling me and spoke with Rishi. Open the gates and let me in!'

The old man looked expressionlessly, staring at her and then his face lit up. He grinned as she noticed the missing teeth and the cataract. She looked for the scar on his right cheek but even that looked both magnified and mellow on his shrivelled and ageing face.

He jumped off the chair and rushed to the gates with the energy of a much younger man, the arthritic limp gone. 'Baby, it is you! I cannot believe it,' he said, unlocking the gates for the car. 'You never came for years and my malkin kept telling me that you were well. And now she has gone to the island and says she will be back only next year!'

The car manoeuvred its way along the driveway, circling a majestic mango tree while Sammy cautioned the driver, 'Careful, do not to collide into it.' It was considered a symbol of prosperity and was so revered that the family chose to negotiate their way around it rather than trim the branches. Better bang the car than touch the tree. She chuckled as the memories came back to her.

The house held all kinds of memories. There had been fights. Reasons for Sammy never coming back. Reasons for the house eventually ending up with Maasi ji. And now who knew when she would be back from Langkawi, with or without her new man.

She thought softly to herself, 'The fight was worth it and so was the struggle. It made me independent and the future became mine to make what I did with it. No glass ceiling, just a blue sky of opportunity.'

She looked up at the sky, smiling as the cadmium yellow sun winked back, shining through the canopy of the mango tree. How well she remembered this place. But she had never come back. Never since her mother had tried to use her own daughter as bait to close a business deal with a 'valued' client. Not since her brother had slapped her across the face because she had shouted at her mother. Not since her mother had forged her signature and tried to make her the perfect patsy in a complicated Ponzi scheme.

With a trembling hand, the old man unlatched the front door for her to enter. Maasi ji was stylish but this house was no longer either majestic or beautiful. The house looked as if it has been attacked by an army of white ants and had been buried under a mountain of dust. Half-eaten food, unwashed mugs and empty bowls could be seen everywhere. And all in a matter of weeks, for that was all the time that her aunt had been missing.

The house was dead; it was as silent as a graveyard. Sammy drew her shawl around her, tighter and closer for comfort.

'Hush,' she whispered to herself. 'Houses can hear and have a soul. I love this house and it has always owned a part of me. I feel a belonging, a kinship with this place. This used to be a house full of life. It was once a sprawling, living, vibrant, noisy house, with its gardens and long verandas. It was our home. My home.'

She turned to the retainer as she stepped in. 'So, what was it about my mother that you wanted to talk to me about?'

He hesitated. The old man wasn't quite sure how to express himself. 'I remember you, baby, running around barefoot in the *aangan*, smiling happily. We all knew what happened, why you left and never came back. *Majboori thi*, where did we have the position or place to say anything?

'But,' he carried on softly, 'This house has its secrets and its ghosts. Things happened here that we saw. Things I can't even talk to you about.'

A blush came to Sammy's cheeks as she remembered the many scandals and hidden dalliances. The old man's words had brought back memories. The hushed moans, the pleasure. The sex in which the people of the house revelled unabashedly.

'Your mother...' he said, and then stopped.

Sammy thought he was hesitating because he didn't want to discuss her mother's sex scandals with her. She recalled whispers because sex was talked about all the time, in bursts of laughter and often while teasing a new recruit, a new daughter-in-law ... the jokes were carefree and even obscene. Women of the house spoke about it openly and loved it, not simply as a way of quenching lust but because sex, and their husbands' greed for it, made the boring routine interesting and gave the women power over a part of their lives, their destinies. It was that power and its impact that made Sammy shudder, shudder with the memories of how her mother had destroyed Sammy's relationships within and outside the family.

But the hesitation was not due to embarrassment. Maasi ji's house servant went on. 'I wait for malkin. She will come back to me one day. I know she will. This house has seen ghosts. I see your mother every day ... my malkin too will come back!'

It was a bit anti-climatic, but Sammy wasn't quite sure what she had actually been expecting. As far as she could gather, her mother was haunting the house and the old man, clearly distraught about Maasi ji not returning from her holiday, was waiting for his beloved malkin to come back too and be reunited with him.

Sammy, too, was emotional and misty-eyed. Through her tears, she saw the house as it once was, majestic with manicured lawn dotted with frangipani trees and endless beds of flowers. She remembered the vibrant colour of the

Canna lilies as she watched a row of Ashok trees sway in the breeze, rain-washed and emerald green, a sharp contrast to the gunpowder red Gulmohar and the brilliant yellow Laburnum that lined the driveway.

The old man thrust a glass of water in front of her and she took it with gratitude, sipping mouthfuls. Sammy walked out of the house and looked around. No longer were there spacious verandas, the large garages, the huge unending gardens and the extra spaces in the house and heart for relatives that had fallen on bad times. The house it seemed to her was gutted with fungus. This house and the life it represented was an anachronism. When Maasi ji also went, it would truly be the end of an era.

'She, your malkin, is alive. She will come back,' she told him, rummaging in her bag for the postcard and letter. But her chain of thought was broken as the old retainer began gesticulating wildly.

'Look, look,' the old man told her, his voice full of excitement, waving at a shadowy figure on the sidewalk.

Sammy gasped as the person came forward. Front teeth missing, dressed in rags, barefoot but with the gait of a queen, albeit a bit exaggerated.

She watched mesmerized as the apparition walked towards her. Heavy eyes, long flowing hair, thin leering lips, an oversized bindi stuck on her large forehead. The resemblance was striking. Her eyes blinking myopically, her face dragged down with pain and effort.

The retainer then explained with greater clarity why he had called her now that Sammy could see for herself. 'She comes here every day, begging for food. Stealing from the labourers, scolding, cursing, laughing hysterically. They run away, scared. Some offer her food but most avoid her because she screams abuses, chasing them away from her house, as she calls it. But I have been watching her. She is her *bhoot*, her ghost,' he told Sammy.

'No ghost!' thought Sammy, as she watched, mesmerized. A surging jumble of memories from various milestones in her life poured into her head, like water gushing out of a dam and breaking free, unrestrained.

Emotions. Her brother's turmoil. His questions. His searching. His quest. Was all of it a pretence?

Her mother, she had been told by her sanctimonious sister-in-law, was dead, lost at sea. Her brother had inherited her mother's wealth and spent his days whiling away time, cocooned in opiate fumes while his wife changed partners with the same speed as she upgraded her designer hand bags. 'Need excitement in life, that good-for-nothing is a lost cause,' she had winked and told a common friend, referring to her husband, Sammy's brother. 'He fulfils only one need ... no, no, not that one ... the ability to sign the cheques, darling. He is a lost cause like his mother. He turned his back on her when she showed signs of senility and raised the boundary walls so that she would not run away. But then, poor thing was lost at sea. Sank without a trace, like the USS Wasp.'

'Sank my foot!' whistled Sammy under her breath. She did not have answers, only possibilities.

With tickets booked for the US and life sorted out, she stood there, lost in thought. The tragedy of life was not lost on her.

She wanted to ask the apparition on the sidewalk, 'Was it worth it?'

She wanted to ask her mother about the greed, the avarice, the running after important people. Wealthy people. 'The manipulation to claw your way into and to remain relevant in society, on its Page 3 circuit … was it worth it? Where did it get you? Why did you try to sell your own daughter?'

The mind, she remembered from *Paradise Lost*, can make a hell of heaven and leave you abandoned.

The silly grin, the soiled clothes, the smeared lipstick, the lost youth told a pathetic story. A story of a life wasted and a society's indifference. For time, in its arrogant or perhaps merely its sluttish way, had jerked its hand from her clasp and moved on.

'What should I do?' Sammy asked herself as she stood there. She whipped out her mobile phone and dialled the doctor.

'Most families have secrets – skeletons in the closet that are never spoken of. Sometimes the secret is so painful, and buried so deep, that it becomes "forgotten" by the family.'

– CATHY GLASS

ACKNOWLEDGEMENT

The idea for this book was sparked by a short newspaper article I had read. A young American had stepped across the racial divide to protect a fellow high school student and had ended up in coma for his troubles. The news may not have made such an impression on me, but I met the head of an Indian school soon afterwards, who told me about the rampant bullying he was dealing with at his institution. The thought then came to me – what would be the power equations that might play out in such a situation in India? Would the caste and class structures of society replicate themselves in schools as well?

I want to thank the teachers, students and parents who have spoken with me. The doctors and nurses who patiently answered my questions but chose to remain anonymous, and the psychologists who helped me understand the mindset of teenaged bullies.

Thank you Pranav Kumar Singh, at Pan Macmillan India, for believing in the story. Diya Kar Hazra, thank you for giving it life. Sushmita Chatterjee, you are an editor after my heart; thank you for your professional edits and focus that pushed me to meet deadlines.

I would not have been able to write this without the support and encouragement of my friends. The novel took shape when I discussed the idea with Amrita Bhalla. Anita Srivastava was the first to read the manuscript and her reaction convinced me that I had a story worth telling. Arti Mathur Lall and Jeevesh Nagrath helped keep the pace in the narrative with their insightful comments. Monika Kashyap and Divya Oswal were important readers. Hema and Vivek Gandhi have seen this book develop over their dining table in London.

Lisbeth Westberg tirelessly read the manuscript in its various stages and gave me her perspective. Sammy's character has grown because of the inputs given by Vaishali and Samir Jasuja. Romonika Dey Sharan spotted gaps in the narrative and the story is tighter as a result.

A big thank you to Rohini Punj, Radhika Chopra Bahl and Sanjay Bahl, Sushma Narain, Sajan Narain, Ingo Schweder and Josephine Leung, KR Sridhar, Rahul Sharma, Inderbir Sandhu, Ajay Srivastava, Sanjeev and Dawn Kumar, Shawn and Mark Runacres, Priyanka Jain, Manek Shergill, Rashmi Khatpalia, Shruti Diwedi Sodhi, Gaurav Sabharwal and Shikha, Rajiv Batra, Gautam and Puja Khattar, Karan Bhagat, Madhav Saraswat, Samir and Tandip Kuckreja, Jaya Bhattacharji Rose, Tanya and Ashwajit Singh, and Neeraj Bawa.

MQ Baig, my agent and friend: you remain a support.

To my new friends at The Magnolias and old, dear friends from Beverly Park.

The friends of my children were always there with their ideas and support. I want to specially mention Aishwarya

Kakkar, my intern over the summer. The comments by Ishan Gandhi were incisive and detailed. Soham Dalwani patiently listened to me as the ideas developed.

And most importantly, my children Suhasini and Shauryya. Suhasini, thank you for working on the poetry in this book, and Shauryya, for your research and verification of each quote.

Shashank without your inputs this book would have remained a manuscript.

To Baba and Ruzbeh, who gave me faith.